S.T.O.R.M.

THE VIPER CLUB

'Andrew was already pulling a pen from his pocket. He grabbed the printout of Chen's first email and started to scribble down the names at the bottom.

It was possible, he knew, for emails to electronically self-destruct. In this case, he had no doubt it would happen. Because this, he'd realized at once, was a *hit list.'*

Also available in the S. T. O. R. M. series:

S. T. O. R. M. – The Infinity Code
S. T. O. R. M. – The Ghostmaster
S. T. O. R. M. – The Black Sphere

Coming soon:

S. T. O. R. M. – The Death Web

E. L. YOUNG

MACMILLAN CHILDREN'S BOOKS

First published 2008 by Macmillan Children's Books
a division of Macmillan Publishers Limited
20 New Wharf Road, London N1 9RR
Basingstoke and Oxford
Associated companies throughout the world
www.panmacmillan.com

ISBN 978-0-330-45416-2

1 3 5 7 9 8 6 4 2

A CIP catalogue record for this book is available from
the British Library.

Typeset by Intype Libra Limited
Printed and bound in the UK by CPI Mackays, Chatham ME5 8TD

For S, R, S, C and James –
for Icebergs and Il Locale

Prologue

Chen Jianguo rubbed his mottled hands together. They were stiff with age. Wormed with blue veins. 'Friends,' he rasped, 'welcome to my home. Follow me.'

Chen coughed and turned. He felt adrenalin course through him. It made his heart flutter.

Behind him, the four men shuffled along the dim jade corridor. They were apprehensive. With good reason, Chen thought. But he had assured them of their safety. He had even allowed them to keep their firearms. 'As befitting gentlemen of such stature,' he had purred.

When it came to the first man, stature – at least of the physical sort – was not in doubt. He was well over two metres tall, with bamboo-thin arms and legs. Privately Chen nicknamed him the Stick Insect. The second was squat and round. The Dung Beetle. The third was the Chihuahua, because of his small head and pointed ears. Last came the Giraffe. Not on account of his neck, which was non-existent, but his eyelashes, which were longer than any girl's.

Each was hugely ambitious. And highly dangerous.

They obeyed Chen because they had to. He was the boss of the Shanghai criminal underworld. If you listened to back-alley rumours – which Chen paid his people to do – one thousand murderous henchmen were at Chen's command. Close, he thought. At the last count it was more like nine hundred and thirty-nine.

Recently, however, the talk had started to take a darker turn. *All reigns come to an end, Chen Jianguo is not a god, he is eighty-nine years old, he cannot live forever* . . . This talk was especially concerning because Chen knew it to be true. The previous week his personal physician had given him one month to live. Maybe two.

Each of the four men, in *his* house, heading now to eat *his* food, thought they could take his place. And Chen Jianguo was determined to teach them a lesson.

Tonight, he told himself, I must be satisfied with that. Only a lesson.

Ahead, the golden door to the banqueting hall stood open. But first Chen had something to show them.

On the wall was a diamond switch. He flicked it. Light flooded from three rosewood display cases mounted on the jade.

Chen jerked a crabbed forefinger towards them. 'Here, gentlemen, are some of the highlights of my collection.'

Inside the first case was a black velvet stand and an

old-fashioned record card, which read: *Proximal phalange, Deschapelles, Haiti.*

On the stand was a small, single bone.

'This is a thumb bone,' Chen said, his voice low and excited. 'It was once owned by a man named Claude Narcisse. He was a *houngan*. A Voodoo priest. Using this very bone, Narcisse cursed four men. Two days later, they died. The cause? A mysterious wasting disease . . . Such power. Can you imagine it?' His arch gaze suggested his guests could not.

The Stick Insect grunted. He edged past Chen to peer into the second case. Inside was an antique Chinese text framed in gold. The Stick Insect's eyes narrowed. 'What is this?'

'*This* describes a technique for triggering *commotio cordis*,' Chen said. He rolled his withered tongue around the Latin words.

The Stick Insect looked blank.

'I admit, it is a dry term for such a mortal terror. For the collapse of the regular beat of the heart into *chaos*.'

'But how—' the Dung Beetle started.

'Technically it is not difficult,' Chen interrupted, his pulse quickening. 'A light blow, directly above the organ, at a speed, ideally, of sixty-five kilometres per hour. If the timing is right, death is instant.' He fixed his gaze on the Dung Beetle, who paled and shuffled in his black silk suit.

Resisting the urge to smile, Chen hobbled on to the

final case. It was filled with water. Piled near the back were rough pebbles and sand.

'Stones?' the Chihuahua said.

Chen hesitated. He shouldn't tell them. He really *shouldn't* . . .

'Somewhere in that pile of stones is a snail,' he said at last. '*Conus textile*. The textile cone snail. Twenty-eight point five millimetres long. Normally found in the Indian Ocean.'

'But what,' the Chihuahua said, 'is dangerous about this snail? Tell us, Mr Chen, how can a snail like that hurt a man?'

'Its poisoned tooth,' Chen said simply. These men were strong and powerful, but beside him, they were fools! They knew nothing of the world! 'This snail preys on fish. It propels a tooth on a jet of seawater. The tooth strikes the victim. The venom is transferred.'

The Chihuahua grunted. 'And the death, it is also instant?'

'For a fish,' Chen replied, his rheumy eyes gleaming, 'undoubtedly. For a man? The strike is painless. The victim may have no idea it has happened. Until his muscles grow weak and his lungs strain. These symptoms may not develop for minutes or even hours. But by that time, death – it is inevitable.'

'Huh,' the Dung Beetle said, folding his fat arms.

The lesson was over, Chen decided. It was time to move on to practicalities. 'Come.'

The corridor opened into a lavish hall. Carved jade

screens semi-circled a polished dining table laid for five people.

'Please,' Chen said. 'Sit. Eat. *Enjoy*.'

For the first course, the men were served with an assortment of appetizers, arranged into the shape of dragons. They looked uncertainly at their plates.

'I can assure you,' Chen croaked, 'it is not poisoned. From what you know of me, am I a man who would use such a crude technique?' He laughed.

No one else did. But they picked up their chopsticks.

Next came Peking duck. Now, the Dung Beetle raised the Meeting of the Tigers, which was scheduled for a fortnight's time.

This meeting was held once a year. Crime bosses from all over China would get together to discuss business, do deals, form alliances – and break them.

At this year's meeting, Chen knew, the Giraffe and the Dung Beetle were conspiring to kill him. The Stick Insect had so far been silent on this matter – or so the back-alley talk said – but Chen was a gambling man, and if he had to set odds that the Stick Insect would support the others, he would put them at . . . 1:2. A *dead cert*. And as for the Chihuahua . . .

The porcelain dishes were cleared away.

Next came sweet and sour spare ribs. A quartet of waiters brought out gold finger bowls, one rimmed with diamonds, another with sapphires, the third with rubies, the fourth with pearls. In the bottom of each bowl was a rubble of precious stones. They shone in the lemon-scented water.

And Chen's failing heart began to tremble.

He watched the waiter set the pearl-encrusted bowl before the Chihuahua, and he nodded to himself.

At last, the Chihuahua finished eating. He lowered his sauce-slathered fingers into the water.

Chen's eyes narrowed. Would he see the movement? Would he observe the strike? The odds that the Chihuahua would escape being hit were, Chen thought, *conservatively* . . . none.

An instant later, as if on cue, the Chihuahua gave a yelp. He jumped up, sending the finger bowl tumbling – and the other men reaching for their weapons. Water and precious stones sloshed on to the table. Not only that. A tiny snail, with a mottled brown shell. It had been hidden in the rubble.

'Chen!' the Chihuahua spat.

The Dung Beetle, the Giraffe and the Stick Insect stood up, their faces red, handguns at the ready.

'Sit down,' Chen said. 'Please, *honoured guests*, sit down.'

'The snail!' the Chihuahua exclaimed. 'A snail – a –'

'Yes,' Chen said, and his thin lips twitched into a smile. 'It is *Conus geographicus*. Known colloquially as the cigarette snail. An unfortunate name. But one which has stuck.'

'The cigarette snail?' the Chihuahua said. *Why?'*

'Why?' Chen snorted. 'Because in the time it would take someone to smoke a cigarette, *you* will *die.'*

'You assured us we were safe!' the Dung Beetle said furiously. 'You told us—'

'What can I say?' Chen interrupted. 'I lied.'

The Chihuahua started to aim his gun.

Chen clicked his fingers, and thirty men erupted from behind the screens. They were expert in kung fu and armed – for good measure – with .45 closed-bolt, semi-automatic pistols. Chen's personal bodyguard.

'No one will shoot me,' Chen whispered hoarsely, his eyes glittering. 'Not if that man wants to live.'

Again, Chen clicked his fingers. One of his men dropped an MP3 player with a miniature speaker by Chen's plate. He picked it up. Pressed PLAY. A moment later, the Chihuahua's voice boomed out:

'Yes, yes, I am invited to dinner. He intends to talk. I intend to kill him. He will not make the Meeting of the Tigers, I assure you.'

Chen pressed STOP. 'So, it is not murder that I have committed. It is self defence. The only interesting question is, to whom were you speaking?'

The Chihuahua said nothing. The faces of the other guests grew redder.

Chen squeezed his eyes shut. He barked: 'Get them out!'

He heard scuffling. Shouting. Token attempts at defiance, as his men *escorted* his guests from the room.

The Chihuahua yelled: 'You will die for this, Chen!'

'We all die,' Chen replied. 'Some sooner than others.'

When the door banged closed, Chen opened his eyes.

He took a deep breath. And he sighed.

The evening had gone as planned.

And yet, somehow, he felt . . . unsatisfied.

Chen's weary gaze fixed on the delicate brown and white patterned shell of the snail, surrounded by diamonds and pearls. Its potent toxin would already be attacking the Chihuahua's muscles. His death was inevitable.

This species contained one of the deadliest agents known to man. And Chen knew them all. Every single one.

A moment later, a thought fireworked in his mind.

Later still, when Chen was back in his dark, ornate study, surrounded by the rest of his precious collection, that thought started to scratch at his brain.

He had to itch it. He had to!

There were risks, of course. But he was eighty-nine years old. Numerous people already wanted him dead. His own doctor had told him he was dying. Just how risky could life get?

And *if* it could work, *if* he could do it, his enemies would believe him to be a god, after all!

From a silk cushion on a chair beside him, a slender

yellow snake stirred. Striking brown spots formed a chain along her body. Her eyes flashed, and she lifted her arrow-shaped head. Around her jaws was a filigree golden muzzle, hand-made by a jeweller who had worked for the last emperor.

'Yes,' Chen whispered to her. 'Yes, my beauty. *Yes.*'

He turned to his computer and composed an email. Then he tapped in a password to access an encrypted file. It contained the top secret names and contact details of all eight members of the Viper Club.

Before he could change his mind, Chen copied every email address from that list into the *Bcc* box of his own mail.

Blood jolted in excited bursts through his decaying body.

Chen took a shallow, shaky breath. And hit *SEND*.

Old San Juan, Puerto Rico. 26 August. 13.10

A tall man with a taut face and slicked back hair sat in the corner of the bar, picking at chicken wings. A baseball game was showing on the TV. He did not understand the rules. In fact the game was of no interest to him at all. Yet he fixed his cold, steel-grey eyes on the screen.

This was a technique for maintaining his isolation, while he waited for his contact. The last thing he wanted was for a stranger to accost him. He detested small talk.

The man yawned. He needed rest. He was half-tempted

to check the time of the next flight to Azerbaijan, to Irkutsk – to *anywhere*. But this meeting could be useful. He glanced at his gold watch. *Five more minutes.*

He pulled his new smartphone from his pocket and selected *Email.*

A moment later, his inbox updated. There was one new message.

The man registered the name of the sender – and he stiffened. Quickly he opened it.

As his eyes scanned the text, they widened.

Was this *genuine*?

No! It couldn't be!

And yet . . . If it was . . .

The man racked his brain. After a few moments, he jumped up.

He left the bar and hurried around the nearest, darkest corner. His meeting was forgotten, no longer important. Still gripping his phone, he scrolled through his list of contacts until he found *Evangeline de Souza.*

In his mind, he saw her. She had auburn hair, rich skin, honey-coloured eyes. But her beauty wasn't the reason why he wanted her.

The man waited. After a few moments, he heard: 'Hello? Who is this?'

She had a soft accent. It betrayed her Brazilian roots.

'Eva, it's me.'

The man heard a sharp intake of breath.

'Listen,' he said, 'I have a proposal.'

'But –'

'I said *listen*. When I've finished, you can speak. So long as all you say is *yes*.'

Watson's Bay, Sydney, Australia. 6 September

'Are you ready?'

Gaia was crouching at the edge of the jetty. Her hands were cupped together. Bright sunshine made her brown eyes squint.

For the past few minutes, she and Will had been surveying the bay.

On the beach, a small girl dug in the golden sand with her dog. Behind her, tourists strolled along the esplanade, eating lobster and chips. In front of them, the sparkling green-blue water was dotted with moored boats.

Will had counted nineteen. Old sailing yachts, with tattered covers. Power cruisers. And fishing boats, their fixed lines bristling like antennae.

'Will?' Gaia said. *'Are you ready?'*

She'd raised her voice. At the end of the jetty, a group of men was gathered outside the Sydney Game Fishing Club. They were shouting to each other, lugging bream, holding a tournament.

One man yelled: 'Take a look at this, Shane! It's a beauty!'

A jet ski sped past, its engine roaring.

Will looked back at Gaia. Nodded. 'Make sure you do a full systems test.' He pulled his mouthpiece from a front pocket in the vest and bit down on it.

'Right,' she said. 'But if we get in trouble, you can do the talking.'

With his mouthpiece in, Will couldn't say a word. He shrugged helplessly. She smiled.

He turned to the water. It was clear, and deep. On the bottom, he could see rocks and weed, and a rusty bicycle wheel.

Gaia held her hands over the edge of the jetty. 'Three,' she said. 'Two. *One!*'

Will dived. Instantly, his muscles contracted. For a few moments, he flailed in the cold. He peered around, urging his retinas to adjust.

Where is it? he thought. *Where is it?*

Then he saw it, shimmering over the rusting wheel. A flash. A sliver of silver. It was fast.

Will kicked his fins. Took a deep breath. His lungs filled. *He had air.* The vest was working. But right now, the vest wasn't his focus of attention.

Will swivelled his head. The flash was streaking away from the beach, heading right for the shadowy hull of one of the yachts.

Will kicked. He sliced through the water, feeling his heart start to race.

At last, he reached the hull – and rounded it. Right into a shoal of tiny fish. They blasted apart and vanished.

Will glanced down. Made out only rocks and sand. His head jerked. He could hear a low rumbling. The jet ski, he guessed, further out in the bay.

Will panned his head.

Got it!

A quicksilver object was spiralling out of the depths, ten metres away. It started to arc through the water, then zipped back on itself. It moved effortlessly. And Will almost smiled to himself. He'd *made* this. It was his creation.

That morning, on the deck of the rented house, he had shown Andrew and Gaia.

It was robotic, remote-controlled and modelled on a salamander. Which meant it could run, crawl and swim. The artificial spine was based on the genuine article. Instead of flesh, it had a slim eight-centimetre long nickel-titanium body. This shape memory alloy could remember its geometry. If it was bent, upon release it would bounce back into its original shape.

Miniature artificial muscles, powered by methanol, could propel the robot to a maximum twenty kilometres per hour on land. Right now, it was swimming at half that speed, Will guessed.

Gaia was doing exactly as he'd asked: testing its underwater speed and manoeuvrability. His job was to follow – and to try to grab it.

Up ahead, the robot seemed to be slowing.

Will kicked hard.

Six metres.

Four.

Two metres.

The robot was maintaining a straight course, parallel to the beach.

Will stretched out his finger tips. *Almost there.*

Suddenly a beam of light flashed from the nose and the robot's alloy tail flicked. It darted away.

Will let his arm drop, relieved. The impact-avoidance system was working. It had *known* he was close. The torch flash had been for the benefit of the built-in camera. But the sonar alarm would also have been blinking away on Gaia's screen.

This sonar system was advanced, with multiple capabilities. But the bones had come from a helmet Will had invented six months ago. Miniature units in the robot's head and tail emitted pulses of sound. If those pulses hit something, they bounced back. The robot's on-board computer could use the returning signals to build up a picture of its environment.

Gaia had been letting him get close, Will decided. Playing with him. An image of her suddenly appeared in his mind. Crouching on the jetty. Her curly brown hair tied back. Goosebumps on her bare legs.

Focus, he told himself.

So far, Will thought, both the robot and the vest were performing well.

Back in England, Will had been allowed to sit in on a class run by the advanced diving consultant.

Anti-Frogman Techniques had been scrawled across a digital whiteboard.

The man was ex-SAS. His tone had been dry. First, he'd gone through everything that wouldn't work.

'Judo throws are unlikely to be successful, due to low gravity underwater. Water resistance would require a baton to be jabbed' – he demonstrated the movement with his hand – 'or thrust. Swinging would be ineffective.

'Rubber bullets, pepper balls, beanbag rounds – forget it. You've got two inches of penetration, at most. So now, we'll move on to the interesting stuff. And if it *sounds* good, that's because it is . . .'

Will kicked harder. He was swimming as fast as he could.

Ahead, the robot was steering a slalom course through the boats. It ducked under the crusted hull of an old sailing sloop and on, until it reached the biggest of them all. A thirty-seven-metre triple-decked yacht with a huge stainless steel propeller. The anchor chain dropped down – and vanished.

Fear suddenly sparked along Will's spine. He was way out in deep water.

It's all right, he told himself.

And he tensed. He could see something.

Dim shapes, just past the entrance to the bay. They were gliding slowly. According to his guidebook, at least fifteen species of shark had been spotted in the harbour, including the deadly bronze whaler and tiger sharks. But these weren't sharks.

They were small. Flat-bodied, with a forked tail and a jagged fin. They couldn't weigh much more than a couple of kilos. And they were familiar. Will had seen them before.

They were *bream*, he realized. The same fish the men had been weighing back at the jetty. Only some of these looked bigger.

Then, out of the corner of his eye, he saw something flash. The salamander started to veer away to the east.

Will followed, breathing hard. Again, he heard the rumbling. It started to get louder. Ahead now, he made out white turbulence. The jet ski.

No, he thought suddenly. *No*, surely Gaia wasn't going to do that. He *had* to talk to her.

Will kicked for the surface. Spat out the mouthpiece. Rocked in the waves. The jet ski was close. Like Gaia, he was wearing a toothphone. It was one of his earliest inventions.

'Gaia,' he hissed, and his voice was sent by radio waves to the tiny device slotted over her molar. 'Don't hit him!'

His own toothphone vibrated, transmitting her reply through his jawbone to his inner ear: 'Jet skis aren't allowed in the inner harbour, Will. I read that in your guidebook.'

'If you hit him, he could drown!'

'I won't hit him hard. I'll just *nudge* him.'

'No!'

'Then what?' She sounded exasperated. '*You* wanted a full systems test – what do you want me to do!'

He should have given her better instructions, he thought. He searched for an answer. Something struck him.

'There are bream out here.'

'*Bream?* You want me to kill a fish?' Gaia was vegetarian. She sounded indignant.

'No, just *nudge* it. Stun it. The lowest setting. And go for the biggest one you can find.'

'I don't even know what a bream looks like!'

'I'll show you!'

Will slipped the mouthpiece back in and ducked under the water. The robot shot to his side. It swam beside him, its silver tail flicking. Will headed back towards the yacht – and he found them. Six shadows. Barely moving.

Slowly Will reached in front of the robot's camera, and pointed.

A split second later, the salamander bolted. One of the fish jerked, and went limp. The others fled.

In his mind, Will heard the voice of the advanced diving consultant:

'High-power, low frequency sonar. Now we're in business. It can rupture a frogman's eardrums.' On the whiteboard was a diagram of the human ear. He crossed a red strike through it.

'Bloody SAS,' someone had murmured behind Will. 'Is he an idiot, or does he just think we are?'

'Even if the eardrums escape serious damage,' the instructor had continued, 'your target will be dizzy. He might panic. Best case scenario – for you – he drowns.'

That was *under* water. Sound didn't travel as well in air. But even in air, the salamander's highest weapons setting could disorientate a man for a few minutes. If he fell into water, he could drown. Yes, Will thought, he wanted a full systems test. But he didn't want to kill someone in the process!

He kicked hard. If Gaia had done exactly as he'd asked, the fish would be knocked out for no more than five minutes.

Will grabbed its yellow tail, and pulled it towards him.

Then he swerved, and headed right for the jetty.

In less than two minutes, he was there. Clasping his prize with one arm, Will snatched the gleaming salamander from the water and slipped it inside his vest. Then he reached for the wooden ladder. Awkwardly he started to climb it.

Gaia was crouching at the top. She was frowning. 'So long as I don't have to touch the fish, do you want some help?'

Will spat out his mouthpiece. 'You've been helpful enough this afternoon,' he said, his chest heaving.

Her eyes widened. 'I *have* been helpful.'

'Yeah,' he said, deadpan, 'that's what I said.'

He staggered on to the jetty. At the far end, the fisher-men had gathered around a digital weighing machine. A glistening fish lay on the metal tray. Beside the machine, a grey-haired man in shorts and a flapping shirt held a small brass trophy. A young man with bow legs stood beside him.

As Will started to hurry over, the man with the trophy coughed and announced: 'Well, fellas, we have a champion. Barry here has landed himself a brute of a bream. The official weight is one point seven kilos.'

The men started to clap.

'Hey!'

Their heads turned.

Will was walking fast towards them. 'What about this one? I just caught it. It's got to weigh more!'

The grey-haired man raised his eyebrows.

Will ran to the scales. Still dripping, he dropped his fish beside the one already on the tray. He checked the read-out. Three point eight kilos. So his weighed two point one. Will glanced back. Gaia was still back by the ladder, her arms folded, shaking her head.

The men didn't look impressed.

'Where'd you buy that one?' one of them shouted.

'Are you a member of the SGFC?' the bow-legged man asked. He had to be Barry, Will thought.

The other man raised a hand for silence. 'Maybe we should be asking: would you like to be a member of the SGFC?' He crouched down, touched the fish. It was obviously a fresh catch, its gills gently flicking, its beady eyes bright. 'This is a big fish, mate. Fair dinkum, you caught it yourself?'

Will wiped water from his face. He jerked his head towards Gaia. 'My friend helped.'

The man nodded and stood up. 'Well, I don't know fellas, what do you think?'

Whatever the fellas thought – and Will thought he could make a fair guess – was drowned out by a voice suddenly bursting through his toothphone.

'Will, Gaia!'

Will's gaze shot back, past Gaia, to the beach. To a whiteboard house, halfway along the esplanade. On the wooden deck, something glinted in the sun. The lenses of Andrew's binoculars, Will guessed.

'If you've finished showing off, can you come back to the house?' Andrew said. 'I think I've found him!'

Watson's Retreat was on the books of a rental agency that specialized in short-term executive lets.

It had white marble bathrooms, walk-in wardrobes and a brushed steel door that opened right on to the esplanade.

Through that door, a neat path wound through a lush sub-tropical garden to an open garage half-filled with jerry cans of marine diesel, an old inflatable rubber dinghy, wind surfers, four red kayaks and a wooden crate. At the back of the garage was a set of concrete steps that led up to the kitchen.

The house was unlike anything Will had ever seen before. In fact, the same was true for Sydney, full stop. It was so different from London. People laughed on the streets. Everyone seemed friendly. Even bus drivers told jokes. Perhaps it was small wonder, he thought, when the skies were blue, the water was clear, the sands shimmered and the local fish-and-chip shop sold *lobster*.

The house had been rented for Will, Gaia and Andrew by Shute Barrington. Until recently, Barrington had been head of the Science and Technology Arm of the Secret Intelligence Service, aka MI6. In July, he had been promoted to C, the agency's chief.

Will, Andrew and Gaia knew Barrington well. They'd met him the previous Christmas in St Petersburg, on the first official mission for STORM, their secret organization. Its aim was to use Science and Technology to Over-Rule Misery. At least, that had been Andrew's original plan.

Andrew was a software millionaire, and the computer expert. Gaia had a photographic memory. She was also brilliant at chemistry. Which so far had translated mostly into making explosives. Will invented things.

After a successful mission to Switzerland in July, Barrington had offered them a reward.

Six weeks later, in his new, modern office, with a postcard view of Tower Bridge, he repeated the offer. 'How about that holiday I mentioned? *With a twist.*'

'What twist?' Gaia asked, shuffling.

Barrington tapped a pen against his desk. There was no point beating about the bush. And it wasn't his style. 'There are rumours Sir James Parramore has fled to Sydney.'

'*Really?*' Andrew asked.

'Hmm. Has the meaning of the word *rumour* been revised without my knowledge?' Barrington chucked the pen back into its pot.

'I meant –' Andrew started.

'Relax, I know what you meant. The intel seems reasonably sound. But then so do some of the other tip-offs. What can I say? At the risk of sounding like a TV cop, *we have to follow every lead*. Now, how much do you know about Parramore? How can I fill you in?'

In fact, after St Petersburg, STORM had learned quite a bit about him. Parramore was a British billionaire businessman, the owner of a string of shadowy multi-national corporations involved in oil, satellites and weapons development. The weapons arm had started out developing nerve agents. Recently the projects had become a lot more experimental, dangerous – and illegal.

Parramore had been identified as the source of the funds for a potentially catastrophic weapon being developed in Russia. STORM had thwarted the plans to test the weapon but Parramore had evaded arrest. Then, in July, it had emerged that he'd been paying the corrupt, previous C handsomely in return for his freedom.

Parramore's assets had finally been seized – but he had vanished.

'We know about the weapons work,' Will said. 'And we know that even after C was arrested, no one could find him.'

Barrington nodded. 'Various bits of intelligence suggest he flew to Sydney. For the past six weeks, ten of our agents have been working with the Australian Federal Police to conduct a manhunt. They've identified several possible Parramores, but none has checked out. Now we've had new reported sightings in Buenos Aires,

Istanbul, even Cardiff. So I'm re-deploying eight of the agents to follow up the other leads. But Matt Walker and Ben Marshall will stay in Australia. Do you three want to join them?

'You could have your own place,' Barrington continued. 'I'd ask a member of our embassy staff to drop by each morning. Greet them warmly, assure them you're *bonza*, and that would be the extent of your obligations. The rest of your time would be, well, *yours*.

'Sydney has some excellent restaurants,' Barrington told Andrew, knowing it would tempt him. 'The best seafood you'll ever eat. As well as some surprisingly decent meat pies.'

'*Pies?*' Andrew had said, smiling. 'Well, obviously that clinches it.'

Gaia had been unsure. Will had said nothing. Only Andrew had been pleased at the prospect.

'Imagine,' Andrew had said to Will. 'What if we did actually find him? And while you're waiting, it would take your mind off things . . .'

While he was waiting . . .

On the narrow white sofa, Will had shaken his head. 'No. I can't leave London now. Not even for Parramore.'

That evening, Andrew had phoned Gaia at her flat in Charlotte Street. Will needed to get away, Andrew told her. It wasn't doing him any good, hanging around in London.

Waiting.

In July, Will had finally met David Allott, the MI6 field officer who'd claimed to have information about Will's father's death. Jonathan Knight had also been a field officer. He'd been killed nearly a year ago, while on active duty in eastern China.

But the meeting with Allott had only thrown up new questions. Barrington told him there had been a full inquiry after his father's death. Those questions had been asked at the time – and gone unanswered. He'd see if there was anything else he could do. But Will shouldn't expect immediate results.

Andrew had home tutors. Will and Gaia were enrolled in a special unit at school. For these students, September was Research Month, when they were supposed to work independently on their own projects. There was nothing to keep them in England, Andrew had argued on the phone.

'For his sake,' Andrew had said. 'Try to persuade Will to go. He'll listen to you.'

'*All right.*'

And so, here they were, at Watson's Retreat.

Matt Walker and Ben Marshall, the two MI6 field officers, were somewhere way out west, chasing a tip-off. Gaia, Will and Andrew were free to follow their noses in Sydney.

For the past three days – practically since the moment they'd touched down at the airport – Andrew had been obsessively on the look-out for men who might be Sir James Parramore.

Now, he thought he'd found him.

Gaia slipped through the gleaming kitchen, heading for the deck.

'Tell Andrew to wait for me,' Will called after her, and detoured into his bedroom. It was also painted white, with bright prints of yacht races on the walls.

He dropped the salamander back into his compact black rucksack. Then he slipped the two toothphones into their box, took off the vest and folded it carefully.

Will had shown the vest to Gaia and Andrew that morning, along with the robot.

Seawater flowed through valves into a network of tiny tubes. Then the pressure in the tubes was lowered until the dissolved air became a gas once more. That air was pumped directly to Will's mouthpiece.

The system was battery-powered. So long as you had enough batteries, it could work forever.

'Artificial gills!' Andrew had exclaimed, his blue eyes wide with amazement.

Will had nodded. With the vest, he could breathe like a fish. If only he could swim like one, he thought. The trip round the bay had been the most exercise he'd done in weeks. His body was aching.

Will pulled off his T-shirt and shorts and dried himself with a beach towel. As he walked into his wardrobe, he caught a glimpse of himself in the mirror fixed to the wall.

His brown hair, cut short, had bleached a little in the sun of Switzerland, and now Sydney. His face, neck and forearms were tanned. He was still thin. But the muscles in his arms and his legs were stronger than they had been a year ago. His face wasn't as gaunt. His mother's Russian cheekbones were less pronounced.

Will turned away from his reflection. He pulled on a pair of jeans and a clean T-shirt. And he strode out, through the living room, on to the deck.

Andrew and Gaia were sitting at a wooden table, under a large canvas sun umbrella. Behind them, the bay and sky stretched, in two-tone blue.

On the table, Will noticed, was a pot of coffee, three cups and a newspaper.

'Here comes the great fisherman!' Andrew exclaimed, his bright blue eyes smiling behind his frameless glasses.

Andrew was smaller than Will, and thinner. Like Gaia, he was wearing shorts. Flowered boardshorts, Will realized. And a yellow T-shirt with a black embossed outline of a surfer. The clothes didn't sit easily with Andrew's heavy gold watch and neat haircut. Andrew had gone out alone that morning. He must have been shopping, Will thought.

'I heard you returned your catch,' Andrew said, as Will pulled out a chair.

'Yeah.'

'Shame.' He tapped the newspaper. 'I've just seen what looks like a very good recipe for harissa barbecued fish.'

Will raised an eyebrow. 'So, apart from new recipes, what have you got?'

Andrew reached for the pot. 'Would you like some coffee?'

There had been a curious note in his voice. Will glanced at Gaia. Who shrugged slightly. He understood what the shrug meant. *This is Andrew. Humour him.*

'All right,' Will said. 'Thanks.'

As Andrew started to fill the cups, he smiled conspiratorially at Gaia. 'I read a very interesting paper in the *European Journal of Social Psychology* last week. It concluded that caffeine makes people more open to persuasion.'

Will smiled faintly. 'So you think it's going to make us go along with your latest James Parramore?' he asked. But he took the proffered cup.

Andrew held up his hands defensively. 'Just hear me out. Both of you. That's all I ask.

'If you remember from Barrington's file, one of Parramore's bank accounts was accessed from Bali early on the morning of 28 August, then again near Bondi Beach here in Sydney later that day. I thought perhaps I should trawl through news archives from around that time, on the off-chance I'd find something interesting.'

'Britain's Most Wanted Man Spotted Surfing?' Gaia said.

Andrew adjusted his glasses. 'Gaia, you can mock,' he said, 'but I did find something. The online story didn't have the photo – but I found the original in the re-cycling bin in the garage.' He picked up the paper and flopped it open on the table. 'Here it is. This is from the 29th of August.'

Will took the paper and angled it so Gaia could also see.

At the top of the page, in large black type, were the words: *Sydney Sauce!*

Below were six short articles, accompanied mostly by shots of glamorous women and tanned, smug-looking men in suits. A diary page.

Half way down, Will noticed a picture of a woman with spiky hair, bright red lipstick and what looked like a studded collar around her neck.

Mayor's fashion sense goes to the dogs! ran the strap line.

Andrew pointed to the story below. 'It's this one.'

Secretive Scientist Reveals All!

Underneath was a photograph of a woman with dusky skin, auburn hair and amber eyes. A low-cut red dress clung to her body. Next to her, a black-haired man was raising his fist. Angry at the paparazzo, Will guessed. The man had fleshy lips and cold, silver-grey eyes. A white mansion was blurry in the background.

Will and Gaia read:

Stunning psychologist Evangeline de Souza has been snapped in the company of a new man. Frederick Broadstairs is an English associate who flew into Sydney yesterday, according to a spokeswoman for Phoenix House.

'Mr Broadstairs is an old friend of Ms de Souza,' the spokeswoman said. 'He's been holidaying in Indonesia and will be staying at Phoenix House for the next few weeks.'

De Souza, 34, who trained in psychology and biochemistry in Rio de Janeiro, is the proprietor of the exclusive psychological retreat, located in Sydney's east. According to the Phoenix House website, her specialities include 'life-coaching, guided meditation and relaxation/stimulation therapy for the body and mind'.

De Souza is famously reluctant to reveal any further detail of her techniques. Her clients are just as tight-lipped. But whatever she's doing, she's doing it right.

Actors, television presenters and even athletes have been booking in for her 'mind/body refreshment programme'.

Last month, former Olympic long-jump gold-medallist, Sheila Barlow, made a spectacular return to form after months of poor performances. Barlow credited her six-week stay at Phoenix House for the turnaround.

'I went in exhausted – and came out restored in every way,' Barlow commented.

Sydney Sauce can only hope de Souza will work her magic on Mr Broadstairs. Hasn't anyone told him the pale, angry look went out years ago?

The article finished.

Gaia looked up at Andrew. She couldn't help feeling a little disappointed. The link with Indonesia and Sydney seemed pretty tenuous. Then there was the photo. 'Obviously Parramore could have had plastic surgery,' she said, 'but this man looks nothing like him.'

Will had to agree. Back in London, Barrington had dug out an MI6 archive shot of Parramore. He was tall and slim, and grey-eyed. So far, so good. It was a black-and-white picture, so it was hard to be sure about the eye colour, but Frederick Broadstairs seemed to fit that bill. Parramore, though, had a long nose, a square jaw and a puckered mouth. The newspaper shot showed plump lips and a dimpled chin. The two faces were very different.

'I have to agree with Gaia,' Will said at last.

Andrew didn't look put out. From the pocket of his shorts he pulled two folded sheets of A4 paper. 'Plastic surgery can change a face hugely, you both know that. But,' and he lowered his voice, 'it can only do so much.

And appearances can be deceptive. Now look.'

Andrew pushed the coffee pot out of the way. He laid flat a printout they all recognized. The MI6 archive photograph of Parramore. The other sheet of paper, which Andrew held out to Will, was covered with neat lines of numbers.

Gaia's gaze flicked between the MI6 picture, the newspaper photo, and Andrew's handwriting. 'What do your numbers mean?'

'Well, as I said, plastic surgery can only do so much. It can change the size and shape of your nose or your mouth, even your cheeks. But it can't alter things like the distance between your eyes, or the ratio of the width of the eyes to the width of the skull. Here –' Andrew tapped the sheet of numbers – 'I've compared some of the key ratios from the two pictures. And guess what?'

From Andrew's tone, it was clear he was building up to a triumphant conclusion.

'They match,' Will said.

'Yes. *All of them.*'

Will's pulse started to race. Had Andrew actually done it? Had he found Parramore? *Wait*, he told himself. *Think.*

'Just because the ratios match, that doesn't prove it's the same person,' Gaia said.

She was right, Will thought.

'No,' Andrew agreed. He pushed his glasses back along his nose. 'But it makes it a real possibility. And this Broadstairs *is* English, and he arrived in Sydney from Indonesia on the same day as Parramore – or the same day someone accessed one of his accounts.

'While you were out, I Googled Frederick Broadstairs and I came up with *nothing*, apart from this article. Then I tried to hack into the Phoenix House network, and I got nowhere – the firewall is state-of-the-art.' Andrew sighed. 'I know the story only says Indonesia, not Bali, specifically. And Bali isn't far from Australia. Presumably lots of British men make the trip between the two. I'm not saying it's conclusive. But it's *something*. The MI6 bank records put Parramore in Sydney. And the face ratios fit. *What if this is him?*'

Andrew really believed what he was saying, Will could see it. From Gaia's expression, he knew she could see it too.

In fact, this was the third man Andrew had identified as a potential Parramore. The first, a pony-tailed chef in a restaurant they'd visited on their first night, had turned out to be a well-known face in Sydney. The second had been on the beach at Watson's Bay. He had borne a physical resemblance to Parramore. But he'd acted and sounded like a German tourist.

'Remember Ockham's Razor,' Will had said to Andrew. The rule held that the simplest explanation was usually the right one. 'The man's a German tourist,' Will had concluded.

So the first two potential Parramores hadn't seemed particularly promising, and they'd quickly been eliminated. But Broadstairs was at least worth checking out, Will decided.

He swilled the remains of his coffee around his cup. Had the caffeine worked as Andrew had intended?

'So, where is Phoenix House?' he asked.

Andrew grinned. From another pocket of his board-shorts, he produced a map of Sydney and spread it on the table.

'This is Watson's Bay – here. If you follow the coast towards the Opera House, Phoenix House is *here*. It isn't far. Not if we go by water . . . There are some rather interesting items in our garage. I thought we could try our hand at kayaking.'

Will looked surprised. 'Have you ever done it?'

'Well, no. Have you?'

'Once, on a school trip to Cornwall, last year. Gaia?'

She frowned. 'I went on the same school trip, *remember*?'

Will coloured, embarrassed. Had she? 'I didn't really know you then.'

'*No*,' she said. 'Apparently you didn't notice me, either.'

'Gaia –' he started.

'It's all right.' She picked up the map and pretended to study it.

Andrew searched for a diversion. How could Will not remember a thing like that? 'Do you think we should tell Walker and Marshall?' he asked.

'Tell them what?' Will said. 'If we find anything solid,

we'll tell them then.' He got up. He still felt bad about Gaia. Especially as . . . Well, he noticed her now. She knew he did. And back then, he'd talked to no one, been interested in no one. She'd changed that. Her and Andrew. He headed for the door. 'I'll meet you in the garage.'

'Where are you going?' Andrew asked.

'To get my kit.' Will stopped. Glanced back. 'Gaia – I'

'It's all right,' she said. Her brown eyes flashed. *'Really.'*

Andrew watched them. He wasn't quite sure what was passing between them, but Gaia didn't look so hurt any more, which was good news. Even better, he couldn't help thinking – and felt bad about it – was the news that Will was getting his kit.

So far, Will had shown them only the vest and the salamander. But the black rucksack, which had been delivered by Marjorie Blaxted, their curt embassy contact, the morning they'd arrived in Sydney, had come with a note from Barrington:

Will, am sending contents of your STASIS locker by diplomatic bag, in case they prove useful. Inconceivably, it seems you and STASIS are functioning adequately in my absence. Have borrowed one of the little seeds. SB. (PS. Looked into sending your rat, but Australian quarantine rules are strict. Can bend them, but can't entirely break them. Sorry.)

3

Matt Walker ran a hand across his sweaty face. Spread over the rickety termite-holed desk were two bulging blue folders and a dozen photographs.

The photographs were all of the same man. Jonathan Simpkin. He had to be Parramore, Walker thought. He just *had* to be. Certainly, he was their best contender yet.

The room was stifling. Walker went to the window and hoisted it open. Smoke and noise drifted in. On a patch of scrubby earth in front of the pub, a local band had drawn a motley crowd. Walker watched men in check shirts and riding boots queue up at a barbecue for what a hand-painted sign advertised as a *Sausage Sizzle*.

He turned. Ben Marshall had just walked into the room. His pale eyes were serious, his blond hair ruffled. He was waving his mobile phone.

'I've got a confirmed sighting on Simpkin. A place called Coober Pedy. A local cop called it in.'

'Where's Coober Pedy?'

'North somewhere. Middle of nowhere. It's an opal

mining town. People go there to disappear. Or so the cop says.'

Walker headed back to the desk. He leafed through the top folder, and shook out a map of Australia. After a few minutes they had it. It was about 685 kilometres south of Alice Springs, and 845 kilometres north of Adelaide.

'It's the middle of nowhere, all right,' Walker said. 'If you were James Parramore, would you head there?'

'Bottom of an opal mine would feel a whole lot safer than Sydney,' Marshall said.

'Yeah.'

Outside, the band's amp kicked up a notch. A shaky version of a 1980s Bruce Springsteen hit filled the outback air.

'You ready to go now?' Walker asked.

'You mean you don't want to stay for the rest of the set?' Marshall sniffed. The scent of burning sausages was wafting in through the window. 'Or a sausage?'

Walker smiled. But he realized he was hungry. And the trip would take seven hours, at least. He swept an arm across the desk, shoving the Parramore documents into his bag. He zipped it shut. 'Last one to the car buys the sausages.'

'Ugh!' Andrew jumped back. 'I just put my hand through a cobweb!'

'Any spiders?' Gaia asked.

The kayaks were strapped to aluminium racks. They were red moulded-plastic single seaters, three metres long, with large, open cockpits and double-ended paddles. Gaia was kneeling on the ground, undoing metal clasps. Andrew had been releasing the one beside her. Will's was already in the garden. He was out there now, bending over it, fiddling with the mooring rope.

Andrew replied at last: 'Not that I can see.'

'Then you're all right.' She paused. 'Unless of course you were bitten by the Australian garage spider.'

Andrew blinked at her. 'I've never heard of the Australian garage spider.'

She looked at him. 'They're tiny. Practically invisible. No one ever feels the bite. But the venom's slow acting.' She lowered her voice. 'After an hour, your cells start to swell. In minutes, you're literally three times your normal size. After two hours, you *burst*.'

Realization struck. '*Gaia!*'

She smiled.

Australia *was* full of dangerous animals – at least according to Will's guidebook, which Andrew had read on the plane. For a few moments, he'd actually believed her. Also, he thought, in his defence, it was unlike Gaia to be so light-hearted.

But her father, who had been very ill, was surprising the doctors. They were even talking about 'remission'. And, she and Will . . . well, despite Will's slip earlier, it was obvious how they felt about each other. Even if they seemed somehow reluctant to actually do anything about it. In general, he thought, Gaia did seem much happier.

Sighing now, Andrew undid the straps of his kayak and gently lowered it to the ground. He felt in his pocket for his zinc cream. It was thick and white, and promised total protection from the sun. Andrew daubed thick lines along his nose and cheeks.

'Gaia?' He offered her the tube.

Her smile became a grin. 'You look like one of those tribal psychiatrists in your dad's albums.'

Andrew opened his mouth to protest – and looked round.

Will had just walked back into the garage, his rucksack on his back. He headed past the cans of diesel, to the far corner, to the wooden crate.

That first morning, the embassy official had told them they were free to use any of the equipment in the house or the garage, except the contents of that crate. It was the personal property of the owner of Watson's Retreat. He was storing it here while he sailed around Antigua.

'You're not thinking of borrowing it?' Andrew asked. 'Though it might provide a useful view of Phoenix House . . .'

'Yeah,' Will said, 'it would.' And he had been contemplating it. 'But there is another way.'

Andrew's eyes shot to Will's rucksack. Will smiled. 'Let's get the kayaks to the beach, and I'll show you.'

Will went back outside and grabbed the nylon rope

secured to the nose of his kayak. Andrew and Gaia followed.

Will checked his watch. It was ten to five. The bay was quieter now. The fish-and-chip kiosk looked closed, and the tables outside the restaurant at the end of the esplanade were empty.

He looked up. Andrew and Gaia were watching him expectantly. He jumped back up on to the esplanade and slipped the rucksack from his back. 'So you already know about the vest and the salamander.'

'You didn't tell us their names,' Andrew said, as he and Gaia followed him.

It was a tradition of Will's to name his inventions only after they'd been successfully tested. 'The vest is Breathe Easy. The robot is . . .' He paused, thinking.

'How about Sam?' Andrew asked.

'*Sam?*' Gaia said.

'Well, it sounds a bit like a shortened form of sala-mander. Don't you think? Will?'

Will hesitated. He'd allowed Andrew to christen one device after Venice – the original sonar helmet – and Andrew had chosen his own name. With that as a prece-dent, 'Sam' was a significant improvement. And a better option hadn't occurred to him. He was about to agree, when he noticed a hint of a smile on Andrew's face. In fact, he thought, Sam was a surprisingly simplistic choice for Andrew, who went in for puns and acronyms.

'Andrew –' he started.

Andrew held up his hands. 'All right, I confess, my middle name is Sam. Samuel, actually.'

'*Samuel?*' Gaia said.

'After a great, great-uncle who ran away to America and found gold.' He looked at Will. 'But it is also sort of a shortened version of salamander. Or it could stand for Salamander Action Machine. Or maybe—'

'All right!' Will interrupted shaking his head. '*Sam.*'

Andrew beamed.

Will dug into the side pocket of his rucksack. He glanced around. There was no one else on this stretch of the esplanade. Only a couple of tourists sitting on a wooden bench beyond the kiosk, gazing at the water. He brought out a small plastic box. 'I call these Spy Seeds,' he said.

These had to be the *seeds* Barrington had mentioned, Andrew realized. He and Gaia edged closer, for a better look.

Inside the box were ten blue objects, about five centimetres long. Apart from their colour, they looked like sycamore seeds, with a small spherical pod attached to a single wing.

'What *are* they?' Gaia asked.

Carefully Will pinched a wing, and took one out. He handed the box to Gaia. 'There's a screen built inside the lid. Watch it.'

Will set the seed on the ground. Then he reached over Gaia's shoulder and hit the touch-screen. A set of icons appeared at the top. Will tapped one marked FIRE. Instantly, the seed shot upward.

Andrew and Gaia stared, following it until it merged with the sky and vanished.

'What just happened?' Andrew asked.

'There's a tiny rocket thruster in the tip of the wing,' Will said. 'It sends it spinning up at about ten metres a second, to a height of one kilometre.'

Andrew's eyes widened. 'Then what?'

'Once the fuel burns up, that's it. Everything that goes up must come down . . . Watch the screen.'

Gaia and Andrew focused on the display. It was showing a blur of mostly blues. But after a few moments, an image began to form. Gaia saw flashes of green. *Trees*, she guessed. And dark inlets. 'It's the harbour.'

Will nodded. 'There's a camera in the pod. It streams wide-angle footage as the seed falls. The wing makes it spiral. It slows its descent.'

Gaia made out North and South Head, the two jutting outcrops of land that formed the entrance to Sydney harbour. Then the tiny island of Fort Denison, and gleaming cross-shaped objects dotted in the water. The seaplanes moored at Rose Bay, she realized.

As the seed fell still further, the camera picked out their wooden jetty, and the Sydney Game Fishing Club. The corrugated iron roof of the restaurant, painted in white and blue stripes. Seagulls, foraging in rubbish bins.

Then the ocean rushed. As the seed hit water, the screen went black.

'Rocket-powered Spy Seeds!' Andrew said excitedly. 'How did you think them up?' He held up a hand. 'Don't tell me, it was a Newton moment. Like when the infamous apple fell on his head. Only while you were lying under a sycamore tree a seed twirled down –'

'It wasn't quite like that,' Will said.

He didn't seem keen to elaborate. But Will could often be cagey about his devices, Andrew thought. He still wasn't sure whether this was down to a natural inclination in Will to modesty – or grumpiness.

'Well, they're amazing,' Andrew said warmly.

'They're useful for a quick blast of aerial reconnaissance,' Will acknowledged. He hesitated. 'But if you want amazing, I've got another device to show you.'

Andrew glanced at Gaia. 'If Will says this is amazing, it has to be pretty special.'

Will put the box back in his rucksack. After a moment, he produced another. 'These are just the toothphones,' he said. 'But I have made a modification.'

'What modification?' Gaia asked. 'You didn't tell me earlier.'

'There wasn't any point.' Will lifted out the tray of four toothphones. Underneath were what looked like electronic car key fobs with five small buttons on the front. One red, one blue, one green, one yellow and one black.

'Now they can transmit on different radio frequencies,' Will said. 'It means more than two people can use them without hearing everyone else talking all the time. You press a button to decide who you want to talk to.' He handed out the toothphones and key fobs. 'Gaia, you're red. Andrew, you're blue. I'm green. If you press black, everyone wearing one of these four units hears.'

'Very clever,' Andrew said, as he slipped his in. 'It gets so annoying listening to Gaia gabble on all the time when I'm right in the middle of an important mission.'

She pulled a face. She was, they all knew, the least talkative of the three. He smiled at her. 'But that isn't the amazing bit?' he asked cautiously. He'd been expecting something more.

Will shook his head. 'I've got one last thing to show you.'

He pushed the toothphone box back in his rucksack. Then he dug around and pulled out a red plastic canister. It unscrewed in the middle. Clipped inside the bottom half were three small flip-lid display screens. Will removed one. Then he opened up the top section, and withdrew a small vial, filled with liquid. He turned his back to Andrew and Gaia.

'Aren't we allowed to see what you're doing?' Andrew asked.

'Wait,' Will said.

A moment later, he was ready. He handed the screen to Gaia. 'When I tell you to, turn it on.' He began to stride off along the esplanade.

'Where are you going?' she called.

'You'll see,' he said. And he smiled to himself.

After a few moments, he stopped. He faced the beach. 'Turn it on.'

Gaia did so. And a grainy, low-resolution image of the beach appeared on the screen. Slowly it shifted to show the esplanade, and then her – and Andrew. Gaia looked round. Will was watching them.

'Well, obviously, you've got a camera attached to you,' Andrew said. 'The image quality isn't the best.' He bit his lip. He hadn't meant to sound so unimpressed. But was this really the amazing device?

Will walked right back to them. 'All right,' he said. 'Where is it?'

'It could be anywhere,' Gaia said, as she handed him the screen. 'Attached to your T-shirt?'

Will held his arms at right angles to his body. 'Go ahead, see if you can find it.'

Andrew bent his head close to Gaia's. 'Go on. Will's asking us to frisk him. Now's your chance.'

She shot him a black look. Perhaps he'd over-estimated her newfound light-heartedness, he thought.

Andrew went to Will. Methodically he started to inspect Will's clothing, from the neckline of his T-shirt right down to his trainers. At last, he stepped back. 'I give up.'

'Look closer,' Will said.

'I have,' Andrew said. He adjusted his glasses, and blinked at him. 'I can't see anything.'

'If you use this, you can see *exactly* what I see,' Will said. He held up the screen.

What was he talking about? Andrew thought. Suddenly he grabbed Will's shoulders and scoured his face. 'You don't mean . . . but I can't see it. I can't see anything!'

Will smiled. He'd left the canister on the ground beside his rucksack. Gently he pushed Andrew's hands away and crossed to it. He pulled out another vial. Held it up. A translucent disc-shaped object floated in the liquid.

'Contact lenses!' Andrew exclaimed.

'Yeah – and look,' Will said. Just off the centre of the lens was a dark fleck, slightly bigger than a grain of sand. Will pointed to it. 'That is actually a digital camera. When you're wearing the lens, it just looks like a mark in your iris. The resolution isn't great. But this is the smallest camera anyone has ever made. I call it Second Sight.'

'You made it?' Gaia asked softly.

'With some help from Thor at STASIS. I came up with the spec. Thor helped me build it.'

'Well, I agree,' Andrew said. 'It is amazing.' He smiled.

'Do we each get one?' Gaia asked.

Will nodded. 'I've got three waterproof displays. You can set them to show one other person's camera feed, or you can split the screen, so you can see everyone's.'

He crouched and started to remove the other screens and the vials from the canister.

Will handed out the lenses and screens. Andrew slipped in his lens, and blinked until it settled. He focused on the screen. Checked Gaia's feed. She was watching Will. No huge surprise there. Then he flicked to Will's. And he saw sand – and a kayak. The kayak got bigger. He looked up. Will had just jumped down on to the beach, Gaia behind. Andrew turned off his screen and slipped it into one of his zip pockets.

He hurried after them. 'So who's going to teach me how exactly to do this?'

'There's an old saying,' Gaia said, as she picked up her paddle. 'You might know it. *Sink or swim.*'

'I didn't realize kayaking involved swimming.' Andrew smiled at her. 'Please, Gaia. I need your help.'

She shook her head, in mock despair. But she went over to him. 'How do you think it works? You use the paddle.'

'It's got two ends.'

She took it from him. 'It's not like rowing. You hold the shaft in the middle, like this. You dip in one blade and pull it, then you twist the shaft with your wrists, so the opposite blade's at right angles to the water. Then you dip that end in.' She traced the movements in the air.

'That's all there is to it?'

A splash made Gaia look round. Will had just dragged his kayak into the water. He jumped in.

'Watch Will,' she said. She went to grab her mooring rope.

Beyond her, the harbour stretched. Andrew blinked at the blue expanse, and then back at his kayak. Yes, he'd said he wanted to try it. But mostly because he'd thought it would help to encourage Will and Gaia to investigate Broadstairs. Now, he was faced with all that water, and the creatures that inhabited it.

'If you don't hurry up, we might get Parramore without you,' Gaia called to Andrew. '*Come on.*'

Evangeline de Souza slipped on a pair of sunglasses and hurried outside. She'd been down in the labs for four straight hours, and she needed a break.

She strode past a marble statue of a dog, and around to the east lawns. From here, she had a view down the hill to the private jetty and beyond, to the sparkling harbour.

Ten minutes ago, Frederick Broadstairs had come to check on their progress. They were close now, she was sure of it. The latest results were due – she glanced at her watch – within the next half an hour. And then? Well, there was the night's business to conclude. And *then* they should be ready.

Broadstairs.

He hadn't so much asked for her help as demanded it, she reflected.

It had come out of the blue. And she had been unable

to refuse. He had such charisma. Such brains. Such unpredictability. Such *brilliance*. Also, he had promised that after this was over, he would take her away with him.

She would appoint a manager for Phoenix House, and they would sail together into one of those perfect Sydney sunsets. Though, technically, the sun didn't actually set over the water. And perhaps they should fly. There was a private jet she'd had her eye on for some time.

'Eva!'

Annoyed at the interruption, she turned.

It was Tench. He was an ape of a man, all thick red hair and bulging muscles. When it came to brains, he wasn't well endowed. But he had his uses. And he was besotted with – he was *addicted* – to her. Like Hutt. Tench and Hutt. Her two faithful servants. What would become of them, when all this was over?

Who cares, she thought.

Tench hurried towards her. His blotchy pink face was wet with sweat. De Souza did her best to hide her disgust. For the moment, she still needed him.

'Eva!' He staggered to a halt. 'The latest results are in.'

Her honey eyes widened. She started to reach into her pocket for her phone. 'Why hasn't the lab called me? Why have they sent you?'

'I was down there, Eva. I thought maybe I should find Mr Broadstairs –'

'Never mind,' she snapped. And took a deep breath. In a gentler voice, she asked: 'Tench, what are the results?'

'An improvement. Of seventy-eight per cent.'

Her excitement vanished. 'Seventy-eight per cent! You think Mr Broadstairs will be pleased with *seventy-eight per cent*!'

Tench looked alarmed.

De Souza exhaled hard. She turned to head back to the house. As she did so, her gaze swept the harbour. She briefly registered a yellow ferry, gliding towards the northern beach of Manly. A yacht, its sail juddering.

And three kayaks, jack-knifing over a wall of wash.

'Gaia! Will! What do I do?'

Gaia yelled over her shoulder: 'Point your nose right at it! Go head on into it, Andrew!'

A double-decker ferry had just thundered past them, creating a huge wave. Now that wall of water was coming right at them. Gaia knew what to do, in theory. Go at a wave side on, and you'd be rolled. To have any chance of staying upright, you had to aim right at it.

But theory was one thing. In Cornwall the waves had been much smaller. In fact, the word *wave* had been an exaggeration. There was no exaggerating this. It was two metres high, at least. And it was about to hit them.

'Gaia!'

'You'll be all right!' Will called. 'What's the worst that'll happen? You can swim!'

His heart racing, Andrew wedged the paddle across his chest, under his arms, and clutched the sides of the cockpit. Suddenly he felt himself thrown back. Saw sky. His stomach lurched. He was going back too far!

Then he was thrust forward as the kayak breached the wave and slid down the other side. It bounced.

Spray drenched him. But he still had the paddle. And he hadn't gone under.

Ahead, Will was already pulling himself closer to the shore.

Gaia called, 'Andrew – are you all right?'

Andrew's glasses were blurry with water. He took them off. Blinked. 'I think so.'

She smiled. 'See – it's fun.'

Andrew didn't reply. He wiped his glasses, replaced them, and took a deep breath. Maybe she was right.

They were out in Sydney harbour. Around them, the water was so dazzling he could hardly open his eyes. He saw holiday-brochure beaches, and mansions along the coast, with glass-fronted swimming pools. And ahead, not far now, was Phoenix House.

Andrew dipped his paddle in. And out. Twist. In, and out. As Gaia had shown him. He soon settled back into a rhythm.

They were moving quickly. Rose Bay, broad and beautiful, was behind them, and they'd just passed another beach, backed by a park. Ahead, a small head-land jutted into the harbour.

Will raised his paddle. He bobbed in the water, waiting for Gaia and Andrew to catch up. 'Is it just after this headland, or the next one?' he called.

'This one,' Andrew said. He wiped his forehead on his shoulder. His kayak gently butted Will's. Gaia drifted to his left.

'So when we get there, what exactly are we going to do?' Gaia asked.

'Let's get a bit closer, see what we can see and then decide,' Will said.

Before she could say anything else, he dipped his blade back into the water.

Gaia and Andrew followed. They hugged the rocky shore. The trees were becoming denser. Ferns and palms jostled for space.

As they rounded the headland, the tops of four white towers came into view.

'That has to be it,' Andrew said.

The Google photo had shown a towering white mansion, surrounded by emerald lawns, on top of a lofty hill. But, Andrew realized now, the hill was only a low rise, just above sea level. Beyond the house, the ground sloped on up to what he guessed was a road.

That road wasn't the only access route to the house. Jutting out into the water was a small wooden jetty. A white speedboat with a 200-horsepower engine was tied to it. To the left was a tiny U-shaped beach, almost covered with tough-looking vines.

Will dug his paddle into the water to slow him down, and drifted into the shadows of the trees. Phoenix House disappeared behind their branches.

'We could drag the kayaks up the beach and go in on foot,' he said quietly.

'Into the wood – or into the house?' Gaia asked. She sounded wary.

Which was understandable, Andrew thought. But they had to try to at least locate Broadstairs.

'The trees first,' Will said. 'Then we'll see if there's a way in.'

'And if there is?' Gaia said. They should have decided on a plan before they left Watson's Retreat, she thought. Andrew had got them carried away. 'If we actually get in and find Broadstairs, then what will we do? Ask him nicely if he's Parramore?'

'I might be able to come up with something more subtle,' Will said.

In fact, he had an idea. It wasn't elegant. It wasn't even subtle. But it could be their best shot at finding out if Broadstairs really was Parramore.

'We've got Spy Seeds and Sam,' Will said. 'Sam's mouth was designed to retrieve, but it can also bite. It can cut through soft things.'

'What exactly are you thinking of cutting?' Andrew asked, one eyebrow raised.

'If we can find a hair or something, great, we can get it tested for DNA. But if we can't find anything like that, and we do actually find Broadstairs, *we* could stay well back and use Sam to cut ourselves a sample.'

Gaia looked incredulous. 'What sort of sample?'

'Whatever you like. A hair. A scraping of skin.'

'That's *insane*.'

'Is it?' Will asked. He looked at her evenly.

Andrew adjusted his glasses, smearing his zinc cream. 'For what it's worth, Will, I think it's a good idea.'

And he couldn't help feeling slightly relieved that the danger implicit in the plan would be faced by the robot, rather than themselves.

'Andrew's being nice,' Gaia said. '*Anybody* else would say it's a crazy idea with no chance of coming off.'

'Does anybody else have Spy Seeds and a robotic salamander?' Andrew asked. 'Does anybody else have our *Will*-power?' He smiled.

Gaia groaned.

Hidden behind a frangipani tree, a girl watched. And waited.

She had a clear view down the drive. And she could see that the front door to Phoenix House was still ajar.

Four minutes earlier, a squat red-haired man with bulging arms had trotted out past the marble dog, around the side of the house, and vanished.

Two minutes later, he'd returned with a woman. The girl had recognized her at once. *Evangeline de Souza.* The pair had hurried inside.

Should she move now, the girl wondered.

Or continue waiting?

For what, exactly, she asked herself. For her courage to fail?

Her digital Dictaphone was in her hand. She pressed the record button. '5.34 p.m. Phoenix House. *Going in.*'

A mosquito landed on Will's cheek. He swatted it, and kept moving. It was hard-going, forcing a path through the vegetation. Branches and roots snarled everywhere. At least the kayaks, which they'd left down near the beach, would be well-hidden.

The wood seemed to spread up along the eastern boundary of the lawns of Phoenix House, all the way from the beach to the road. As soon as they were on a level with the house, he'd send up a Spy Seed, Will thought, and prepare Sam.

He glanced over his shoulder. Gaia was close. Andrew was trailing behind. 'Andrew, keep up,' he whispered through the toothphone.

'Will, roger,' Andrew replied.

But he was treading slowly – and carefully – on purpose. The thick ground cover might easily conceal dangerous animals, he thought. He'd considered warning Will and Gaia, but held his tongue. After the incident in the garage, he'd be asking for trouble from Gaia, he decided.

According to the guidebook, though, there was no end of deadly snakes, spiders and sea creatures in Australia. A male red kangaroo could spill a man's guts with its hind claws. So too could a cassowary – a large, pre-historic-looking flightless bird. Thankfully, cassowaries lived only in northern Queensland. And Andrew doubted wild kangaroos inhabited cities.

'Andrew!'

He'd just stumbled right into Gaia, who'd stopped.

'Sorry,' he whispered.

They were in a ditch, Andrew realized.

Will was picking his way to the top, to the very edge of the wood. In between the trunks, Andrew saw flashes of grass.

He clambered up after Gaia, and lay flat on his stomach beside her. Twigs and pine cones dug into his legs. He did his best to ignore them and to focus on the view: the eastern side of Phoenix House.

Behind a sweeping half-moon balcony were shuttered windows. Below was a pair of slender wooden doors. To the left, a path led past a marble dog, to the front of the house.

Andrew's gaze jerked. Will had been quietly digging in his rucksack. Now, he was holding a Spy Seed.

Will set it right at the edge of the lawn. He gripped his touch-screen. Hit FIRE.

Andrew wriggled closer to Gaia, so he could see.

The screen showed a murky blur. Then sky. It was blindingly blue. As the seed stabilized and began to fall, they saw the outline of Phoenix House.

It was roughly square-shaped, with bulging, convex sides. There were three balconies, and two entrances: the one they were looking at, plus front doors which opened on to the drive.

'I can't see any security,' Andrew whispered, as he removed a sharp twig from under his thigh. 'If there are guards, they must be inside.'

'Yeah,' Will replied. Then he tensed. And stared.

Someone was running out of the front door and stumbling on to the drive.

Will's gaze flew up – to the real world.

He saw a dark-haired girl. She gazed around wildly, then swerved, and started to race to their side of the building.

From inside the house, someone shouted. A second later, a stocky red-haired man thundered out after her, his legs a blur.

As the girl ran, she scanned her surroundings.

Clearly she was searching for an escape route or somewhere to hide, Will thought.

He snatched up Sam and flicked on the torch. The narrow beam was powerful. He aimed it. Caught her in the eye, and she blinked. Saw him.

Will beckoned her over. Then he slumped back down beside Andrew and Gaia.

'What do you think's going on?' Andrew whispered.

No one answered.

Will's eyes were on the girl. She was glancing over her shoulder. The man was still behind her. Then he slowed to talk into a radio. He glanced back at the house. And she took her chance and sprinted for the trees.

'Get down into the ditch!' Will said.

Andrew and Gaia obeyed, scrambling to the bottom. Will stayed where he was. Waiting.

A second later, the girl reached him. He grabbed her arm, pulled her backwards with him.

She rolled, and slithered. Twigs and leaves flew up into the air. At last, she came to a stop beside Andrew.

She was breathing hard. Her olive face was glistening with sweat.

She stared at Andrew, then Will and Gaia. Her black eyes were huge. She opened her mouth –

'*Quiet*,' Will whispered.

A bag was slung across her shoulder. She pushed it out of the way so she could turn and try to climb back up the ditch, to see over.

'*Don't move*,' Will hissed.

Above them now, they heard a voice.

'Hey!'

The red-haired man, Will presumed. He was panting. 'Where did she go?'

After a moment, they heard the thudding of feet, and then: '*Who?*' Another man. He had an eastern European accent.

'A girl! There was a girl! I saw her coming out of the library. Now she's bloody vanished!'

'You are sure she is not a client?'

'It's my business, Hutt, to know the clients. Remember? And if she was a client, genius, why would she run?'

'The sight of you,' Hutt said, 'it would be enough –'

'Oh, can it! Where *is* she?'

There was a pause.

Will held his breath.

Andrew watched the girl. She seemed to shrink back into the leaves.

Above, heavy feet stomped along the edge of the wood.

At last, the man called Hutt said: 'She has gone. And why should we care? A *girl* – exploring. Perhaps she did not know this is private property.'

Another pause. Longer this time. 'You think we should tell Eva?'

'It will be your look-out.'

'But what if she saw something, what if –'

'*What if, what if,*' the other man mimicked. 'You think Eva will be impressed with your report? If I were you, Tench, I would keep my mouth shut.'

Will's legs were twisted under him. They were starting to ache. *Go*, he urged silently.

Then he heard Tench curse. And a scuffing sound. Shoes on grass. Then nothing. Silence.

The girl started to move. He grabbed her arm to stop her. The men could still be close. They had to wait.

Seconds ticked past.

Then a minute.

And another.

A bug landed on Andrew's cheek. He slapped it.

'Andrew!' Gaia hissed.

'Sorry, but I think they must have gone now. Don't you?' Andrew sat up. He reached behind him, to brush leaves and twigs from his back. His eyes were on the girl.

She was about their age. Her long brown hair was twisted back and tied. She had an open face. Huge, jet eyes. A Roman nose. Olive skin. She was slim, but she looked sturdy. She was wearing shorts and a white T-shirt. The muscles in her legs were well-developed. Her arms looked powerful. He was staring, Andrew realized. He couldn't help it.

'What just happened?' Will asked her quietly. 'Who are you?'

She took in the three faces.

The girl looked vaguely hostile, she thought. The first boy – the one who'd just asked her who she was – was clutching what looked like a metal lizard. The other boy's expression was earnest. He was blinking at her through thick glasses. His cheeks and nose were smeared white with sunscreen.

What else? she thought.

They sounded English. Clearly they were surprised to see her. The feeling was more than reciprocated.

'My name's Lydia,' she said.

Andrew dabbed at his face, suddenly remembering the zinc cream. He hoped it didn't look as bad as he feared.

'I'm Andrew,' he said. 'This is Will, and Gaia.'

Lydia watched as Will slipped Sam back into his rucksack.

It *was* a metal lizard, she thought. Who *were* these kids? What were they up to? What were they doing, hiding out in the woods? Lydia was sorely tempted to ask them those exact questions. But the temptation to get out of there *fast* was even stronger.

'OK,' she said. 'Well, nice to meet you, and thanks for your, er, help. I'd better get home.'

She jumped into a crouch.

'Wait,' Andrew said, surprised. 'What were you doing in there? Why were those men chasing you?'

Lydia stood up. 'Look, I mean it – thanks. But I *do* have to go.'

Andrew's surprise deepened. And he couldn't help feeling a little put out. 'Surely the least we deserve is some explanation,' he said. 'We did just save you from being caught. Without us, you could be in serious trouble.'

Lydia frowned. She could do without this. After what she'd heard in the library, there were things she had to think about. 'No offence, but get over yourself. This is Sydney, not Manchester or wherever. They weren't going to *shoot* me.'

Andrew stiffened. *Get over yourself.* Had she actually said that?

Will glanced at Gaia. She was watching Lydia stonily. But he was curious.

'Did you break into Phoenix House?' Will asked. He paused for effect. 'Because that's what we had in mind.'

Lydia had been about to head off. Now she froze.

They'd been planning to break in?

She hesitated, torn. But she knew there was no way

she'd be able to leave without an explanation. She fixed her black eyes on Will. '*Why?*'

For a moment, Will considered what to say.

He could make up a story. But why not tell her the truth? Or at least part of it. That way, if the girl knew anything interesting about Phoenix House, she'd be more likely to share her knowledge with them. If she didn't, she'd leave anyway. They wouldn't have lost anything.

'We belong to a secret organization based in London,' Will said quietly. 'We're on the trail of a man we think could be living at Phoenix House under the name Frederick Broadstairs. If Broadstairs is really who we think he is, he's a dangerous criminal, and he's wanted by MI6.'

Will's gaze was fixed on Lydia, but he could feel Gaia glaring at him. Andrew was blinking, surprised.

Lydia's expression flickered. And settled on stunned. She barked a short laugh. '*Right.*'

'No,' Will said. '*Really.*'

Her eyes narrowed. '. . . You're actually not joking.'

Will shook his head.

'And this isn't all in your head? You're not *mad* or anything?'

'No.'

'That's a matter of opinion,' Gaia said.

'I'm telling you the truth,' Will said, trying to avoid Gaia's gaze.

Lydia took a deep breath. Re-ordered her thoughts. 'OK . . . *OK.*'

She glanced through the trees, towards the main road. Then she fixed her gaze back on Will.

'You have to tell me all about this organization and what you know about Broadstairs and Phoenix House.'

'All right,' Will said. 'But first, you tell us why you were inside Phoenix House and what you know about it, and Broadstairs. That's if you actually know anything.'

Lydia opened her mouth to protest, and stopped herself.

If this boy was serious – and he certainly seemed it – she just couldn't pass this up.

Broadstairs was potentially much more interesting than she'd imagined. She had to find out what they knew.

'I won't tell you,' she said. Paused. 'I'll *show* you.'

6

The shutters kept out almost every scrap of light.

If they'd been open, Frederick Broadstairs might have seen movement on the lawn. He might have noticed Tench and Hutt, and the girl.

But he was preoccupied. And he wanted darkness.

He crossed to the fireplace and lit a match. Instantly, flames billowed. Sweat prickled his forehead, and he backed up.

Broadstairs needed this fire, but not for its heat.

On the desk was a mass of papers. *Research.* Which had kept him awake for seventy-two straight hours. De Souza had only her project to worry about. He had the rest of the plan to put into place.

Now, he was almost ready. And he would win. If this was a chess game, Broadstairs thought, he held the killer pieces.

'Ha,' he murmured to himself. 'How apt.'

He went back to the desk, grabbed his phone and dialled a number. After a few moments he heard:

'*Chen.*'

'It's Broadstairs. I thought I should give you advance warning that tomorrow you can expect—'

'*Expectations,*' Chen interrupted, 'are, I find, so often dashed. When you have something to tell me, then you should call. In the meantime, I do not expect to hear from you. From any of you.'

Anger pulsed in Broadstairs's veins. *How dare he?* But Broadstairs contained his fury. He had no choice. 'Very well.'

He pocketed his phone. And his gaze jerked across the papers. They contained special knowledge. *Secret* knowledge.

It was for her knowledge, and her skill, that he needed de Souza. But when she had done as he asked, he thought, when he had sucked her brain dry – what would be left to interest him?

Broadstairs gathered the papers in his arms. He went to the fire, and shoved them hard into the grate. He watched, transfixed, as they started to blacken and curl.

$100 million.

It was not a trifle. Even to him.

'Will!'

Gaia stumbled through the trees after him. Lydia was racing on ahead, with Andrew at her heels.

Lydia had told them she had transport. The kayaks would be all right, Will had decided. They could pick them up later, when they had finished with Lydia.

'Will!' Gaia called again.

He stopped. As she reached him, she wiped sweat from her face. 'I thought we were going to try to find Broadstairs.'

He nodded. 'But we can do that later. We can do it tonight. But Lydia was leaving, and I want to know what she was doing inside Phoenix House, and what she knows. Don't you?'

Gaia caught her breath. 'She might not know any-thing.'

'Then we'll be back here tonight,' he said.

She sighed.

Will pushed a branch out of his way and held it for Gaia. She took it, and followed him up between the trunks, to the main road.

Thirty metres along it, Gaia noticed, was a side road. A white four-wheel-drive truck was parked in its mouth.

As they got closer, she saw that *Australian Institute of Sports Research* was painted in black on the side. Lydia was at the driver's door, waiting for them. Andrew had already jumped in.

'Get in,' Lydia said. 'It isn't far.'

Gaia hesitated. When Lydia had talked about trans-port, Gaia hadn't thought she'd meant her own car. 'You're *driving*?' she asked. 'How old are you?'

Lydia flashed a look that made Gaia colour. 'Dad doesn't know I've borrowed it. *Come on.*'

Gaia had no choice but to get in. She climbed up, and found the back seat covered in litter. Chocolate wrappers, water bottles, crumpled maps. She pushed the rubbish to the floor.

'So what's not far?' Will asked, as he slammed the door shut.

Lydia was behind the wheel. She turned the key. 'Dad's office.' She shoved the gearstick into Drive.

Andrew glanced round. 'Lydia, what's that?'

He pointed at a black tube that poked up vertically beside his window.

'It's a snorkel,' she said, and hit the accelerator, swinging the truck on to the road. 'So you can go through deep water without flooding the engine.'

Andrew's blue eyes lit up. Exotic phrases from the guidebook reappeared in his mind. 'For going through *creeks* in the *outback*?'

To his surprise, Lydia laughed.

Andrew smarted. 'My information might be wrong,' he said, realizing how stilted he sounded and somehow unable to stop himself, 'but don't you have creeks in the outback?'

She smiled. 'Your *information*'s right. It was just the way you said it. Sorry.'

Her open expression was so disarming, Andrew smiled back. He couldn't help himself.

Lydia rolled the truck around a left-hand bend, and they sped past the drive that led to Phoenix House.

The road twisted on, still climbing. It was narrow, and lined by luxurious-looking houses. The afternoon sun reflected off closed shutters, security alarms, high gates and swimming pools.

'So we're going to the Australian Institute of Sports Research?' Andrew asked.

'Yeah. Dad's the medical director.'

'And we're going to talk to your dad?' Will said.

'No. There's some stuff in his office I want to show you. He's got workshops till seven. He won't be there.'

'What stuff?' Gaia asked.

'I'll *show* you.' Lydia glanced in the rear view mirror at Gaia. Smiled slightly.

They passed a small, grey church on the left, and Lydia hit the brakes. She sent the truck swerving in between a set of wrought iron gates. Ahead, a red-brick Victorian building loomed.

The truck rolled over a speed bump and down past the side of the institute. At last, Lydia cut the engine. She jumped down on to the pavement and started to head for a white door.

She'd left the keys in the ignition, Andrew noticed. 'Doesn't anyone worry about security round here?' he asked, as he followed her.

'Dad was always losing his keys,' she replied. 'He's been leaving them in the ignition for three months and no one's stolen it yet.' Her jet eyes glinted. 'Except me.'

The door was marked *AISR Personnel Only*.

Lydia pushed it open.

'Will anyone mind us coming in?' Andrew asked.

Lydia looked round. She took in Andrew, with his

glasses and traces of zinc cream. Gaia, arms folded across her skinny chest. Will . . . Maybe she'd have got away with Will.

She'd been going to tell them to pretend to be visiting junior athletes.

And changed her mind.

Fluorescent lights hummed in the corridor.

Lydia led the way along it, into an atrium. It was empty, apart from a cluttered noticeboard and a steel mesh sculpture of a woman about to hurl a javelin.

Through a set of swing doors, they entered a bright room which stank of chlorine. Hardly surprising, Will thought, as there in front of them there was a vast swimming pool. But it looked like no pool that Will had seen before.

Strung on cables that ran around the perimeter, under the water, and in regular rows about a metre above the surface, were what looked like miniature video cameras.

Andrew noticed them too. 'What are all the cameras for?'

'They help with training,' Lydia said. 'A computer uses the images to create a three dimensional image of a swimmer. And there are sensors in the starting blocks. When someone dives, they measure the force, the speed and the angle of the dive, and obviously the timing. See those pads in the wall at each end? They measure a swimmer's force when they turn, and the angle when they push off.'

'Very impressive,' Andrew said.

Lydia continued walking. 'A lot of money and effort goes into sport in Australia. Why do you think we win everything?'

'Like football?' Gaia asked.

'You mean soccer? Yeah, well give us a chance. We have our own football. We're pretty good at that.'

'You're the only ones who play it,' Andrew said. 'It's hardly fair to compare.' He smiled faintly. 'It's just not cricket.'

Lydia looked at him. To his mild surprise – and pleasure – a grin burst out across her face. 'Come on.'

After leaving the pool, they entered another corridor. Halfway along, Will stopped. He'd heard a muffled thud. A wire mesh window was cut into the wall. He peered in. Two boxers were going at each other. Their kit *looked* normal.

'They've got sensors in their vests, in the gloves and in the head protectors,' Lydia called back.

'They measure their performance?' Will asked.

'Yeah, but not really to improve it. It's a new system. It's designed to stop cheating. Every punch gets registered and goes up on a big screen – it's behind the door there, you can't see it. *Come on.*'

At the end of the corridor was a final beech door. On it was written:

Dr Andy Michalitsianos, Director of Medicine.

Michalitsianos, Andrew thought. So Lydia's origins were Greek.

The office was square, and smelt of flowers. A bunch of them was stuffed in a glass vase on top of a metal filing cabinet.

'From a grateful patient,' Lydia said, seeing Will looking.

She headed past the cabinet and yanked a cord closing the window blinds. Then she sat down at the desk. On it were a laptop computer, a lamp and a plant pot. Lydia rummaged in one of the drawers and brought out a thick cardboard folder. As she opened it, newspaper clippings and a DVD slid out.

Lydia slipped the DVD into the laptop and grabbed a remote from the pot. She aimed it at an LCD TV hanging on the opposite wall.

'What are you showing us?' Will asked, as he moved with Andrew and Gaia to stand by the desk.

'Evidence,' Lydia replied. '*Watch*.'

7

Lydia double-clicked on a file titled *Murray*. A video segment started on the TV. They saw an athletics track. A hurdles race was about to start. Eight athletes were poised on the starting blocks.

'Any moment now, the race will begin and perhaps—'

Lydia hit mute, silencing the commentator.

'It's over four hundred metres,' she said. 'Watch the man in lane six. His name's Neil Murray.'

As she finished speaking, the athletes burst from the blocks. They sprinted and launched themselves over the first of the hurdles.

Soon, the pack began to string out. By the 200-metre mark, Murray was in fourth place. A close-up showed his teeth clenched and his cheeks turning red. At 220 metres, he slipped to fifth. Then to sixth. His arms flailed, his legs shaking as they pounded the track.

On the home straight, Murray dropped to last place. He finished almost a whole second behind the man placed seventh. The camera closed in on the winner's jubilant face, and the clip ended.

'That was in April,' Lydia said. 'And that was the fifth

race in a row he'd come in last. He's thirty-two years old. Everyone thought he was past it. Now watch this.'

She nudged the cursor to a file titled *Murray2*, and hit PLAY.

The screen showed the start of another hurdles race. Again, Neil Murray was in lane six.

This time, he quickly took the lead. By the halfway mark, he was five strides ahead of the next runner. Down the home straight, he stretched his lead to a clear seven metres. His legs were flying, his arms pumping – until he crossed the finish line, and they shot up in the air.

New Commonwealth Record flashed up at the bottom of the screen.

'That was in June,' Lydia said. 'And you want to know what happened between April and June?'

They could guess the answer.

'Yeah,' Lydia said. 'He went for "therapy" at Phoenix House.'

She patted the thick folder. 'There are another four examples in here. Six years ago, an athlete called Sheila Barlow won an Olympic gold medal in the high jump. Four years ago, she stopped competing at an international level. Until this March. Then she set a new Australian record, *four weeks* after she'd spent a fortnight at Phoenix House.'

The newspaper story Andrew had shown them on the deck had mentioned Barlow, Gaia remembered. 'So you're thinking Phoenix House can't just be giving therapy?' she asked.

'*Therapy* doesn't turn someone ready for the glue factory into a record-breaking athlete,' Lydia said. 'It just doesn't. Dad knows something's going on there, but all these athletes are passing their drug tests.'

'They could still be taking drugs,' Will said. 'Just not ones the authorities know about.'

'Yeah,' Lydia said. 'Obviously Phoenix House must be handing out some new kind of drug. And it isn't showing up in the standard tests.'

'So why are you interested?' Gaia asked. 'Your dad's the sports doctor.'

'You don't have to be a sports doctor to be interested.'

'No,' Will said, still bristling at her *obviously*. 'But why are *you* interested. Why were you there today?'

'I –' Lydia hesitated. 'I wanted to get in. I thought if I could find their store, or their lab, I could get samples of whatever drugs they're using, and I could bring them back to Dad and we could work out exactly what's going on.' A pause. 'Then I could write it all up and get the front page of the *Australian*, so when I leave school, they'll take me on as a cadet.'

'You want to be a journalist?' Andrew asked.

'I think that's what I just said.'

Andrew's hand went to his glasses. A nervous gesture.

Lydia sighed. 'Look, I don't mean to sound rude. It's just, I know what you're thinking. I'm fifteen, I want to be an investigative reporter, so do loads of people, I've got my head in the clouds, it'll never happen – and all the rest of it.'

'I wasn't thinking that,' Andrew said.

'No?'

Andrew's hand dropped from his glasses. 'Lydia, I'm a multi-millionaire software developer. Gaia is brilliant at chemistry – and I mean *brilliant*. Will is a genius inventor. *MI6* invites him to work with them. Why shouldn't you get the front page of the *Australian*?'

For a moment, Lydia said nothing. Then, very slowly, she nodded. The combative expression on her face disappeared. In her own way, she really was incredibly beautiful, Andrew thought.

'I *see*,' Lydia said quietly, half to herself. 'Multi-millionaire. *Right*.'

She wasn't sure what to make of Andrew. Of any of them. Was Andrew trying to impress her with their achievements? It hadn't really sounded like it. More like he was just making statements of fact. Putting her in context.

'But you didn't find any drugs in Phoenix House?' Will asked now.

'No,' Lydia said. 'I didn't really get chance to look.' She sighed again. 'Since you're taking me seriously, I don't have much of a file on this, but I know they don't just treat athletes. Look at this.'

Lydia's bag was still on her hip. She pulled out a bulging notebook, and from that, she produced a newspaper clipping.

It was another excerpt from *Sydney Sauce!*

The memoir of Sydney actress Sunny Bell has rocketed to the top of the best-seller lists. Her 'insight and intelligence' have been praised around the globe.

It's a remarkable turnaround for a woman who, last year, gave an astonishing interview in which she confessed that years of excess had left her brain 'like a rusty sieve'.

Bell herself is quick to give the credit to top psychologist Dr Evangeline de Souza. 'After six weeks at Phoenix House, I emerged a new woman,' Bell says.

'A girl at school, her mum spent two weeks there,' Lydia said. 'Apparently she kept forgetting things. She thought it might be stress. Anyway, when she came out, her memory was perfect. *Better* than perfect. I asked this girl if her mum had taken any drugs, and she said she hadn't. But she might not have been telling the truth. Or she might have been given something while she was staying at Phoenix House.'

Lydia took the clipping back and slipped it into her book.

'So,' she said, 'I've told you everything I know. It's your turn. What do you know about Broadstairs and Phoenix House? What exactly is this secret organization?'

Will, Andrew and Gaia exchanged glances.

Gaia shrugged. Andrew nodded.

So Will filled her in.

He didn't have to, he thought. But after Lydia had been so forthcoming, he felt obliged to. Also, she was clearly smart, and she was no coward. Maybe she could help them.

Lydia listened, her eyes getting steadily wider, as Will talked about STORM, and how they had already worked in Russia, Italy and Switzerland. He told her much of what they knew about Sir James Parramore.

'We don't know if Broadstairs is Parramore,' Will said. 'But that's why we're interested in him. Now it sounds as though he's interesting whether he's Parramore or not. Him and Evangeline de Souza.'

'Yeah,' Lydia said quietly. She rocked back in her chair. She looked as though she was pondering something. Then she said: 'So what do you want to do now?'

Again, Will glanced at Gaia and Andrew.

Yes, he thought, they had Sam. And they could still send him into Phoenix House to search for Broadstairs.

But while recon robots were useful, there were certain things they couldn't do. Like ask questions. Or open closed doors.

STORM had got used to having to break into buildings. But there were risks involved. Perhaps, this time, there might be another way.

'We need to get inside Phoenix House,' Will said at last.

'Lydia did,' Andrew said. 'And look what happened—'

'I don't mean break in,' Will interrupted. 'I mean, get invited in.'

'*How?*' Gaia said.

'I could ask for an appointment.'

'For what?' Gaia asked.

Will hesitated, thinking. And Andrew's gaze flickered to Lydia. Will always took the lead. At first, Andrew had fought against it. Now, he felt happy with the way they worked together. But he didn't want Lydia to see him take a back seat.

'Perhaps I should go,' Andrew said, and felt his heart start to thump. 'I could tell de Souza I want help with my memory for the Science Olympiad. It's coming up soon, and I've competed in the past, so if she asks me about it, it won't be a problem. I could see what I could get out of her and maybe poke around a bit.'

After a moment, Will nodded. 'That could work.'

'And, if I can somehow get her out of the way and get access to a computer, I might be able to slip some spyware on to their network.'

'Which would mean what?' Lydia asked.

'Well, I've already checked their network, and the firewall was impenetrable. But if I could get on to the network from the *inside*, I could easily transfer a bit of software that would give me access from home.'

'Good idea,' Will said.

'Won't they be suspicious?' Gaia asked. 'A fifteen-year-old girl gets caught in Phoenix House. Then the same day a fourteen-year-old boy asks for an appointment. Why should they give him one?'

'You heard the men,' Will said. 'It didn't sound like they were even going to report seeing Lydia. And even if they did, Andrew's English. He can say he's here on holiday. Why should they make any connection?'

'But what if Broadstairs is Parramore?' Gaia asked. 'And what if he's somehow seen a picture of Andrew?'

'Why should he?' Will said. 'The official line was that MI6 sabotaged the lab in Russia. Parramore wouldn't have even heard of us. But Andrew could use a false name to be on the safe side.'

'Obviously it is risky,' Andrew said, for two reasons. First, because it was. Second, because he wanted Lydia to appreciate the fact. 'But I think it's worth a try.'

Will nodded. 'Yeah.'

'What's wrong?'

Gaia had spoken. She was watching Lydia, who looked as though she were weighing something up.

'Lydia?' Andrew asked.

'There's something I haven't told you,' she said at last. 'I wanted to keep it to myself, in case I found out something useful. I wanted the scoop –' She stopped.

'You can have all the scoops you like,' Will said. 'So long as you keep all of this to yourself, for now. What haven't you told us?'

Lydia bit her lip. 'When I was inside Phoenix House, I overheard something. De Souza walked right past me when I was hiding in the library. She was talking. I couldn't hear anyone else, so I thought she had to be on the phone. I heard her say she'd be leaving at eight, and Broadstairs would make the other pick-up.'

'Leaving to go where?' Gaia asked quickly. 'What other pick-up?'

'I don't know, that's all I heard. But from the way she was talking, I think she meant tonight. I thought maybe they're going to pick up new drugs – I don't know – something to do with what's going on at Phoenix House, anyway. I was thinking I could try to follow her.'

Gaia's eyes shot to Will. It wasn't hard to guess what he was thinking. He looked at Andrew. Who nodded.

'So you agree we *should* try to follow her?' Lydia asked.

'I think we have to,' Will said. 'And Broadstairs, if we can.' If he'd had any doubts about telling Lydia about why they were in Sydney, he didn't any more. This could be an important break. Whatever the pair were 'picking up', it had to be related to what they were up to at Phoenix House.

He checked his watch. 'We should aim to keep Phoenix House under surveillance from seven thirty – which gives us one hour. We're staying in Watson's Bay. I need to go back to get a few more . . . items. Then we'll get a taxi and we'll meet you. Here?'

Lydia nodded quickly. 'I'll wait here. I'll make up some excuse to Dad about where I'm going. I should be able to use the truck again. I can drive us.'

Lydia had caught Will's hesitation over the word

items. She knew now that Will invented devices. And she remembered the lizard. She still had to ask him about that. 'When you say items, what do you mean?'

There was no time to explain now, Will thought. He thought of her words back at Phoenix House. Threw them back at her. 'I won't tell you,' he said. '*I'll show you.*'

8

Chen Jianguo coughed into his silk handkerchief and inspected the contents.

Disgusted, he threw the bloody mess on the floor.

Four days, he thought. In four days, the Meeting of the Tigers would begin. So far, what progress had there been? One phone call.

Frederick Broadstairs was no fool. He had the capability and the audacity, Chen thought. But would he succeed?

'*Could* he?' he whispered to his snake.

Her half-metre long body was coiled on his desk, her eyelids flicking. A Russell's viper. Cold and sleek as a dagger, and at least as deadly. The muzzle was regrettable – but this was a weapon that had to be sheathed.

Chen's head jerked up. Into his study walked his personal assistant, a tall young woman with a plain face, special forces training and a capable brain. Mei wore a skin-toned earpiece and a black jacket. A microphone and a GPS transmitter were sewn into the lapel. Chen could communicate with her – and track her – at all times.

Mei crossed to his desk, bowed neatly, handed him a package, and left.

Chen checked the postmark, and his breathing became hoarse.

This was not a communiqué from a member of the Viper Club. Still, it was a very welcome delivery.

Chen sliced open the seal with his fingernail. Out fell a plastic folder. Inside was a sheet of dusty vellum. Grains of sand scattered from it to his desk, and a thrill electrified Chen's stiff veins.

He scanned the ancient writing.

It was in Aramaic. Chen did not understand the words. But the archaeologist who had reported the discovery of the document had told him what it *meant*.

These *very words* would have been read at a *pulsa dinura*. A *rod of fire*.

A rabbi would have led the call for God to curse the sinner, for the angels of destruction to wreak their worst, to tear life from the living. This was a death curse. An ancient Jewish rite. And Chen's latest trophy.

It was an invaluable addition to his collection.

And yet, naturally, it was not practical.

He could not read this curse out loud and truly *expect* a man to die.

Again, Chen coughed. Blood spattered on to his desk, narrowly missing the vellum. He grimaced.

The Viper Club could not fail him. Time was running out!

On the deck at Watson's Retreat, Andrew paced.

He was nervous. Which was ridiculous, he told himself. This was only a phone call. Albeit an important one.

Through the plate glass window, he could see Will and Gaia in the living room. Will was packing up his rucksack. Gaia was talking. Smiling. Gaia smiling! It was a rare sight, though thankfully less rare these days.

Sighing, Andrew dialled the number. He faced the bay. The sun was setting, turning the sky sci-fi lurid.

'Good evening, Dr de Souza's office.'

'Ah.' Andrew's voice had squeaked. He coughed. 'Hello, I wonder, is Dr de Souza available?'

'I'm afraid she's with a client. Can I help?'

'Well, I was wondering if I could make an appointment. It's rather urgent.'

'This would be your first consultation, Mr . . .?'

Andrew realized he hadn't thought of a pseudonym. 'Yes, er, Jason. Jason Argo.'

Jason had been a hero of ancient Greece. The name had popped into his head. Clearly his subconscious was trying to tell him something, he thought. He wanted to be a hero. Specifically, *Lydia's* hero.

Again, Andrew sighed. His father had once told him that you ignored your subconscious at your peril. But there was no more time for self-analysis because the receptionist was talking:

'I do have a cancellation tomorrow at 2 p.m., Mr Argo. Would that suit?'

Footsteps behind made him turn. Will was at the door, watching him.

'Two o'clock tomorrow would be perfect,' Andrew said.

'Very good, Mr Argo. May I give Dr de Souza an indication as to the nature of the consultation?'

'Ah – well, I –'

'That's quite all right, Mr Argo. For so many of our clients, privacy is paramount. You can rest assured that here at Phoenix House we understand that perfectly.'

'Excellent,' Andrew said, relieved. 'Thank you.'

He flipped his phone shut and pushed it into one of the pockets of his wicking trousers. The boardshorts and T-shirt were on his bed. The evening was getting cool. He zipped up his fleece.

'Two o'clock tomorrow,' Andrew said to Will, in case he hadn't heard. 'A visit will be useful, won't it?' he added. He'd offered to go, but he couldn't help being apprehensive.

'You can ask questions, and you can use your initiative,' Will said. 'Sam can't do that.'

'Sam *can* defend himself, though,' Andrew said.

'So can you.'

'With what – my right-hook?' He looked down at his body unhappily. 'Lydia seems very sporty.' *Lydia*. There she was again.

'Yeah,' Will said.

'I wonder what she thinks of us.'

Will knew what Andrew was really thinking: *what she thinks of me.*

'I'm not exactly sporty,' Andrew persisted.

'What do you call swimming into submerged dungeons in Venice?' Will said. 'Or hydrospeeding through underground caverns in the Alps?'

'That? Oh, I call that foolhardy,' Andrew said and smiled slightly. The smile broadened. Gaia had appeared behind Will. She stepped past him, on to the deck.

She was dressed in black jeans, black trainers and a black zip-up jacket. Her hair was scraped back.

'Gaia, you look like a ninja,' Andrew said, impressed.

'Well, if you don't want to be seen at night, black is slightly better than *yellow.*'

She was right, Andrew thought. But this was the only really warm top he had.

'You'll be all right,' Will said. 'If we all wore black, we'd be more obvious.' He checked his watch. 'Four minutes till the taxi's due. You've got your toothphones and your lenses?'

Andrew and Gaia nodded. Then Andrew reached into a pocket for his toothphone keypad. He pressed the red button. 'Gaia,' he whispered, 'will you swap jackets with me?'

She pressed her blue button. 'What do you think?'

Will smiled. And a thought that had been at the back of his mind shot to the front. The smile became a frown. 'There was a speedboat at the jetty at Phoenix House,' he said abruptly. 'What if de Souza or Broadstairs uses it tonight?'

'I suppose it's possible,' Andrew said. 'What do you want to do?'

Will thought for a moment. 'You meet Lydia as we planned,' he said. 'Get to Phoenix House and find somewhere safe to watch the road.'

'What will you do?' Andrew asked.

'I've got an idea,' said Will. Given what he had in mind, it would be easier if he went alone, he thought. But easier wasn't necessarily better. 'Gaia, you could come with me,' he said. 'If you want.'

Gaia had no idea what he had in mind. Did that matter? She looked at Andrew. 'Will you be all right?'

All right, with Lydia? Andrew thought. *Alone* with Lydia. His pulse quickened. But he'd talked about her too much already that evening. And presumably, Gaia had meant *all right* trailing de Souza or Broadstairs without them, rather than *all right* with Lydia. 'You are talking to someone who's swum into submerged dungeons in Venice,' he said.

Gaia looked confused. But Will smiled.

Andrew was about to press Will to explain his idea when a car horn sounded three times. 'That must be the taxi,' he said. He held up a hand in farewell. 'Good luck. And be careful.'

'You too,' Gaia called after him.

Andrew hurried through the living room to the hall. As he opened the back door, he felt a rush.

Nerves and excitement. STORM. *On a mission*. And he was going to meet Lydia. Lydia Michalitsianos with her jet eyes and her strong, olive limbs. An Australian-Greek goddess. And he was –

Andrew's daydreams short-circuited. He certainly wasn't a god. Or a hero, despite his pseudonym. Not unless gods and heroes had thin white arms, glasses and wicking trousers.

But he was on the other side of the world. Everything was upside down. Perhaps anything was possible.

Will was running, dragging the last of the kayaks across the esplanade.

Gaia followed him. 'We can't both fit in this,' she said, for the second time. The first time, he'd been busy tying a loop in the mooring rope and he hadn't responded.

'Yeah,' he said now, 'I know.' He jumped on to the beach. The sand looked dark in the half-light. 'Go and wait for me on the jetty. On the other side, where the ferries stop.'

'Can't you just tell me what you're going to do?'

'If I do, you might try to stop me.'

'*Will –*'

'Gaia. Trust me.'

'How can I do that if you think I'd stop you?'

'*Try* to stop me, I said.' He smiled.

Gaia rolled her eyes. But she knew Will well by now. She could argue, which would be a waste of time, or go to the jetty. Annoyed, she jogged away.

Will heaved the kayak to the water's edge. He glanced around. Voices and light drifted from the tables at the restaurant along the esplanade. But there was no one on the beach.

Ahead, the bay stretched, black and glassy. Waves lapped gently against the sand. Mooring ropes strained. It was an eerie sound.

Will dropped his rucksack into the kayak. Then he pushed it free, grabbed the paddle and jumped in.

Quickly, he pulled away from the shore. His muscles strained, making his vest feel tight.

Ten strokes. He was in among the boats.

Twenty. He steered around a bobbing cruiser.

Now his target was dead ahead.

Curtains were drawn across the windows in the main cabin. But light seeped out around them. The rest of the boat was dark.

Will paddled on, barely making a sound. Cloud covered the rising moon, and the red kayak was almost invisible. Perfect for a stealthy approach.

When he was close, he eased up on his strokes. And he heard something. Music. Rock. A song he didn't recognize. Then a man's voice over the top. So there was at least one person in that cabin.

After another four strokes, Will lifted the paddle and let his momentum carry him on. As he was about to hit the hull, he dug one blade hard into the water and twisted it. The kayak spun. It came to a stop parallel with the boat.

Now Will was close enough to his target to touch it.

The music was loud. *Good,* he thought. If he made a mistake, it would help to cover it.

Will reached for his rucksack. He slipped it on to his back and tightened the straps. Then he collected the coiled rope from the nose of his kayak. He felt for the loop. Aimed. And threw.

The coil unravelled through the air. And the loop landed neatly around the tow bar of the jet ski. The same jet ski that had been cutting up the harbour that afternoon. It was held against the stern by a winch.

Gripping the rope, Will pulled himself, hand over hand, to the ski. He reached behind him and slipped the paddle through the straps of his rucksack, wedging it in place. Then, very slowly, he stood up.

The kayak wobbled. Will froze. He waited until it stabilized, and glanced behind him. The bay was still quiet. Nothing moved. But he'd have to. *Fast.*

Will bent his knees. Reached out. Jumped.

His left hand closed tight around the tow bar. His right flailed. Will's heart thudded.

Inside the cabin, the track changed, and the singing got louder. Will made out a second male voice. Taking a deep breath, he heaved himself up – and on to the back of the ski.

For a few moments, Will just sat there, listening, and running his eyes over the machine.

It was red, with a motorbike handlebar, a black double seat and a narrow platform that ran all the way around the base. For diving off, he guessed.

Will had messed around with a jet ski during the school trip to Cornwall. But the engine on this machine was 215 horsepower. Much more powerful than the one he'd used in England.

He scanned the dash. Saw a speedometer and a rev counter, and a red button marked START. By his left leg was the gear stick, with three positions: FORWARD, NEUTRAL and REVERSE. The accelerator lever was inside the right handlebar. But where was the key?

Then Will saw it, dangling from an elastic wrist strap that had been pushed along the left-side handlebar.

Will pushed the strap over his hand. He looked over his shoulder, and spotted the clasp that held the ski to the winch. He was about to reach back to release it when from inside the cabin one of the men shouted: 'I'll get the beer!'

Will tensed. That voice had been loud. And close. He held his breath.

The music suddenly got louder. A door must have had opened, Will realized. He craned his neck. He could see about ten metres along the starboard deck – and he noticed a cardboard box. What was in it? Beer?

If he could see the box, anyone picking it up would be able to see him. *If* they looked around. Why would they? He asked himself.

But if they did –

Perhaps he should release the ski now.

Perhaps he should just stay still, and wait.

Then he heard another voice. *Much* closer. In his ear.

'Will?' Gaia said.

Will didn't respond. He heard footsteps, and he hunched over, his heart starting to thud.

The man was singing to himself: '*And the last train out of Central's almost gone* – uh.'

There had been a clunk. He must have stumbled.

'*Will?*'

Her voice seemed impossibly loud. 'Shh,' he whispered, under his breath.

Will wanted to look round, to try to see if the man was still there, but he didn't dare to move.

Then he heard a soft rushing noise. Out of the corner of his eye, Will saw an arc of water curve up away from the yacht, and into the harbour. Not water, he realized.

A voice from inside called: 'Where's the beer?'

Will heard a belch. Then the sound of a fly being zipped up. Another clunk. Then a scraping. Cardboard against wood. The man was picking up the box.

'*Will, are you all right? Where are you?*'

Will gritted his teeth.

'Uh,' the man grunted. Unsteady feet started to stumble away.

Then there was a bang, and the volume of the music halved.

Will breathed again. 'I'm fine,' he whispered. 'If I don't respond, it's because I can't! Why didn't you check my video?'

'I did! All I can see is black. It isn't working.'

'It is working,' Will hissed. 'I'm looking at the water, and it's black!' He glanced back along the deck.

'What's that?' Gaia asked.

'*Shh.*'

'Are you on a *boat*?'

Will didn't reply. He reached back, grabbed the winch clasp. Released it.

The ski dropped half a metre. And bounced.

Will's pulse raced. The splash had seemed loud. He listened hard. But he heard only the music, and the two voices. *Singing.*

Will yanked the paddle free and dug it into the water. Every second stroke, he switched sides. Steadily, he pulled away from the yacht, dragging the kayak behind him. The longer he used the paddle, the smaller the chance the men on the boat would realize it was *their* jet ski when he started the engine, he thought.

But the clock was ticking. They had to get to Phoenix House.

When he was thirty metres from the cruiser, Will slipped the paddle into the kayak. He gripped the magnetic key and pushed it into the slot. Then he hit START.

The engine roared. After the silence of the kayak, it seemed ear-splitting.

He shoved the gear stick into FORWARD and squeezed the accelerator. Instantly, the ski responded, skidding across the water, dragging the kayak behind him. Will glanced back. There was no one on the deck. He squeezed harder, aiming for the jetty.

'Gaia, get ready,' he said.

'Where are you?'

Will didn't reply. He concentrated on maintaining a straight line. The wind whipped his face. The engine vibrated through his body. And he grinned.

The jetty was dead ahead. He'd be there in seconds.

'That isn't *you* on the jet ski!' Gaia said suddenly. 'You remember you're not actually allowed to use them in the harbour!'

'Weird, I thought I had Gaia with me, not Andrew! Do you think we could trail a speedboat in a *kayak*?'

'What use will it be if we get *arrested*?'

Will held his tongue. He'd reached the end of the jetty. He swerved around it, heading for the stone steps that descended into the water. A yellow water taxi with inflatable sides was usually moored here, waiting for customers. But it wasn't here now.

Gaia was waiting, hands on her hips. Will manoevred the ski as close as he could to the steps. The water churned.

He reached out.

Gaia hesitated. Then she grabbed Will's hand, jumped on to the platform, and threw her right leg over the seat.

Will squeezed the accelerator hard.

They blistered away from the jetty, heading west. He checked the speedometer. 113 kmph.

He bounced on the seat, his heart still pounding, but from triumph and exhilaration. They were racing across

Sydney Harbour on a stolen jet ski, on the trail of –
what? An illicit drugs gang? Sir James Parramore?

It didn't matter, Will thought. What mattered was that
he could feel his blood crashing through his veins. Every
nerve in his body, every atom of his flesh, was *alive*. And
he could feel Gaia, her arms pressed tight around him.

10

A power boat screamed past. Will steered into the wash. It acted like a ramp, and the jet ski took off, the kayak flying behind them. Stars glinted. They cleared a metre of water and slammed back down. Spray soaked them. Gaia's grip tightened. She blinked water from her eyes.

For at least the tenth time, Will checked over his shoulder. There was still no sign of the cruiser. Or police. They'd got away with taking the ski. So far.

Only one more headland to go, and they should glimpse Phoenix House.

Just what were de Souza and Broadstairs planning to collect, Will wondered.

Ingredients for a new drug? Or were they paying someone else to do the chemistry – and collecting their latest cache? If that was the case, why two separate pick-ups?

'Will, slow down,' Gaia said.

They were rounding the headland. Will eased his pressure on the accelerator.

Gradually the speedo dropped down to ten kilometres per hour.

Around them now, the harbour was dark. Apart from the engine, they could hear only the regular wash of waves against the shore. The half moon was dim, cobwebbed with light cloud.

Will turned the handlebars, sending the ski curving gently to the south. And there, through the trees, he saw the white-lit tips of the towers of Phoenix House. His gaze jumped down to the jetty.

Clearly Gaia's had done the same, because she whispered: 'The boat's still there.'

'Yeah.' Will checked his watch. 7.48 p.m. He took his toothphone keypad from his jacket pocket and hit the blue button. 'Andrew, where are you?'

After a moment, they heard:

'Will, Gaia, we're in position. I am eyeballing the driveway of Phoenix House. Confirm your location. Over.'

Will looked round at Gaia, one eyebrow raised. She was smiling. Andrew had a tendency to use military vocabulary – or what he imagined to be military vocabulary – when he was talking into a toothphone. Especially when he was nervous.

Will replied in kind. 'I'm eyeballing the jetty of Phoenix House. Boat still in position. Over.'

'You and Gaia are in a kayak? Over.'

'Negative.' Will paused. 'We have requisitioned a vehicle.'

Will expected further questions, but Andrew exclaimed: 'Will, the gates are opening! A black car

– a Bentley – is leaving Phoenix House. I think Broadstairs is driving. Over!'

Will whispered hard: 'You know what to do.'

Brakes screeched.

Andrew glanced uncertainly at Lydia.

Yes, he thought, they were on the tail of a man who a) just might be Sir James Parramore; b) even if he wasn't, in all likelihood was involved in something seriously underhand, if not downright illegal; and c) could be en route to collect a new consignment of whatever revolutionary new drugs were being used at Phoenix House. But, still, they were barrelling around blind corners – and they were doing it without headlights.

Andrew didn't want to criticize Lydia. Neither did he want to die. 'Lydia, do you think you should put the lights on?'

Her eyes didn't budge from the road. 'I can see him. This way, he can't see us.'

'But with our lights off, we're actually more noticeable. If a police car drives past –'

'This is a 4.8-litre engine. I'll race away,' Lydia said, flashing him a smile.

But she did slow down. After a moment, she flicked on the side lights.

'Who actually taught you to drive?' Andrew asked, trying to sound casual.

'My grandparents have a property in northern New South Wales. On private land, you can do what you want.'

Andrew resisted pointing out that this road was not private land. 'And your dad doesn't mind you driving?'

'He doesn't know,' Lydia said.

'*Really?* What if you get stopped by police?'

'What'll they do? I'm only fifteen.' She smiled again.

They swept downhill, along the curving coastal road.

To their right, the harbour was a black void, dotted with an occasional light. Ahead – and getting closer – skyscrapers looked two dimensional against the sky.

'Looks like he's heading for the city,' Lydia said. And flinched. Bright headlights had just reflected in the rear view mirror, half-blinding her.

In his wing mirror, Andrew saw a sedan swerve. He realized he was gripping tight to his seat. He ordered himself to let go.

Perhaps, in fact, it would be better to die than for Lydia to think him a coward. He considered telling her about hydrospeeding through underground caverns in the Alps. *Later*, he decided.

The road began to level out. Lydia kept her foot down, and they shot down a street lined with boutique clothes shops and cafes. Then the clothes shops became bars and, as they sped across a square, Andrew noticed men with bottles in brown paper bags. Neon restaurant signs advertised tapas, pizza, even Balkan cuisine. 'Where are we?'

'Taylor Square,' Lydia said. 'Darlinghurst.'

'So this is the rougher end of Sydney.'

'Sydney isn't all paradise.' She slammed on the brakes. A white pick-up with three spotlights mounted on a bar above the cabin had just swerved in front of them. 'Hoon!' she yelled out of the window.

'Why has that pick-up got spotlights?' Andrew asked.

'That *ute*,' Lydia said, 'has got spotlights because that's what *hoons* use when they're standing in the back in the bush finding roos to shoot.'

Andrew stared at her. 'You're serious?'

'*Deadly*.' Lydia rolled the steering wheel, hit the accelerator, and overtook the ute. Now there was only a motorbike and a green SUV between them and the Bentley.

The men with bottles in bags had vanished, Andrew noticed. To his right, he saw an elegant park with silver birch trees. To his left, Victorian buildings loomed.

Suddenly the Bentley's brake lights flashed. Broadstairs – at least, Andrew hoped it was Broadstairs – cut across a lane of traffic and came to a stop.

Lydia slowed.

'Keep going,' Andrew urged, 'or he'll know we're following. There! Stop in front, here!' He jabbed his finger at a large white truck parked on the left.

'Make your mind up!' Lydia said, but she took the spot in front of the truck. It looked like a refrigerator lorry. And it hid them perfectly.

Andrew jumped down on to the street. It was

crowded. Couples ambled past. A group of office workers tumbled out of a bar.

Lydia ran to join him. She followed his gaze, to the Bentley. They could just see the driver's door. It was opening. Andrew wondered if he should get out his binoculars.

No need. The driver was tall. Black-haired. Before the man turned away, Andrew registered the small nose and fleshy lips. *Broadstairs.*

'Will, Gaia, am eyeballing Frederick Broadstairs,' Andrew whispered excitedly. 'Continuing pursuit on foot.'

Lydia shook her head. It was still hard to believe these toothphones actually existed.

Andrew had told her about them while they'd watched the drive at Phoenix House. He'd even taken out his contact lens to show her the miniature camera. If she'd had any doubts about the story Will had told her in her dad's office, she didn't any more. These *items*, at least, were real. She set off after Broadstairs.

'*Will?*' Andrew said. '*Gaia?*'

There was no response.

As he followed Lydia, Andrew took the contact lens display from his pocket, flipped it open and selected Will's output.

'*Andrew,*' Lydia hissed. She was hurrying along the pavement. Like almost every other man on the street, Broadstairs wore a dark suit and she was afraid of losing him. 'Andrew, hurry up!'

Andrew nodded, but he was frowning. What *was* that? What on earth was Will doing?

Thirty seconds after Andrew informed them that a black car was leaving Phoenix House, Will and Gaia got an *eyeball* of their own.

A woman in a black skirt and jacket and a floating black headscarf walked out on to the jetty. They couldn't see her face. But her legs were bare. They were slim and tanned.

'De Souza?' Gaia whispered.

'It has to be,' Will said. She *was* going to leave by water.

After a moment, Gaia whispered: 'So maybe it was worth stealing the jet ski.'

He smiled. 'I did tell you to trust me.'

Gaia pulled a face. But Will didn't see it. He was watching de Souza step into the speedboat. She lifted the mooring rope free and sat down at the wheel. A second later, the engine fired. The boat turned, heading west.

Gaia had been resting her hands on her knees. Now she wrapped her arms back around Will. He squeezed the accelerator and steered a zig-zagging course. He raced in one direction, then doubled back, trying to make it seem to anyone who might be watching that his only purpose on the water was *fun*.

Gaia held on tight, trying to get comfortable. Her wet

jeans were clinging to her skin. Andrew's wicking trousers might not look good, but they were a lot more practical, she thought.

Suddenly Will u-turned the ski. Over her shoulder, Gaia saw the speedboat had changed direction. It was moving away from the coast. Going *where*?

Gaia extended its course, and her eyes hit a shadowy island.

It was smack bang in the middle of the harbour. Long, and narrow. And dark, apart from the boating lights that blinked from a jetty. Gaia couldn't see any houses – only vast Norfolk pines.

The speedboat was heading for the jetty.

'She's going to the island,' Gaia whispered.

'Yeah,' Will let go of the accelerator. The last thing he wanted was for de Souza – or anyone waiting for her – to spot them.

The ski rocked gently in the swell.

'What are you doing?' Gaia whispered. 'Aren't we following her?'

'I'm going to kayak in,' Will said. 'I'll need you to wait out of sight with the ski. Keep an eye on my camera feed. If I get in trouble, I'll call you in.'

'Wait *where*?'

'Anywhere, but not too far away. And stay out of the way of the ferries.'

'But I don't know how to drive this thing!' she said. 'Not that you'd remember, but I didn't do the jet ski course.'

'It's easy.' Will showed her the gear stick. 'Forward. Backwards. Squeeze this lever to accelerate.' His gaze shot back to the speedboat. It was almost at the island. 'I have to go. We *have* to try to find out what she's picking up.'

Gaia took a deep breath. Nodded.

Will swung his left leg over the seat. He edged along the platform, to the tow bar. Then he grabbed the rope and pulled the kayak alongside.

Will picked up the paddle. Very carefully, he stepped into the cockpit. The kayak rolled hard to the right. One blade of the paddle was sticking up in the air. Gaia grabbed it. She held it until the kayak stabilized.

'Thanks,' Will said.

Gaia nodded. She slid forward and clutched the handlebars.

She was looking anxious, Will realized. 'I'll be fine,' he said.

'It's not actually you I'm worried about.'

He smiled. 'You'll be fine.' He dipped a blade into the water, and started to paddle away.

Gaia glanced up. A silver streak of cloud was moving from the moon. When she looked back, she noticed a sign nailed to the jetty. She shuddered.

Shark Island.

Andrew and Lydia walked quickly, staying close to the shops. It wasn't easy to keep track of Broadstairs. The street was poorly lit, and men with dark hair and suits seemed to be out in force.

Broadstairs crossed a side road, into shadows. Lydia started to hurry past Andrew.

He touched her arm. 'We have to stay well back,' he whispered. 'He might see us.'

'But we'll lose him!'

'Lydia, please, I have some experience of this.' Before the sentence was even out, Andrew knew it sounded patronizing. He bit his lip. His gaze was still on their target, so he couldn't see Lydia's expression. In fact, he wasn't sure he wanted to. 'I mean, it's rule one of surveillance. You don't get too close.'

'What's rule two? Wear a yellow top?' Suddenly Lydia rammed her back against the wall. 'He looked round!'

A scene from a film shot into Andrew's mind. A man and a woman had been following someone. Afraid they'd been spotted, they'd flung themselves into an embrace, as cover. Now Lydia was looking at him with her liquid jet eyes.

But the idea of grabbing a girl and kissing her was ridiculous. At least, for him, Andrew thought. He wrenched his gaze from Lydia. Thankfully, Broadstairs was still walking, and he was maintaining his pace.

'We're all right,' he said. 'But if he looks round again, don't over-react. Look in a shop window.'

'The shops are closed,' Lydia whispered hotly. 'The windows are dark.'

Andrew glanced at her. Perhaps Lydia hadn't liked being told she'd over-reacted. He changed the subject. 'Where are we, exactly?'

'George Street. The main shopping street. If we keep going, we'll get to Circular Quay. Where the Opera House is.'

Andrew had seen a map of Circular Quay in Will's guidebook. It was shaped like a horseshoe. The Opera House was at one end. From the other, the Harbour Bridge sprang across to the north shore. In the curve of the horseshoe were the city's main passenger ferry terminals.

'What's he doing?' Lydia whispered.

Broadstairs had slowed. He raised something to his ear. A mobile phone, Andrew guessed. After a few moments, Broadstairs started to stride away, even faster than before.

'Who do you think he was talking to?' Lydia whispered. 'His contact for the pick-up?'

'Perhaps,' Andrew said.

They hurried on, keeping to the shadows.

After a few minutes, the street opened out. Andrew smelt salt in the air. Ahead, he saw globe lights, people milling, and black water. He glanced up. They were passing beneath an iron railway bridge.

Broadstairs turned right. They followed, on to a paved esplanade.

Suddenly noise surrounded them. People thronged the ferry terminals, eating pies, swigging water, queuing for tickets. An Italian ballad blared from a busy restaurant.

Andrew and Lydia pushed their way around past a busker on a unicycle, and hit a tour group.

Andrew could just make out Broadstairs. He was striding on, past two men sitting on the ground playing didgeridoos. Andrew's gaze caught. The breathing action required to produce the continuous hum took years to master, he'd read. But there was no time to look now. Broadstairs was moving fast. His dark suit kept merging with the backs of other people.

At last, they cleared the ferry terminals. Ahead, to the left, a string of globe lights lined the water's edge, all the way to the Opera House. It glowed, moon-bright. *No time to look.*

Andrew dragged his gaze away.

At a roundabout ahead, people were streaming from a tour bus. A woman pushed a pram. Three Chinese tourists were grinning for a photo. But where was Broadstairs?

'*Where is he?*' Andrew whispered.

'He was right in front of us!' Lydia cried.

No, Andrew thought. *No!* They *couldn't* have lost him.

He pushed his way into the crowd from the tour bus, muttering, 'Excuse me, excuse me.'

Where was he?

Andrew nearly tripped over an old woman in a wheelchair.

'Watch where you're going!' a man yelled.

'Sorry!' Andrew called.

At last he broke free of the crowd.

And he saw it: a flash of black. A dark suit. Slick hair.

Andrew's heart rushed.

Here, the esplanade was lined with kiosks selling tickets for tourist cruises. Wooden jetties floated behind them. Broadstairs was stepping off one of these jetties on to a gangplank.

The gangplank led to a triple-decked white boat with a huge red paddle wheel at the back. *Sydney Showboat* was painted on the hull in red.

At the other end of the gangplank, a man in a blue uniform urged Broadstairs on.

Andrew heard him call: 'All aboard, we're about to leave!'

Broadstairs waved a hand in response. He strode on

to the deck, ducked his head and vanished into the saloon.

This was no time to weigh up potential options, Andrew decided. He ran along the esplanade and across the jetty, to the gangplank.

The deck-hand was securing a rope. His head jerked up.

'Sorry,' Andrew puffed. The paddle wheel started to churn the water, and Andrew raised his voice above the noise: 'My parents are already inside!'

'You're just in time, mate. Go on in.'

Andrew smiled. Partly in relief. Partly at being called 'mate'. As he stepped on to the deck, he turned. The man was yanking in the gangplank. He dropped it by the rails and leaped up a flight of metal steps.

Andrew looked back. And realized two things. First: Lydia was only just emerging from the coach-load of tourists. Second: the boat was on the move.

Lydia raced to the water's edge, seeking Andrew. Found him! She ran along the jetty. Backed up a few paces.

'No!' Andrew called, as he realized what she was planning to do.

It was too dangerous! Already, there was a clear metre of frothing water between them.

Lydia paid no attention. She ran – and jumped.

Her right foot hit the deck. Her left slipped. Andrew had reached out, and now he grabbed her arms. For a moment, Lydia seemed to sway. Then she toppled, collapsing against him. Her cheek slammed against his arm. He didn't fall. He held her. Andrew's heart pounded. He didn't move.

Lydia regained her balance. She pulled back, smoothing her hair. She was breathing hard. Her eyes gleamed. 'Thought you were going to get away and follow Broadstairs on your own, did you?'

Andrew's heart sank. 'No –'

'I'm kidding!' She grinned. 'We made it.'

Relief washed through him. 'You must have jumped more than two metres of water. Even Sheila Barlow would be impressed.'

'Before or after she went to Phoenix House?' Lydia asked, still smiling. She peered past him, and into the saloon.

Two women with fur-cuffed scarlet coats and black feathers in their hair were escorting late-comers to tables. At the far end of the room was a stage. An overweight old man in a red fez and a three-piece suit was performing a card trick.

Andrew and Lydia scanned the tables. There was no sign of Broadstairs. But it was impossible to make out the people at tables on a gallery above the main saloon.

'Shall we go in?' Lydia whispered.

'We have to be very careful,' Andrew said. 'We just can't risk Broadstairs seeing us. Especially if I'm meant to be going to Phoenix House tomorrow.'

Stealth was of the essence, Andrew told himself. And glanced down at his yellow fleece.

Lydia followed his gaze and nodded. Andrew coloured. She'd realized what he was thinking.

One of his first tasks was to find something less conspicuous to wear.

Will rocked gently in the darkness. He was about thirty metres from the eastern point of the island. The speedboat had slowed. It was closing in on the jetty. Will couldn't see any other boats. Nor, he realized, could he see Gaia.

He set his toothphone to transmit to hers. 'Where are you?' he whispered.

There was a pause. Then: 'Near the fort.'

Will's gaze shifted to the lights of Fort Denison, to the west. According to the guidebook, it had been an island convict prison. Now it was a tourist destination.

'OK,' he whispered. And he saw the speedboat stop. De Souza tossed a rope around a mooring post. 'Stay there, I'm paddling in.'

Will pulled hard. The kayak glided through the water, barely making a sound.

Where was her contact? he wondered. Perhaps they'd already found a concealed spot to pull in. He'd have to do the same.

As Will rounded the island, he kept his head low, and he scanned the rocky shore. In among the pines, he made out wooden picnic tables. And what looked like a small bandstand with a domed roof. There were no houses. Clearly, the island was uninhabited. Now, where was de Souza? And where could he land?

Then his eyes narrowed. Just past a rocky outcrop, he saw an inlet. It was edged with a narrow band of sand. At the back was a low cliff.

Perfect.

But before he pulled in, perhaps he should try to locate de Souza, he thought. Andrew's binoculars were equipped with night vision and they would have come in handy. But at least he had Sam.

Will shrugged the rucksack from his back. Holding it between his knees, he pulled the robot and its screen from a side pocket. Will flipped the screen open. He selected *Night Vision*, and activated the robot. Its alloy head twitched.

To keep Sam small, Will had been forced to use a low-resolution infra red camera. The sensitivity was poor. But it should still be enough to detect de Souza's body heat, he thought.

Starting at the western tip, Will began to pan the robot's head along the length of the island. A series of small red blips showed up on the screen. Animals, he guessed.

The camera passed the dense, cool structure of the bandstand. And there she was! A hot strip, on the move. She was heading away – towards the other side of the island.

And Will's hand froze. A faint hum came through the

trees. Was it an engine? Could it be her contact, arriving? Was de Souza going to meet them?

There was no time to lose.

Will dropped Sam and the screen in his lap. He grabbed his paddle and pulled as hard as he dared.

Twenty seconds later, there was a thud as the hull hit sand. Will stepped into the water. Icy fingers crept up his legs. For a moment, he stood still, listening. He heard waves against the rocks. Breeze in the pines. And that engine. *Getting louder.*

Quickly Will dragged the kayak in between two boulders. He wrapped the mooring rope three times around the biggest rock, and wedged the end underneath. His thoughts raced. He *could* send Sam overland to spy on de Souza and her contact. But the robot would make a noise in the pines and twigs. And it would be slow going.

Instead, Will zipped Sam and the screen into the pocket on the front of his vest. He slotted in his mouthpiece, biting down hard on the plastic. Then he turned. Crouched. And slipped into the black water.

Andrew shoved his yellow fleece behind a fire extinguisher and gratefully took Lydia's jacket. It was dark brown, and smelled faintly of vanilla. Though it was a little too tight to be comfortable, it would keep him warm.

'You're sure you won't be cold?'

'I've got two jumpers on, Andrew. I'll be fine.'

They had their backs to the saloon. Inside, the evening was in full swing.

Andrew sneaked a glance through a window. He saw waiters in white jackets pouring wine. The diners were tucking into oysters and smoked salmon. 'He *could* be up in the gallery. But I don't think we can risk going in. At least, I can't.'

'I could,' Lydia said. 'If he sees me, it won't matter.'

'It could be dangerous. What if he saw you at Phoenix House today?'

Lydia shook her head. 'The hairy guy saw me, and maybe his friend. No one else.'

'Broadstairs might have been watching from a window.'

'Look, even if he did see me, and *even* if he sees me

now and gets suspicious, what's he going to do – throw me overboard?'

'Well, yes, he might.'

Lydia's black eyes widened. 'Do you always worry this much?'

Andrew flushed.

She checked her watch. 'Give me five minutes. I'll take a quick look, and I'll be right back. If we stay hanging round out here, someone's going to notice us anyway.'

'Wait.' Andrew wished he'd brought the last toothphone for Lydia. But he did have something to offer her. From a zip pocket, he produced the binoculars. He held them out. 'They might come in handy.'

'For knocking Broadstairs on the head?' Lydia said, but she took them and started for the door.

Andrew whispered: 'Lydia –'

She turned.

'Be careful.'

The faint exasperation on her face vanished. She winked.

Andrew sighed. He really shouldn't be letting her go in on her own. But what else could he do? If Broadstairs saw him, his chance to question de Souza and access the computer network at Phoenix House would be ruined. Will and Gaia would rightly be angry.

But just because he couldn't go inside didn't mean he should hang around and wait for Lydia, of course. He could at least thoroughly check the deck.

Andrew set off. At each window, he paused, ready to duck out of sight. But no one seemed to notice him. The diners seemed happily occupied with their companions, or the food. Or the stage. Andrew did a double-take.

The magician had gone. In his place, heavily made-up women in stockings and ruched lemon skirts were performing the can-can. Was Broadstairs in there, watching them, he wondered. Had Lydia spotted him? Why hadn't he brought another toothphone!

Andrew reached the bow.

He found a lone couple leaning against the railings, taking in the night-time view of the water and the houses along the far shore.

Andrew turned the corner, and started along the starboard deck. As he closed in on the red wheel, the churning steadily got louder. Soon, he couldn't hear anything except the whack of the paddles and the rush of water.

It was dark back here – and very noisy.

Cautiously, Andrew peered around the edge of the metal wall, on to the stern deck.

And he jumped. His heart palpitated.

A large black sports bag had just been dropped on to the deck. Andrew saw a large, rough hand reach down to grab the zip. And he saw something else. His eyes were cold, his hair slick. *Frederick Broadstairs.*

Andrew stared.

The hand belonged to a stubby man in a black T-shirt. He was opening the bag. Broadstairs peered down into it. Behind his head, the paddle wheel churned. Droplets of water were flung through the air.

Andrew held his breath. This was the pick-up! *What was in that bag?*

Spray coated his glasses, and he longed to clean them. But he didn't dare to move. Simply standing here was dangerous enough. Dangerous, and *useless* from this distance. If only he had Sam. Which he didn't. But he *had* to try to get a closer look.

Andrew stood on tiptoe – and his head hit metal.

He flinched.

His blood ran cold.

Had they heard him?

The stubby man started to turn, and sweat sprung from Andrew's palms. How could he have been so foolish? He'd have to run –

Suddenly, the contact and Broadstairs both looked up.

Andrew knew why. He'd heard it too. A violent groan.

Long brown hair was falling over the railings of the deck above. Lydia was retching hard. She groaned again.

Was she really being sick? No, Andrew thought at once. She must have been watching, and now she was creating a diversion, giving him time to get away.

Andrew backed up cautiously, determined Broadstairs wouldn't hear him. Then he ran.

He slipped around the bow, and down the port deck. When he reached the door to the saloon, he ran through it, into another world.

Warmth and music filled the room. On stage, the six women were in traditional Japanese costume, smiling coyly as they performed a fan dance. Andrew's gaze darted on. Past the bar, he saw a black downward arrow and a sign for *Gentlemen*. A place to hide.

He jumped down the stairs, found a cubicle and locked himself in.

Less than a minute later, the metal door to the toilets banged open. Andrew held his breath.

Was it Broadstairs? Or his stubby contact? Had they followed him?

Then he heard a tap run, and stop. Someone moved about. There was a scratching sound. And a cough. *What were they doing?* After a moment, the door slammed shut.

It was just a diner – and he'd gone. Andrew breathed again.

But this was ridiculous, he told himself. He couldn't spend the rest of the cruise in the toilets.

Thirty seconds later, someone else came in. Andrew froze.

'*Andrew?*'

Lydia! He fumbled with the bolt.

And Lydia was there in front of him, looking relieved.

Her hair hung around her shoulders. 'I've been looking all over for you!'

'I had to hide. I—'

'Can't let Broadstairs see you. Yeah, I know.' A smile crept on to her face. 'You want to know what else I know?' She waved the binoculars. 'They were useful, after all.'

'You didn't see inside the bag?' Andrew said quickly.

'Yep.'

'*Drugs?*'

'Not exactly.'

'*So?*'

'A black briefcase.'

'Which might have held drugs?'

'No. Broadstairs's friend opened it. There was something mounted inside. It looked a bit like a hairdryer.'

'A *hairdryer*?'

'But there was a label on the side. A hazard symbol. You know, the skull and crossbones. Below that, there was another label –'

'Lydia, if you don't hurry up and tell me –'

'It said, *Danger: high-power microwaves.*'

'Microwaves . . .' Andrew racked his brain. What was Broadstairs doing with microwaves? How could *microwaves* improve sporting performance, or skin, or memory? He had absolutely no idea.

Perhaps Will or Gaia might. Andrew checked his watch. 8.27 p.m. The cruise could easily last another hour or more. He couldn't wait that long.

He found his toothphone keypad. Hit the black button. 'Will, Gaia. I have intel. *Do you read me?'*

Will was swimming breast-stroke. He was about a metre below the surface, and he could hardly see anything. Sam had a torch, but he didn't want to risk using it. Besides, he thought, he had to be close.

After another ten seconds, Will stopped. He broke the surface. Water lapped around his nose. And he heard something. A man's voice?

It was faint. And it had seemed to have drifted from over the cliff to his left. It was about three metres high, and glistening with moss. Root tendrils snaked down to the water. But Will couldn't see anyone. Had he imagined the voice?

Then he heard 'bitter . . . you told me . . .' Snatches of words. From a woman with a rich accent. *De Souza*.

Will stared up into the darkness. He grabbed hold of a root, and hauled himself out of the water. And he tensed. He could see the end of a black scarf fluttering above him in the breeze.

Suddenly the breeze blew stronger. Leaves rustled, almost muffling a grunt.

Then a male voice with an Indian accent rang clear: 'Because of the money!'

He sounded angry. *What was going on?*

'I have the money,' de Souza said.

Then silence. What was happening? Will wondered. Was she handing it over? He had to get closer.

His wet trainers slipped on the rock. He had to use his arms to pull himself up the root. He clung on tight, his chest against the cliff, scrabbling for a footing.

And de Souza said: 'All . . . as we agreed!' She seemed annoyed.

So, Will thought, they were arguing about money. But for *what*? He cursed. Five minutes earlier, he might have been in time to get Sam with his camera into position. Perhaps there was still time –

And Will tensed. He'd just heard a metallic click. The wind died.

'Don't be crazy!' de Souza exclaimed. 'If you want more, I can try to get it, but you will have to wait.'

'But what about our deal? Every time, Eva, you play games. I do as you ask, and what do I get?'

'Every time, Sharif, what you deliver is not quite what you promised!'

'*Enough!*'

'Sharif!' A pause. 'If you want more, I can get it!' Her tone had changed. Now she sounded *scared*.

Will hauled himself higher until at last, he could peer over the cliff. And he saw de Souza. Her scarf floated out behind her. Her high heels snapped twigs as she stumbled. She was taking clumsy steps backwards, and raising her hands.

In front of her, a small man angrily waved a gun.

'*Sharif –*'

'No, Eva! My patience is over. It is *too late!*'

He was going to shoot!

Will took his right hand from the root. He leaned in against the rock and pulled Sam and the screen from his vest. Then he aimed Sam's nose at the man, selected maximum power, and hit FIRE.

Suddenly the man groaned. He clapped both hands to his ears, dropping the gun.

De Souza looked startled. Then she darted forward. She grabbed something from the ground. And she pulled off her shoes, and ran.

She was taking her chance and making a getaway, Will thought. He should do the same. Right now, the man's ears would be splitting. But he'd soon start to recover.

Will zipped Sam and the screen back into his vest, and he dropped into the water.

He swam hard. In a few minutes, he'd reached the tip of the island. The inlet was just ahead.

Will hit sand. Panting, he hurried to the boulder, and unwound the rope. And he stopped.

Movement. Out of the corner of his eye. Will looked up. And stared.

De Souza's contact was *right there* at the top of the cliff. Had he followed him around the island? Will made out the whites of his eyes. And the gun. Still in his hand. The man was peering at the water. Had he seen him?

'Gaia,' he hissed. 'Come now! I'm on the other side from the jetty!'

'What's going on? Will – is that a *gun*?'

He ducked low. 'Just come *now*!'

And the man moved. 'Hey! You!'

Crack. A bullet slammed into the boulder beside Will and ricocheted off. Fragments of rock splintered through the air. Fear sparked along his spine.

There was nowhere to hide. He had no choice. He had to run.

Will shoved the kayak into the water and leaped into it. He snatched up the paddle.

'You!'

Will hunched low, and didn't turn.

'Stop! *You!*'

This time, Will heard the bullet whistle. It crashed into the water, sending a plume of spray shooting in the air. Will shook his head, trying to get the water out of his eyes.

'Gaia, be careful! I'm being shot at!'

Will felt his muscles start to burn. A second later, another bullet whizzed past, close enough for him to flinch. Will peered round wildly. '*Gaia, where are you?*'

Then he saw her.

The ski was bouncing. It was coming from the west, hurtling towards the island.

Will checked over his shoulder. Saw the silhouette of the man. How far away was he now? Twenty metres? Thirty? If that was a pistol, the range could easily be two hundred. But how accurate could the shooter be in the dark?

Will kept paddling hard. His gaze jerked back to Gaia. Just how were they going to do this? Somehow, she'd have to slow down enough for him to jump on to the ski without them both becoming sitting targets.

Then she said: 'Get ready. Throw me your rope. I'm going to pull you!'

Will glanced back. The man was taking aim!

But the ski was ploughing on towards him. At last, Gaia was close. Her arm shot out. Will hurled the rope.

She caught it – and looped the end around the tow bar. Then she squeezed the accelerator.

Will waited, his blood rushing. For a split second, nothing happened. Then the slack in the rope was gone – and he felt the kayak leap through the water.

Air was suddenly blasted from his lungs. Spray drenched him. Tension made his limbs feel like rods. He was grasping the sides of the cockpit with iron fists. And he looked back.

Shark Island was merging with the water. The man with the gun had vanished into darkness.

He hadn't found out what de Souza had picked up. But he'd stopped her being injured – and probably killed. And he was safe. And so was Gaia.

Will tilted his face to the sky. Stars glittered, millions of them. He was being dragged across Sydney Harbour. He'd been shot at. He was soaking wet. His back felt like it was breaking. And right at that moment, there was nowhere else in the world he'd rather be.

What would Dad think, Will wondered.

Slam. Gaia smashed through a wave from a ferry. Will's grip was nearly broken. But he was still holding on.

Then he heard Andrew's voice in his ear: 'Will. Gaia. I have intel. *Do you read me?'*

Will watched steam rise as he stirred the coffee.

He wasn't sure he and Gaia needed caffeine. But he wanted something hot.

The kitchen seemed surreally quiet. But only because his body was still recovering, he realized. His senses were on edge, his pulse still fast. In his mind, he could see the man with the gun. The whites of his eyes. The plume of water as the bullet struck.

Will picked up the cups and took them out to the deck.

Gaia was on one of the chairs, wrapped in a blanket. Beyond her, yachts bobbed in the water. A ferry trundled towards the Watson's Bay jetty. Diners strolled out of the restaurant, slipping on jackets and shawls. Everything seemed normal.

Well, it *was*, he thought, as he gave a cup to Gaia. Normal for them. Normal for STORM.

And at least the trip home had passed without incident.

As they'd entered the bay, Gaia had cut the engine. Will had paddled the ski right up to the cruiser. The music had still been blaring from the cabin. They'd connected the ski to the winch and hoisted it back up. Then Gaia had sped away in the kayak, Will swimming underwater behind her.

This time, the men did hear something. They stumbled on to the deck. One even did a circuit. But there was nothing to see. Only a ferry in the distance. And a girl in a kayak.

Now, Gaia loosened the blanket so she could check the time. 9.48 p.m. She turned to Will, who'd taken a seat beside her. 'Shouldn't they be back by now?'

He shrugged.

Andrew had started to fill them in – until their toothphones had speeded out of range.

Will and Gaia had tried to come up with reasons for why Phoenix House might need high power microwaves. And failed.

If only he'd found out what de Souza had picked up on Shark Island, Will thought, they might have an answer. Or at least be closer to one.

Perhaps they should call Barrington to tell him what they'd discovered so far, he thought. But if Broadstairs wasn't Parramore, Barrington wouldn't be interested. Maybe –

Will stopped himself. He knew he wanted an excuse to call Barrington so he could ask if he'd discovered anything more about his father.

Barrington had said he'd call when he had news. But Will hated waiting. And he'd waited long enough.

It had been Easter when David Allott first told him he had 'information' about his father's death. But then Allott had been busy.

Six weeks ago, he'd finally called to say he could meet Will that night.

Gaia had gone with him.

Nine o'clock, and Leicester Square had been packed with foreign students. They'd waited, as instructed, on a bench near the statue of Shakespeare.

The minutes ticked past.

Allott had been twelve minutes late.

He'd looked surprised at Gaia's presence. Then he'd sat next to Will, and said: 'This is what I have to tell you . . .'

On the deck at Watson's Retreat, Will could still hear Allott's voice. Every word had been branded on to his mind.

Allott said he'd known his father for seventeen years. Just before his death, Jonathan Knight had been working near a village called Xidi in eastern China, investigating a secretive research institute.

Allott had been on a job in Beijing. When it had finished, he'd taken the opportunity to fly out to meet his old friend. They'd talked for two hours, and Allott had taken the last flight back to the capital.

'I got the call at six twenty the next morning,' Allott told him. 'It was from the Chinese secret service. The institute had exploded at four twenty-six. I checked with MI6 Operations Control. At four twelve, your father had sent a coded signal to say he was going in. That was the last message they got from him.'

Allott had flown straight back to Xidi to investigate. But the institute had been obliterated. There was only rubble, and police, who'd erected a security cordon.

'Your father had told me he was working with a CIA officer,' Allott went on. 'So I tried to track him down. But the CIA had no record of any agent working in the region. Either this man had never been employed by them, or his file had been deleted.

'Neither was there any record, anywhere, of what the institute was – or what research it was involved in. In your father's latest assignment report, he said he was still trying to find that out.'

'*What else?*' Will had asked, his voice raw.

'I'm sorry. I tried to find out more about the institute, about the CIA officer, and every time, I hit a brick wall. I know all this is probably no comfort. But I wanted you to know.'

On the deck, Will shook his head. Allott had been right. The conversation had been no comfort. It had thrown up more questions than answers, and it had stirred up a mess of feelings he'd hoped had been laid to rest. How could they rest now?

But Barrington's security clearance went much higher than Allott's. Surely he'd be able to discover *something*.

Will looked up. He'd realized Gaia was watching him. Sydney rushed back.

She lowered her cup. 'Are you thinking about your dad?' she asked softly.

After a few moments, he said: 'Is it that obvious?'

'Barrington's on your side, remember. When he gets answers, he'll let you know.'

'*If* he gets answers,' Will said.

He fixed his gaze on the black ocean. He'd been focusing on Broadstairs. Phoenix House. De Souza. Before that, school, and STASIS and his devices.

But all that other *stuff* was still there. Every so often, it took over. Like it was *now*.

Gaia's chair was close. She put her cup on the ground. And she touched his arm.

Will hadn't noticed her move, and he tensed. He looked at her. His head was raging. He wanted it to stop. His gaze ran over her face. Her forehead, her bright brown eyes, down to her mouth. He was about to reach out – and he froze.

Gaia had heard it too. Wheels on the gravel at the front of the house.

Lydia and Andrew. They were back.

The front door slammed.

Andrew called: 'Where are you?'

'On the deck,' Will shouted. He was watching Gaia, who was wrapping the blanket tighter and avoiding his eyes.

Andrew and Lydia dashed out. Andrew swiped a

hand through his hair. It looked wild. Half on end. He dragged two chairs over to Will and Gaia. But while Lydia sat, he stayed standing.

'So,' he said, 'I don't think Broadstairs got a good look at us. Possibly only a glimpse of Lydia, when she was pretending to be sick, so I could get away.' He shot her a quick smile. She flashed one back.

Gaia noticed. In normal circumstances, she'd have glanced at Will, to check his reaction. But she kept her eyes on Andrew.

'Unfortunately I did have to stay in the toilets for the rest of the trip,' Andrew added, pulling a face. 'Lydia pretended to be genuinely ill. They let her into the crew's quarters. And we told you the rest, I think. So there you have it.'

Lydia waited. But Will and Gaia weren't exactly letting the compliments rip. Even though, according to Andrew, they had come up with nothing. 'So you didn't manage to find out what de Souza was picking up?' she said evenly.

'. . . No,' Will said. 'I heard de Souza talk about something being bitter. But I don't know what. It could have been her contact. He did almost shoot her.'

'But de Souza didn't see you?' Andrew asked.

Will shook his head. 'I hit the man with Sam's sonar. I guess she thought he suddenly wasn't well. And she decided to run. But he must have seen me. Or he must have heard me when I dropped back into the water.'

Andrew shook his head. 'I can't believe he *shot* at

you. You didn't see where he went when he left the island?'

'It was hard to see much when I was being dragged behind the jet ski.' Will looked at Gaia. This time, she met his gaze. But she didn't smile.

Andrew nodded. 'Right.' At last he sat down. 'Well, I've been trying to think about microwaves. I still can't come up with anything that makes sense.'

'We need more information,' Will said. 'Which hopefully you'll get tomorrow.'

'You think I should still go for the appointment?' Andrew asked, surprised. 'Do you think de Souza will really keep it, after tonight?'

'I don't know,' Will said. 'But I hope so.'

'*Or* we could call Matt Walker and get him to try to organize a police raid on Phoenix House,' Gaia said.

'Who's Matt Walker?' Lydia asked

'An MI6 field officer,' Andrew told her. 'He's here in Australia, with another agent. But they're somewhere in the desert, I think.'

'But why would the police want to raid Phoenix House?' she said. 'We haven't got any proof of anything yet. And there's no law against meeting people on islands and paddleboats.'

'De Souza's contact *shot* at Will,' Gaia said. 'And you've got your file. You could take that to the police.'

Lydia frowned. She didn't want anyone to raid Phoenix House. And she didn't want to take her file to the police. Because *she* wanted to find out the truth. She wanted the scoop. She'd told them that already. But perhaps at this point, it would be better to give a different answer.

'What does the file really *prove*?' she said. 'A couple of athletes have done surprisingly well after treatment at Phoenix House. They're getting drug-tested – and they're coming up clean. What can the police do? They can't just raid private property when they feel like it.'

Gaia looked at Will.

'She's right,' he said.

'But you got *shot at*.'

'I have no idea who the man was. And de Souza would just deny being there.'

'If we think Broadstairs is Parramore, we should tell Walker anyway,' Gaia said.

'We could,' Andrew said, 'but remember that Walker thinks he and Marshall have found Parramore. I have to say, I doubt he'd listen to us when, unfortunately, as yet, we have no evidence that Broadstairs *is* Parramore.'

Will nodded. Walker and Marshall were busy with their own man. But there was more to it than that. Broadstairs was *theirs*, whether he was Parramore or not. *He* wanted to find out what was going on at Phoenix House.

He looked at Gaia. 'I think we need more information before we go to Walker or Barrington, or the police. Maybe Andrew will get it.'

Gaia bit her lip. But Will was being logical. Slowly she nodded.

Lydia didn't try to hide her pleasure. She turned to Andrew. 'When's your appointment?'

'Two o'clock. *If* de Souza keeps it.'

'But we'll keep Phoenix House under surveillance in the morning?'

'We'll meet here in the morning,' Will said to her. 'And we'll plan exactly what to do.'

Lydia was about to protest. Who was Will to be making all the decisions? But she held her tongue. She'd stopped them going to the police. Perhaps she should be content with that victory for now. 'Then I'd better get home,' she said, and got up. 'Dad'll be wondering where I am.'

Andrew's face fell. He felt it happen. And he coloured. He adjusted his glasses. 'I'll walk you out,' he said.

As he followed Lydia, Andrew realized he was still wearing her jacket.

He should return it at once, he thought. But it smelt of vanilla, of Lydia. Perhaps if he didn't say anything . . .

Lydia was already outside. Her trainers crunched in the gravel, and she jumped into the truck. The door slammed.

Andrew waited.

A moment later, the window shot down. Was she going to ask for her jacket?

'I'll be round about ten,' she said.

Andrew felt his heart beat faster – with guilt, and pleasure. 'Aren't you in school tomorrow?'

In answer Lydia laughed and started to pull away.

'Until tomorrow,' he called, as she pulled on to the road.

When, all being well, he'd walk into Phoenix House, charm Evangeline de Souza, make vital discoveries, and get out in one piece.

Less likely things had happened. This was STORM. There were precedents.

Lydia's brake lights flashed. She vanished around the corner, but her olive face was still vivid in his mind. His stomach churned. Was he worried about tomorrow? Yes –

No. It wasn't Phoenix House that was making him feel like this. It was her. *Lydia*.

De Souza stepped out on to the balcony of Broadstairs's study. The still night looked outrageously serene.

'I don't know what happened to him,' she said, 'but I really think he would have shot me. And he brought only half what I asked!'

'But he did bring *enough*? You did get the package?'

De Souza didn't hear him. She was looking at the stars, absorbed in her thoughts.

Sharif was a brilliant bio-prospector. He knew the flora of Asia like no one else. And the product he had described seemed ideal. He had 'discovered' it only last month. No one else in the world knew of its existence.

It was true, she reflected, he had always been an unstable contact. When he had insisted on their island rendezvous, she had felt concerned. But he had never pulled a gun before!

'*You did get enough?*' Broadstairs asked again. This time his tone was sharp.

De Souza looked round. Broadstairs was by the fire-place, his arms folded. His silver eyes were hard.

'Yes,' she said.

A half-smile replaced the glare. At least, de Souza thought it was a smile. The corners of his mouth had twitched.

Broadstairs unfolded his arms, and crossed to her. His gaze seemed to soften. 'Then,' he whispered, 'we have nothing to worry about. Only the latest results . . .'

'I will go to the lab now. I'll work on it myself. Tomor-row, I promise –'

'*Promise,*' Broadstairs interrupted quietly, and he stroked her hair, 'is a word I do not like. To me, it is the equivalent of *try, attempt, endeavour* –'

De Souza couldn't help recalling that when this pro-ject was over, Broadstairs had *promised* to take her with him. She met his eyes. 'I *will* get the results we need,' she said. 'We *will* succeed. And when we have, we *will* fly away together and live happily ever after.'

Again, Broadstairs's mouth twitched. De Souza decided to be optimistic. She took it as another smile.

On the deck at Watson's Retreat, Gaia wrapped the blanket tighter around her.

After Andrew had left to escort Lydia to the front door, Will had got up.

He had to clean Sam, he said. The robot had to be in perfect working order for Andrew's visit to Phoenix House. He hadn't really looked at her. He felt awkward too, she decided.

In London a few weeks ago, Andrew had asked her what was going on *with you and Will*.

Nothing, she'd said, because nothing was *going on*, and she hadn't wanted to discuss how she felt with anyone, even Andrew.

But would anything ever happen? Would the time ever be right?

Maybe, she thought. Maybe not.

Sunlight flooded the corridor. It reflected off the white walls and the shining limestone floor.

The interior of Phoenix House was immaculate, as befitted a centre for relaxation and healing.

De Souza had wanted the atmosphere of a day spa. Clients' bedrooms came with fluffy bathrobes and essential oils. Rainforest birdsong was piped into the Relaxation Lounge.

Everything seemed calm and reassuring. This was in stark contrast to the true heart of the centre: the laboratories, housed in the cellars.

De Souza had spent most of the night in the labs. She was exhausted. And she couldn't help feeling afraid that, after failing in what had certainly seemed an attempt to kill her, Sharif would come after her to try to finish the job.

Nonsense, Broadstairs had told her. He'd be on the first plane back to Delhi. And business must go on as usual. *Nothing* should be different.

Fortunately, de Souza had only two appointments scheduled for that day. The first client had cancelled.

She'd hoped the second would do the same. But he'd arrived exactly on time.

The receptionist hadn't warned her he was only *fourteen*. 'He sounded older on the phone,' the woman had whispered.

But the registration card clearly indicated his age, as well as his name.

Behind her now, Andrew removed his glasses and pressed a hand to his right eye. The contact lens was rubbing. He couldn't stop blinking.

Will's voice came through the toothphone: 'Andrew, I've just lost your video.'

Andrew dropped his hand.

'OK. Got it back.'

It was odd to think that Will, Lydia and Gaia could see what he saw, Andrew thought. But also reassuring. So too was the fact he was wearing Lydia's jacket.

He'd tried to give it back to her that morning. But the afternoon was cool. And he'd left his only warm top on the *Sydney Showboat*. He could have asked Will if he could borrow something, but the jacket smelled of vanilla, and Lydia had offered . . .

But despite all these reassurances, Andrew couldn't help feeling nervous.

That morning, after a brief visit from Marjorie Blaxted, they had worked on their plan. On what they wanted from his visit. And how it might be achieved.

Andrew would arrive by taxi. Will, Lydia and Gaia would follow at a safe distance. They would park the truck in a side road near the woods, and Lydia and Gaia would wait there, close at hand. They would use tooth-phones and a contact lens screen to keep track of him.

Meanwhile, Will would head into the wood, in search of a safe spot from which to deploy Sam.

While Andrew was trying to learn more about what 'treatment' at Phoenix House actually involved, Sam would explore the building, and hunt for Broadstairs.

Ten minutes or so into Andrew's appointment, Will would also use Sam to create a diversion that would – hopefully – require de Souza to leave her office.

Andrew would quickly slip the spyware on to her computer – presuming she had a computer – and acti-vate it. This would give him access to the Phoenix House network from his smartphone.

In theory, the plan seemed sound.

'You've got your toothphone,' Will had told Andrew. 'And you've got a lens. If you get into trouble, we'll know about it. We'll get you out of there.'

Easier said than done, Andrew thought, as he fol-lowed de Souza down another corridor.

Her high heels clacked on the stone. They were red, matching the suit she wore under her white lab coat.

So far, she'd barely said a word to him. This was hardly surprising, Andrew thought. After the events of the previous night, she was bound to be preoccupied. In fact, he thought, if anything was surprising it was that she'd actually kept the appointment.

Just as he was wondering whether he should say

something, de Souza broke her silence. 'So, the reputation of Phoenix House has spread as far as England?'

Andrew cleared his throat. He had prepared an explanation for how he'd heard of her. It was important, he thought, that it sounded as vague as possible.

'Actually, someone here in Sydney told me about it,' he said. 'I was with a family friend, and she was with a friend, or perhaps she was a cousin, I can't remember, and that friend – or cousin – was talking about how she knew someone who'd come to see you, and they were really helped with their memory.'

Hopefully that was obscure enough that de Souza wouldn't ask for any names, he thought.

He pressed on: 'Now, with the Science Olympiad coming up, I thought it couldn't hurt to find out whether perhaps you could give me a bit of a boost in that department.'

Andrew considered pointing to his inability even to remember whether the woman was a friend or a cousin as evidence of his problem. But that would direct de Souza's attention back to his fabricated story, which he didn't want.

'The Science Olympiad?' de Souza asked, one eyebrow arched. 'What is your specialty?'

'Well, I'm quite good at physics and maths.'

'Indeed?' She stopped.

For a moment, Andrew thought she was going to test him. Then he saw they'd reached a glass door etched with: *Dr E. de Souza.*

In any case, he told himself, there was nothing to worry about on that score. He *was* good at physics and maths.

As de Souza stood aside for him to step into her office, Will said: 'Andrew, you're doing well. I'm sending Sam in.'

Andrew nodded slightly. And de Souza's honey eyes narrowed. She had noticed. That had been *stupid*. Andrew's hand shot to his neck. He nodded again, pretending to rub it.

'Please,' de Souza said, 'go in. Sit down.'

The room was sparsely furnished. Andrew saw two metal filing cabinets with an oil painting above them. Along the right hand wall were shelves packed with books and papers. A chrome and leather chair faced the glass desk. On that desk was a *laptop*. Andrew was relieved.

De Souza sat down behind her desk. She steepled her fingers and fixed him with a professional smile. 'So, tell me, Jason – if I may call you Jason – what exactly are your expectations? What do you hope to get out of our time together?'

Andrew took a moment to appear to gather his thoughts. 'Well, I want to improve my memory. That's it, really. That *is* something you can help with?'

'I can help with many things. There are techniques I can teach you. A colour-matching method, for instance, which makes it easier to recall numbers.'

Andrew nodded slowly. There was little point being reticent, he decided.

'Actually, I do already use that method. In fact, I've tried most of the things you can read about in books.' He hesitated. Too pushy, and he might alarm her. Too vague, and she might not see what he was getting at. 'I – I was wondering if you might have *other* methods. If you see what I mean.'

That had been the very definition of *vague*, he told himself.

De Souza's composed expression did not change.

'I read a paper a few weeks ago,' Andrew continued, trying to keep his nervousness from his voice. 'It concluded that when people are hungry, they remember things better. It was talking about ghrelin, a hormone.'

'You are wondering if I have *hormones* that could help you?'

Again, Andrew hesitated. Lydia's voice came through the toothphone: '*Go on.*'

'Or something like that,' he said.

'If it is supplements you are looking for, I will tell you that you are far too young, but many already exist. Creatine, for instance, boosts muscle as well as memory.'

Andrew stiffened. De Souza was giving him a cool look. Was she actually suggesting that his muscles needed developing? And he coloured. Lydia would have heard her.

'I – I was thinking of something *newer*,' Andrew said. 'At the Science Olympiad, you see . . .' He let his sentence trail off, guessing de Souza would grasp his implication.

'They test you for stimulants. For all known drugs?'

Andrew pretended to look bashful. 'Yes.'

De Souza folded her arms.

This was not a good sign, Andrew thought. It was negative body language. She didn't trust him. In fact, her face suggested she was about to show him the door.

He'd pushed too hard and gained *nothing*.

He had to backtrack. In fact, until Will could come up with a way to get her out of the office, it was vital that he kept her talking, in case she used a pause to ask him to leave.

Andrew's gaze flicked from de Souza to the painting above the filing cabinets. A gaunt woman reclined awkwardly in an iron bath. The water was red, he noticed.

De Souza followed his gaze. 'It is the Hungarian countess, Elizabeth de Bathory. She lived in the sixteenth century. In a bid for eternal youth, she bathed in the blood of young girls.'

Andrew paled.

De Souza unfolded her arms. 'Mr Argo, I suspect, I am afraid, that I cannot help you. I am a psychologist. Phoenix House is a retreat. If psychological techniques are of no interest to you—'

Suddenly an electronic ringing blared from her coat pocket.

'Please excuse me,' she said quickly. She checked the

screen of her mobile, and her eyes narrowed. 'I am sorry, I must take this.'

Andrew held his breath. Was this Will's diversion? If it was, it was ahead of schedule – and yet well-timed.

De Souza listened intently. Andrew noticed a gleam appear in her eyes. What looked like relief crept over her face. Had Will somehow managed to create a *welcome* diversion? Andrew wouldn't put it past him.

'Very well,' de Souza said. 'I will try to come down at once.' She flipped her phone shut. 'Mr Argo, I must apologize. I'm afraid I have a client with an emergency. If –'

'No problem at all,' Andrew said, before she could ask him to go. 'Actually, I was about to say, I think you're right. I really want to hear all about your psychological techniques. I'm very happy to wait while you see to your client.'

Andrew got up and went to the bookshelf. He pulled out a large tome titled *Cognitive Behavioural Therapy*. 'This looks fascinating. I'll read it while I wait.'

De Souza was desperate to leave, he could tell. But she looked uncertain.

Andrew smiled sweetly. 'Take all the time you need.'

The door clicked shut behind her.

'Will,' Andrew whispered hard. 'What did you do?'

There was a pause. Then he heard: 'Nothing. But I've found something. Hold on.'

15

Moments after Andrew walked through the front door of Phoenix House, Will spotted an open side window. Two minutes later, Sam was in.

If he could find Broadstairs's bedroom or office, there was a reasonable chance he might find a hair, Will thought. But he also wanted to try to locate the microwave device and the package from Shark Island.

And, if Phoenix House *was* developing new treatments, there had to be a lab, Will reasoned. It wouldn't be somewhere that a guest might stumble across it. So, an attic? A basement?

Neither should pose a real problem for Sam. The robot was fitted with sticky pads inspired by geckos' feet, and it could navigate stairs all right.

Will rested his back against the trunk of a pine tree and slotted Sam's audio earpiece into place. Through the toothphone, he heard Andrew talking about the friend or cousin who'd recommended de Souza, and he turned the volume down. Andrew could brief him later. Right now, he wanted to focus on Sam's feeds.

The camera showed a white-walled corridor. Sam

scurried along it, streaming back images of flagstones and arched windows. Then a door marked *Media Room* and another, *Library*. These rooms were unlikely to contain much of interest, Will thought.

He sent Sam on, keeping him close to the wall. The robot's mike transmitted only the clicks of his feet against the floor. But if someone did appear, there'd be nowhere for Sam to hide, Will realized. He'd have to be ready to put him into a sudden retreat. Or, at the very least, make him freeze. *Or,* at the very worst, order him to shoot.

Will frowned. Sam had reached what looked like a dead end. He nudged the robot's nose, and saw that the corridor right-angled. Will poked Sam's head around the corner – and he tensed. A stocky man with red hair and a blue uniform was striding towards the camera. The man who'd chased Lydia from Phoenix House!

Then Will saw something else: a steel door, on the left. Was the guard heading for the door, or the corner? He had to maintain Sam's position, Will decided. He *had* to wait and see.

A moment later, the man stopped at the door. He tapped at the wall. He was entering a code via a keypad, Will guessed. If he was right, then whatever was behind that door was off-limits to clients. Which meant he had to get Sam in.

The man's arm dropped. He stepped forwards. The door must have opened. Will's heart thudded.

He sent Sam swerving around the man's back and in, just between his legs, then sideways.

The door clunked shut – and Will's display screen went black.

What had happened?

In the wood, Will waited, nerves on edge. The screen still showed nothing. He didn't dare risk trying to move Sam. Had the man *trodden* on his robot?

Then the display flashed. Suddenly Will was looking down a narrow passage, to a short flight of stone steps. The guard must have switched on a light, Will realized.

The man tramped down the steps.

Will sent Sam forwards slowly. Now, the robot's neural network took over. As brains went, it was primitive. But it had been trained on stairs.

Will watched. He saw darkness, and grey, and then a wall, dead ahead.

To the left was an open door. Will sent Sam to it. And he stared.

There was no doubt about it: Sam was in a lab. Will saw three stainless steel benches. On top was a series of cages. Inside those cages, something moved.

The guard had vanished. He must have gone straight on, Will thought, through another door at the far side of the room.

Will lifted the robot's head as high as it would go. And he saw what was inside the cages. They were sniffing the air and jumping at the metal bars, trying to get out.

Lab rats.

They had to be used for testing new drugs, Will thought. But which drugs, exactly?

Will sent Sam pattering past the tables to the far door – and he saw something even more interesting.

Sam was at the edge of an ante-room. An electric bar-heater glowed in the near corner. To the right were two wooden desks. At the rear was a smaller steel table.

Leaning over that table was a slim young man in a white coat. A mobile phone was pressed to his ear. The red-haired guard was at his side. They had their backs to Will. What were they looking at?

Then the young man spoke: 'Eva, we've got it! Six animals. *Forty-six seconds.*'

He sounded excited.

There was a pause. Then the man nodded. 'All right.'

He picked up a notebook and scribbled something down. Then he turned to the guard. Will cupped a hand around his ear. It looked like the guard had said something, but he hadn't caught the words.

Now the guard reached out, towards whatever was on the table. The *six animals*, Will wondered? The scientist batted his hand away.

There were more mumbled words.

And: 'Yeah, she's coming.'

Then, a second later, Andrew's voice burst through his toothphone: '*Will. What did you do?*'

Andrew whispered: 'Will? *Will? Hello?*'

Will had told him he'd found something, and to hold on, and now Will wasn't responding.

'Andrew, is everything OK?' Gaia asked.

'What's going on?' Lydia said.

'I don't know,' Andrew whispered back. 'But de Souza's just left her office. I'm going to install the program. Can you check Will's video and make sure he's all right?'

Andrew crossed to the desk. He perched on the edge of the leather chair and swivelled the laptop towards him. From one of his zip pockets, he pulled a USB memory stick. He slotted it in, opened the F drive and double-clicked on a file called *Phoenix*.

The egg-timer icon flashed – and the software uploaded.

One eye on the door, Andrew removed the memory stick and slipped it back into his pocket. Then he double-clicked on the email icon. As soon as a window appeared, he closed it.

That was it. The software was active.

It would replicate, and distribute itself to every computer on the Phoenix House intranet.

Andrew pushed the laptop back into its original position. 'Will,' he whispered. 'I've transferred the spyware.'

Silence.

'Will?' Lydia said. 'Can you check in?' Then, in a sharper tone: 'Is that *de Souza*?'

This time, Will responded. 'Quiet!' he hissed. 'I'm

trying to listen to Sam's audio. Don't speak unless you've got something urgent to say!'

Will didn't have to sound so irritated, Andrew thought.

In the truck, Lydia was shaking her head in annoyance. She hit the blue button on her toothphone keypad so Will wouldn't hear her.

'Andrew,' Will went on, 'de Souza is still here. As soon as she leaves, I'll let you know.'

'Will – where is *here*?'

'Shh,' Will said. 'Hold on.'

Andrew sighed. But, he reflected, the most important thing at that moment was that Will had his eye on de Souza. So he could start a search of her office.

Beneath the desk was a white plastic unit with three drawers. In the first, Andrew found pens, a stapler, an open pack of nicotine patches and a hermetically sealed bag. The bag contained a rubbery translucent material. Andrew peered hard at it. Was none the wiser.

He shut the drawer and tried the others, but they were locked.

So too, he discovered, were the filing cabinets. He really should ask Will to get hold of some of the more basic technologies, like lock-picking devices and bugs, he thought. There were times when they would be incredibly useful. But Andrew could imagine the response he'd get. Perhaps it would be better to order some online.

Andrew ran his eyes around the office. The only other place left to search was the bookcase.

Eight of the nine shelves held hefty hardbacks with equally weighty titles. *Psychodynamic Psychiatry. Advanced Neurochemistry: A Clinician's Guide. Coaching Psychology: The Mind-Set for Success.* The middle shelf, though, was jammed with plywood files stuffed with journals and papers.

He might as well be methodical, Andrew decided, and he reached for the first paper on the left.

It was a reprint of an article from the journal *Science.*

The title read: *Protein composition of catalytically active human telomerase from immortal cells.*

Telomerase . . . He'd heard the word before. It had something to do with cells. But he was more interested in maths and physics than biology, and he couldn't remember what, exactly.

'Telomerase?' Gaia whispered. 'Andrew, what are you looking at?' She'd just switched from Will's video feed to Andrew's.

'It's a paper on de Souza's shelf. I can't really remember what telomerase is.'

'It's an enzyme,' she said. 'You get it in stem cells. It stops telomeres getting shorter when the cell divides.'

'And telomeres would be . . . ?'

'The caps of your chromosomes! When a cell divides, they get a bit shorter, until the DNA gets so unstable the cell dies.'

'And telomerase stops this,' Andrew said, thought-fully.

'Yeah – it makes a cell immortal.'

Andrew put the paper back, and pulled out the one next to it.

Lessons from mice without telomerase.

He plucked out another paper at random.

'*Telomerase – a death-defying enzyme,*' he whispered.

And another:

Hairs and hairpins: a novel role for the telomere.

All these papers seemed to be about telomeres and telomerase. *Why?*

'The picture!' Gaia exclaimed.

'What picture?' Lydia said.

'Andrew – the picture in the office. Remember what de Souza said: the countess bathed in the blood of young girls *in a bid for eternal youth.*'

Andrew's gaze shot to the painting. The woman's body was old and wrinkled. Her hair was limp. Her flesh sagged.

Eternal youth.

His brain simmered.

Athletes. Models. Telomeres. Youth . . .

'Gaia, you don't think –' he started.

But Gaia didn't hear him. Her clamouring thoughts drowned out his voice.

Institutes all over the world were searching for a 'cure' for ageing.

What if de Souza had actually done it? What if she'd developed a drug that could repair telomeres – that could turn back a cell's clock?

'That could be why those old athletes started improving after they stayed here,' Gaia said. 'De Souza could be making them physically *younger*.'

'That's impossible!' Lydia said. '*Surely*.'

'I don't know,' Andrew whispered, his gaze running over the stacks of papers. 'Maybe not. Maybe Gaia's right . . .'

But if she was, what did all this have to do with microwaves? How did it all tie together? 'Gaia, can you think of a reason why you might need microwaves to make an anti-ageing drug?'

After a moment, she said: 'Even if you did, why not just buy a commercial microwave machine? Why would Broadstairs meet some guy on a boat in the harbour?'

Andrew sighed. It just didn't stack up.

His gaze shot back to de Souza's desk. Perhaps answers would lie on her computer. Or Broadstairs's. And he couldn't help wondering where Broadstairs was. Was he here at this moment, in Phoenix House?

'Will,' he said, 'I know you don't want to be interrupted. But can you give me an update? What's happening?'

There was a pause. Then: 'De Souza's still down here.'

Andrew waited for more detail, but it didn't come. He slipped the three papers back into the file. 'I think I've got all I can from her office,' he said. 'I should probably head back to Lydia and Gaia.'

'Why don't you try some other rooms,' Will said. 'See what else you can find.'

'But if I get caught –'

'Then they'll kick you out. You won't have lost anything.'

It was easy for Will to be cool and logical when he was safe in the wood, Andrew thought. But – Will was right. He had nothing to lose.

'All right, I'll nose around a bit. But can you tell us what you've found? What's de Souza doing? Where's "down here"?'

'Later,' Will said. '*Shh.*'

16

Andrew slipped into the corridor.

He could head left, towards the entrance, and Lydia and Gaia. Or right, deeper into the unknown.

He steeled himself. Turned right.

Yes, he told himself, if anyone did accost him, he could honestly tell them he'd been invited into Phoenix House. And de Souza *had* been called away from their appointment.

He could be simply on the hunt for a toilet. Or the way out. Both should be acceptable excuses. He had nothing to worry about.

So why did it feel as though his heart was trying to break out of his ribs?

Up ahead was a door. As Andrew got closer, he saw it led into the *Relaxation Lounge*. He was half-tempted to see whether it actually worked. But he hurried on.

At the end of the corridor, he turned into a semi-circular hallway, lined with wood panels. At the back was a narrow flight of stairs.

'Go on,' Lydia said. 'See what's up there.'

Andrew blinked. He'd almost forgotten about the

contact lens. It was unnerving, knowing that Lydia was out in the truck, yet she could see through his eyes. And something occurred to him. Should he?

No, he thought, he *shouldn't*. But in the spirit of having nothing to lose . . .

Cautiously, Andrew took the first stair. It didn't creak. As he continued up, he took his toothphone keypad from his pocket and pressed the red button.

'Gaia,' he whispered, 'don't let on I'm talking to you. I've set my toothphone so only you can hear me. I wanted to ask. Well, you're alone with Lydia. I was wondering if – maybe –'

This was harder than he'd anticipated. His gaze darted up, to a landing. It looked dusty and still. No sign of life.

'Well, maybe,' he went on, 'if at any point, you stop transmitting to me, you could talk me up a bit to Lydia.' He paused. 'Actually, I know what you're thinking. It's stupid. I shouldn't have asked you. Forget I did. All right?' Then he heard: 'No.'

'No, what?' Lydia said.

'I thought I heard Andrew say something,' Gaia said.

Andrew fumbled for his keypad. He hit the black button, so Lydia would also hear him. 'I didn't say a word,' he whispered.

'Weird,' Gaia said.

Andrew wiped his palms on his trousers. *No*, Gaia wouldn't forget he'd asked her or *no*, she wouldn't do as he'd asked? He shook his head. He was inside

Phoenix House, and he was thinking about Lydia. Gaia would think he'd gone mad. Perhaps he had.

Andrew reached the landing. Leading off from it were four wooden doors. All closed.

He tried the first. It didn't budge. The second opened into a broom cupboard. The third opened too. And this room was much more interesting.

Andrew saw rich red wallpaper, a mahogany desk, a grandfather clock, another door, a bookcase and a fireplace. The grate was full of white ash. Not only ash, he noticed. Fragments of half-burnt paper.

Taking a deep breath, Andrew pushed the door shut behind him, and headed for the hearth.

Will's back ached. His legs felt cramped. He wanted to stretch, but he didn't dare to move.

Sam's audio was so quiet that if he made a noise he'd risk missing something. And he couldn't do that because what he was listening to was *odd*.

De Souza was in the ante-room. Two minutes ago, she'd dismissed the red-haired guard. He'd stomped right past Sam, who was hiding behind the electric heater.

Now she and the scientist were at one of the wooden desks, bending over what Will guessed from their conversation had to be microscopes. It sounded as though they were doing an autopsy on one of the rats.

The scientist straightened. 'No sign of liver damage.'

De Souza nodded. After a moment, she murmured, 'The heart seems clear.'

Will was itching to send Sam at least part way up the wall, in the hope he'd get a better view. But the robot's feet would make a noise. And what would he see? The insides of a dead rat? In all likelihood, the video would tell him little. It was better to listen, and wait.

The man had gone back to his microscope. Now he turned to de Souza. 'Eva, the lungs are also clear.'

Clear of *what*, Will wondered. What were they looking for? What weren't they finding?

The questions were rapidly stacking up. It seemed about time he got some answers. But perhaps Andrew was having better luck.

Claiming to be looking for an exit or a toilet while crouching over a fireplace could be somewhat tricky to pull off, Andrew thought. But if someone did come in suddenly, he'd think of something. He couldn't pass up the chance to snoop on documents that someone at Phoenix House clearly had wanted to destroy.

Carefully he picked through the ash. Any surviving fragments of paper he pulled out and studied.

After a few minutes, though, Andrew's initial optimism started to fade. Yes, he'd found some words. But he couldn't glean much from them.

The longest continuous stretch of writing read: 'delay of approximately 52 minutes.'

Then, in descending length order, came: 'Viper Club requested to', 'only in South America', 'of molecular biology', 'free radicals' and '*commotio cordis*'. Commotio cordis . . . He should have paid better attention in Latin as well as biology, he thought.

'Andrew,' Gaia said. 'The resolution's not good enough for us to read what you're looking at. What have you found?'

'I don't know,' he whispered. 'Nothing . . . At least, nothing that tells me anything.'

He was far more likely to find answers on the computer network than in this study, he thought.

After entering the words into his smartphone, he dropped the paper fragments back into the grate and stood up, thinking he should leave. Then the bookshelf caught his eye.

The fireplace had grabbed his attention, and he'd hardly noticed the bookshelf. But now he realized that the shelves held not books, but canisters and jars. And a series of small glass boxes containing – *yes*, he thought, as he padded closer – *spiders.*

Andrew peered into one of the boxes.

And Lydia's voice almost burst his eardrum: 'Don't touch it!'

He jumped, one hand on his ear. '*Quietly!* What is it?'

'It's called a funnel web,' she said. 'They live in Sydney. They kill people!'

But the small, hairy spider was trapped behind glass.

And it wasn't moving. It might even be dead, Andrew thought.

He checked the contents of the other boxes. More spiders. When he came to the last, he gasped.

'What?' Gaia said.

'I can't believe it!'

'*What?*'

'I think this might be an extremely rare example of the Australian garage spider!'

'*Andrew!*'

He smiled to himself.

'What's a garage spider?' Lydia asked.

'Ask Gaia,' Andrew whispered. 'They're deadly. Allegedly.'

He adjusted his glasses, and lowered his gaze to the next shelf.

It contained a jumble of glass bottles and plastic canisters. Andrew scanned the labels, reading the names of chemicals. Formaldehyde. Iodine. Potassium permanganate –

'Wait!' Gaia said. 'Back up. The one you just looked at – yeah, that one. Does it say carbon nanotubes?'

Andrew blinked at the label. 'Carbon nanotubes. Diameter: 1 nanometre. Why?'

'Can you fit it in your pocket?'

'Why?'

'Just do it. I'll explain later.'

Andrew shook his head. Sometimes Gaia could be as

bossy as Will. But he plucked the jar from the shelf and zipped it into his trousers. And he froze.

His head snapped round.

The door handle was turning.

'Andrew, hide!' Lydia hissed.

Where? he thought. There was nowhere to hide!

Andrew darted for the other door, praying it wasn't locked, and Will's voice erupted in his ear: 'Andrew, I can't see de Souza. I thought she'd gone into another room down here – but she might have left.'

Thanks for the warning! he thought. Was *de Souza* outside? Was this her study?

Andrew reached for the brass handle. But his palms were sweaty, making it slippery. He glanced back. The other door was opening –

At last, he got a firm grip.

And the handle turned.

There was no time to check what was on the other side. His heart thudding, he slipped through and he pushed the door shut.

He blinked. He was in a narrow passage. Through the door behind him, he could hear footsteps. They were slow. In no hurry. *He hadn't been seen.*

Andrew didn't hang around any longer.

He crept along the passage as fast as he dared. At the end, he found stairs. He raced down them, into a corridor. It had white walls. Gleaming flagstones. The same corridor he'd followed de Souza along to her office?

Andrew wasn't sure. But at least he was back on the ground floor. And judging by the sunlight pouring through the windows, the entrance was somewhere behind him.

He started along the corridor. *Slow*, he told himself. *Nice and slow* . . .

Then a door in the wall opened.

And Andrew's spine seized.

Disbelief broke out through his body. Nausea washed up to his throat.

There, *right in front of him*, was a man.

Not any man.

Black hair. Dimpled chin. Gunmetal eyes.

In the truck, Gaia stared.

'That's him!' Lydia whispered. 'That's *Broadstairs*.'

'*Yeah*,' Gaia said.

What could they do?

Andrew couldn't hide. He couldn't run.

'Andrew, you're OK,' Gaia whispered hard. 'You have an appointment, remember. De Souza invited you in. You can talk your way out of this. *You'll be all right.*'

Andrew swallowed. His brain felt empty, drained of blood.

Frederick Broadstairs was glaring at him. He looked surprised, and hostile.

But was he *Broadstairs*, Andrew thought, or *Sir James Parramore*? And what if Parramore had found out about STORM's actions in St Petersburg, and seen pictures of them? What if the base's surveillance tapes had somehow survived?

The MI6 psychiatric assessment had concluded that Parramore found killing as 'non-emotive' as catching a bus.

'Non-emotive', Andrew knew, meant it *didn't matter*.

Parramore could murder and not bat an eyelid. And if Broadstairs was Parramore, surely he'd leap at the chance to eliminate him!

Andrew forced himself to meet the man's cold gaze.

'Um. Hello,' he said at last.

'Who are you?' Broadstairs's accent was Home Counties English. 'Where are you going?'

Andrew coughed. It felt as though a rock had lodged in his throat.

Broadstairs's eyes narrowed. The irises flashed impatience. Now they looked silver, like a barracuda.

The black-and-white photograph in the paper had done him absolute justice, Andrew realized. The man was monochrome. Black hair, metallic eyes, grey lips, white skin.

'I said: who are you? Where are you going?'

'I – I had an appointment with Dr de Souza,' Andrew managed to get out. His voice sounded like someone else's. 'But she was called away.'

'Your name?'

'Jason. Jason Argo.' Andrew took a deep breath. 'I – she – Dr de Souza said a problem had come up with another client and I said I'd wait, but actually I have another appointment, you see, and I'm running late, so I had to leave –' Andrew stopped. His right hand started to waver towards his glasses. He thrust it into his pocket.

'Dr de Souza is no longer able to keep appointments today,' Broadstairs said sharply.

Questions fire-crackered through Andrew's mind.

Why not – is she dead? Have you killed her? Was it even the tiniest bit 'emotive'?

Stop, he told himself. You're letting your fear dominate your thinking. A classic mistake.

'I see,' Andrew said.

Again, the metallic eyes narrowed. 'Is something wrong?' Broadstairs asked. 'You seem nervous.'

'I – I do?' He could hardly deny it, Andrew thought. But what could he say? Whatever it was, it *had* to be believable. 'Well, actually I am nervous,' he admitted at last. 'That's why I came to see Dr de Souza. I have a condition called social anxiety disorder. A fear of strangers.' He tried to clear his throat, and spluttered: 'Like you.'

But *was he*, Andrew thought? *Was he* a stranger?

Broadstairs grunted. 'The exit is that way.' He pointed along the corridor.

Then, without another word, he stomped away in the opposite direction.

Andrew staggered back, half collapsing against the wall. He felt as though he'd just been dropped from the ceiling.

'*Well done*,' Gaia whispered.

'Now get out of there!' Lydia said.

Andrew didn't need any encouragement. 'On my way! Talk to Will – ask him to get Sam out. We need to de-brief!'

Andrew strode along the corridor. At last, he reached the entrance hall and he hurried to the driveway. He forced himself to walk. But as soon as he was out of view from the house, he broke into a run.

At the main road, he saw the truck, barrelling towards him. It screeched to a stop.

The back passenger door flew open. Will was holding on to it.

'Hurry up,' he hissed.

Andrew threw himself up, and tumbled in.

Broadstairs pushed open the door to his study.

De Souza was at the window. She smiled, and it was dazzling. Her honey eyes glowed. In her hand was a black leather pouch. Now she raised it, letting it dangle.

It was like a piece of meat to a hawk.

Broadstairs dashed across the room and snatched it up. He opened it and saw three plastic vials inside. 'It *works*?' he asked, his voice low.

'Yes,' de Souza whispered. 'Just now, in the lab, we performed—'

'The details,' Broadstairs interrupted, 'do not matter to me.'

He took the bag to the grandfather clock.

De Souza watched him, her smile fading. She knew him too well to expect gratitude. But this aggression . . . it wasn't attractive, she found herself thinking.

Broadstairs opened the belly of the clock. Inside, instead of a pendulum, was an oblong metal door. Set into it was a small screen.

Broadstairs crouched, so his left eye was level with the screen. A miniature camera instantly imaged his iris. Then a computer chip compared it with the one in its memory.

They matched. The door swung open.

Inside the safe was de Souza's tin box and the black sports bag, with its briefcase. The contents had been recently developed by one of Broadstairs's former employees. The man had a mistress in Bermuda and a penchant for high-stakes gambling. In return for the briefcase, Broadstairs had told him, his rich wife would not find out.

Now Broadstairs carefully placed the pouch on the bag. He closed the doors and looked round.

'You have done well, Eva,' he said. 'You have done exactly what I expected of you.'

De Souza's expression wavered between a frown and a smile.

Broadstairs was oblivious.

He pulled a mobile from his pocket and dialled a number. When the ringing stopped, he said: 'It's Broadstairs. I've done it. *I'm ready.*'

Chen Jianguo's gaze settled on his snake. He recalled the dealer's notes: *The Russell's viper is slow and sluggish – unless provoked.*

A dry laugh scuttled up Chen's belly to his throat.

On occasion, he thought, the same might be said of him.

But now?

No!

'Very well,' he croaked into his phone. 'You will receive further instructions in one hour.'

'Further instructions –'

'*One hour.*'

Chen's snake was coiled on a Louis IVth chair. He hobbled over to it. Gently he stroked the chain of scaled diamonds along her graceful spine.

'Broadstairs says he has done it,' Chen whispered. 'Will we believe him?'

The viper's gaze was cold.

'Indeed. Why should we?' He barked: 'Mei!'

The communications console on his desk sprang into life.

'Sir?'

'Prepare the jet. We are going to Sydney.'

'At once, Mr Chen.'

As soon as Andrew was in the truck, Lydia slammed her foot on the accelerator.

They swerved up the hill, across a main road, around two corners and into the car park of a supermarket.

Shoppers wandered by with trolleys. Young kids licked ice creams. It was an abrupt shift back to normality, and for a moment, no one spoke.

Then Gaia turned. 'Right,' she said. 'What did you find?'

Will looked at Andrew. 'You first.'

He nodded. And he couldn't help wondering if Gaia had talked to Lydia about him. If so, had Lydia made any comment in return? He'd have to wait for those answers.

Andrew gathered his thoughts. 'I don't know how much you managed to piece together from my side of the conversation, but I didn't get much out of de Souza. Though probably the most important thing she said I thought was irrelevant at the time. Anyway, I transferred the spyware. Then I searched her office.'

He thought of the rubbery material in the drawer. But if it had any bearing on what was going on at Phoenix House, he had no idea how.

Andrew looked at Will. 'And I found a stack of journal articles on telomerase. As Gaia reminded me, telomerase is an enzyme that can put a hold on the normal ageing of a cell. We think that maybe de Souza has a drug that slows or stops ageing.'

'Or even reverses it,' Gaia said.

Lydia was shaking her head. 'You *really* think that's possible?'

'There are lots of researchers working on anti-ageing drugs,' Gaia said, 'and this is one way you might go about trying to do it.'

'And we have these athletes and models who seem to have had incredibly successful treatment,' Andrew said.

Will frowned. It seemed far-fetched. But that didn't mean it was impossible. 'Apart from the papers on telomerase, did you find anything else?'

'Not in her office.' Andrew told Will about the fireplace, and the papers. 'Then the door opened, and I ran. And encountered Broadstairs.' He pushed his glasses back along his nose.

'Do you think it was him?' Gaia asked, her voice low.

'Parramore, you mean?' Andrew bit his lip. 'I have no

idea. I know, I should have tried to get a hair or *something*, but I'm afraid all I was really thinking about was getting away.' He glanced at Lydia. Was she disappointed in him? It was hard to tell.

'What about the words on the burnt papers?' Gaia said. 'Did you find anything that might be relevant?'

'Well, I saw the words "Viper Club" – and there was a Latin phrase. It could be worth doing a search on them.' Andrew pulled out his smartphone. 'And I need to check the spyware's working. But Will, what did you find?'

So Will told them about the lab, and the rats. 'They talked about six animals, and forty-six seconds. I guess that's the time it took for whatever they were testing to take effect.'

'For the drug to work on telomeres?' Lydia suggested.

'Maybe. Then they did an autopsy. I couldn't see much but it had to be on one of the rats. They checked the heart and the lungs and the liver, and they said all were clear, and they seemed pleased. Then de Souza called someone – Broadstairs, I suppose – and she left.'

Will looked at Andrew. 'Then I checked your video feed and saw Broadstairs, and I pulled Sam out . . . Andrew?'

'Mmm,' he said, absent-mindedly. He didn't seem to be listening. He was focusing on his smartphone.

A woman pushing two screaming babies walked right past his window and he didn't even glance up.

'*Andrew?*' Lydia said.

His head jerked up.

'Did you hear what I said?' Will asked.

'Forty-six seconds, heart and lungs clear,' Andrew said, and he smiled at Lydia. His eyes shot back to his screen.

'Have you found something?' Gaia asked him.

'Nothing on a "Viper Club". I'll search the Phoenix House networks for that in a minute. But there were two Latin words on one of the scraps of paper. *Commotio cordis.'*

Will and Gaia studied Latin at school. 'Commotion of the heart?' Will said.

Andrew nodded. 'It seems to be a medical term. I've found an article all about it. There are case histories here. A baseball player who was struck lightly in the chest, and died. A boy whose brother knocked him in the chest while they were on a climbing frame – he also died.' Andrew looked up. 'It seems even a light blow can disrupt the heart's rhythm enough to kill someone, it if hits at just the right time, and in just the right place. Well, wrong time, wrong place, I suppose.'

Will frowned. 'How might that tie in with what's going on at Phoenix House?'

'I have absolutely no idea,' Andrew said. 'Maybe nothing . . . But I'll try searching their network for any references to any of the words on the burnt papers. At least that will be a place to start.'

'How long will it take?' Gaia asked.

'It depends how many hard drives I have to search,

and how much data's on them. Could be five minutes. Could be fifty.'

'Then let's head back to the house,' Will said. 'We'll see what you come up with, then we'll work out what to do next.'

Lydia started the engine.

For four and a half minutes, they drove in silence.

Will thought about anti-ageing research. There were so many teams working on it, and so much money being thrown at it, someone had to come up with a drug that worked some time. So why not here, and now – at Phoenix House?

Suddenly Andrew's head shot up. '*Very* interesting!' he exclaimed.

'What—' Gaia started.

He held up a hand to silence her. '*Listen.*'

'I've been searching Phoenix House emails using the words from the papers as keywords,' Andrew said. 'My first hit was an email sent to Broadstairs, and to six other people, five weeks ago.'

'Which keyword?' Lydia asked. She glanced back at Andrew, and swerved.

'The subject is *The Viper Club*,' Andrew said, as his shoulder bashed against the car door. 'It's from a man called Diamond Mbama. The original email was encrypted, but Broadstairs also saved a decrypted version.'

'So, what does it say?' Will asked.

'It's about a new type of gun that can fire one million rounds a minute.'

'And?' Gaia said.

'There's a full spec here. A detailed description, mechanism, price, and so on.'

'*And?*' Gaia asked again.

'Give him a chance!' Lydia said.

A sudden smile rushed over Andrew's face. And he bowed his head. He didn't want Lydia to see. Luckily she was driving, and – at least in theory – watching the road.

Gaia rolled her eyes.

'Well, that's it,' Andrew said, 'for another week. Then, exactly seven days later, Broadstairs received another encrypted email with the same subject line – *The Viper Club*.

'This email is from a woman called Dolores Blatt. It discusses in great detail a – and I quote – "little-known radioactive element that can be administered in food to kill a person within hours". A week later, there's another email to the Viper Club, also about death – about a technique for murder.'

'So this Viper Club is interested in killing people,' Gaia said.

Lydia veered on to the coast road. Andrew resisted the urge to grip his seat. 'It certainly looks that way,' he said. 'I did a quick search on Blatt and Mbama. Blatt's the president of an arms company based in Ohio, in the US. Diamond Mbama seems to have made a fortune in Sierra Leone from blood diamonds – hence what must be a nickname – and he's a local warlord. I haven't checked the others yet.'

'And Frederick Broadstairs?' Will asked.

'Well, as you know, there are *no* internet references to Broadstairs, apart from that story in the paper, which in itself is odd.'

'But I thought we decided Phoenix House is making anti-ageing drugs,' Lydia said as she hit the brakes to enter a roundabout. Watson's Bay glittered to their left. 'So what's Broadstairs – or the Viper Club – got to do with all that?'

'Very good question,' Andrew said. 'Which brings me to the latest Viper Club email.'

He scrolled down his list of hits. 'On 26 August, the group received an email from a member called Chen Jianguo. There have been no other Viper Club emails since then. Will and Gaia, if you remember, according to that newspaper article I showed you, Broadstairs arrived in Sydney on 28 August. Coincidence? Perhaps. Perhaps not.'

'So what does this Chen guy's email say?' Lydia asked.

Andrew's buoyant spirits deflated slightly. 'Well, unfortunately Broadstairs doesn't seem to have saved a decrypted version. I can only read the header information – so all I know is that it's from Chen and it's about the Viper Club.'

'But you can decrypt it?' Will asked. 'You've got the other Viper Club emails – can you use those to do it?'

'Yes,' Andrew said. 'But I'll have to write a program. It will take time.'

Will nodded, thinking. De Souza had been treating clients long before Broadstairs arrived on the scene, he thought. So did the Viper Club really have anything to do with her research, or with the packages she and Broadstairs had picked up? And if so, *what*? And how did the dead rats fit in? They needed to know the contents of the last Viper Club email.

Gravel crunched as Lydia pulled up outside Watson's Retreat. Palm trees swayed in the breeze.

As they got out, Andrew glanced up from his smartphone. 'By the way, Gaia, I meant to ask – why did you want me to take the nanotubes? Do they throw some light on all this?'

She slammed her door, and smiled faintly. 'Not really. But if you throw some light on them, you'll see why I asked you to bring them.'

Andrew raised an eyebrow.

Gaia held out her hand.

Andrew pulled the canister from his pocket, and gave it to her.

Gaia removed a small fistful of the powder and re-sealed the canister. Then she turned to Lydia. 'I saw a torch in the truck. Can I borrow it?'

'Why?' Will asked. 'What are you going to do?'

'*Just trust me.*'

Will smiled. While Lydia fetched the torch from the truck, Gaia crossed the road. She emptied her handful on the ground, in the shadows of a pine tree. Her hand still cupped over the mound, she called: 'Lydia, when I move away, can you aim the beam on the pile.'

Lydia nodded.

Gaia backed up, and Lydia flicked the switch. The four-watt beam cut through the shadows. A split second later, there was a flash. Smoke and dust billowed into the air.

Everyone's eyes shot to Gaia. She grinned. 'Shine a bright light on carbon nanotubes and they explode. It's a little-known fact.'

'Which you might have *told* us,' Lydia said, coughing. She glanced at Andrew, who'd pushed his smartphone under his T-shirt to protect it from the smoke. To her surprise, he was smiling at Gaia.

'Well,' he said, 'it wouldn't be a STORM mission without you blowing something up and almost killing dozens of innocent people, would it? At least now I know how you'll do it.' He turned, and headed for the front door. 'In fact, maybe you should join the Viper Club!'

'Maybe if I did, we'd actually find out what Broadstairs is up to!' Gaia called back.

Andrew held up a defensive hand. 'I'm working on it. Just give me a little more time.'

He went inside – and disappeared into his room.

Will, Gaia and Lydia headed into the lounge.

Thirty-four minutes later, Will had shown Lydia exactly how Sam, the vest and the contact lens cameras worked, and he was about to go through the specs for the Spy Seeds.

Gaia had been leafing through Will's guidebook, thinking about telomerase – and Will. He wasn't avoiding her. But after last night, things still weren't *normal*.

She shot him and Lydia another sidelong glance. Lydia was obviously impressed.

And Gaia's gaze jerked to the door.

Andrew had just burst in, a sheet of paper in his hand.

His hair was ruffled, his glasses askew. He pushed them back along his nose.

Gaia sat up straight. She dropped the book. 'You've decrypted the email!'

'Yes.'

'And it's relevant?' Lydia asked.

Andrew fixed his gaze on her. His face showed a mixture of triumph and astonishment. '*Yes.*'

Andrew slapped the printout on the table. Will, Lydia and Gaia crowded round. They read:

From: Chen Jianguo
To: Frederick Broadstairs, Dolores Blatt, Diamond Mbama, Virgil Santander, Dijon Fleiss, Ariana Gamal, Aubrey de Mastadon
Subject: The Ex-Prize
Sent: 26 August

Friends,
There is a grand tradition of prizes for excellence in scientific achievement.
I think, for example, of the Ex-Prize. $10 million to the first private company to put a person into space. The point? I cannot tell. There are agencies that put people into space. And $10 million? To us, what is that sum, if not an insult to our time?

I am creating, then, a prize to win all prizes.

The subject is close to all our hearts.

The challenge:

Create three new, untraceable methods of murder.
The deaths must be inexplicable or – the ideal –
appear to be from a natural cause. Foul play may be
suspected, but **must not** be able to be proven.

If any of you succeed, I will award

$100 million.

You have fourteen days.

C

'Is this *for real*?' Lydia asked, her eyes wide.

Will quickly scanned the email again. 'Who is this Chen Jianguo?'

Andrew adjusted his glasses. He took two quick, excited breaths. 'To answer your question, Lydia, yes, it could be very real. Will, this is the Wikipedia entry on Chen.'

Andrew pulled another printout from his pocket and laid it on the table.

They read:

Chen Jianguo

A Shanghai-born businessman, Chen is CEO and primary stakeholder of Sino Enterprises, which has an estimated value of $1.2 billion.

Chen owns a string of casinos and nightclubs. He has a reputation for ruthlessness in business and has

been plagued by accusations of corruption, extortion,
racketeering and other criminal activities.

In his private life, he is known as a great collector.
In 2007, Chen famously paid $10.3 million for a set
of papyruses from a previously unknown Egyptian
Book of the Dead. A former maid revealed to a
Reuters reporter that Chen, 89, has an 'obsession with
death'.

'An obsession with death,' Lydia echoed. 'Do you know anything else about him?'

'That's it for Wikipedia,' Andrew said. 'But I've just done some searching through the archive of the *China Daily*. Chen's name crops up in court and crime reports again and again.

'He's been accused of the bribery and murder of five Communist Party officials, and for ordering the deaths of competitors. There are also reports that he's branched out into heroin dealing. He's been charged with various offences, but he's never been convicted. One journalist calls him Teflon Chen – no matter what gets thrown at him, none of it sticks. He's so rich, I suppose he's been able to buy people off.'

'So Chen really could have the cash for this prize,' Will said.

Andrew nodded. 'And he really could want those techniques. Look at that Wikipedia entry. The maid says he has an obsession with death.'

'I can't believe this is actually real,' Lydia said. 'I can't believe there's a prize like this. And if there is, I can't believe he's *emailed* people about it.'

'The encryption was first class,' Andrew said. 'Without those other decrypted Viper Club emails, there's no way I could have broken it. And the Phoenix House firewall was impenetrable. Presumably Broadstairs and the others are careful. The Viper Club is obviously meant to be top secret.'

'So how might this prize link in with de Souza?' Gaia asked. 'Why's Broadstairs at Phoenix House?'

Suddenly Will thought of the autopsy conversation. 'When de Souza and the scientist checked the dead rat, they looked at the heart, lungs and the liver, and they seemed happy that all were *clear*. Maybe de Souza's developed a method. They could have been working on something that would kill the rats without leaving a trace, so if it was used in people it wouldn't look like *murder*.'

'I thought de Souza was working on *anti-ageing* drugs,' Lydia said.

'Phoenix House has labs,' Gaia said. 'Perhaps Broadstairs just wanted somewhere safe and out of the way to do the work – or for de Souza to do it, along with whatever other drug work she's been doing. She trained as a biochemist. She could be working on anything for him. But if I had to guess –' She looked at Andrew, who nodded. Had the same thought occurred to him? '*Telomeres?*'

Andrew rubbed a hand across his forehead. 'If de

Souza's found a way to stop ageing, or even reverse it, she knows how to mess around with it at a basic level.' He paused. 'What if she's found a way to speed it up?'

Lydia's eyebrows shot up. 'Make someone grow old fast, you mean?'

'There's a genetic disorder that can do it,' Will said. He'd read about it in a science magazine. 'By the age of four, these kids have wrinkled skin and they're bald. They *look* like old people. They usually die in their early teens of heart disease or stroke. But that takes years.'

Andrew nodded. 'If Broadstairs wanted to win the prize with a drug that accelerates ageing, it would have to work *much* faster. But if you *could* come up with something that somehow got into every cell in a person's body and destroyed telomeres –'

'You'd only know how they died if you looked at their chromosomes,' Gaia finished. 'And why would you do that? Even for a suspected murder – who'd look at chromosomes?'

'It would be just what Chen Jianguo wants,' Will said.

'But he wants *three* techniques,' Lydia said. She paused. 'What if Broadstairs and de Souza picked the other two up last night? Could using microwaves make sense?'

Silence.

Then Andrew looked at Will. 'I don't know,' he said at last. 'High powered microwaves can be used as a weapon, but I'd have thought they'd leave skin blisters.'

Will's eyes went back to Chen's email.

Little more than an hour ago they'd been on the trail of what they'd thought was simply a new drug to enhance physical and mental performance. That drug could still exist. In all likelihood, he thought, it did. But now it was obvious that Phoenix House – and Broadstairs and de Souza – were involved in something much more sinister.

And surely Chen wouldn't have a purely intellectual interest in three new undetectable ways of killing someone, he thought. He'd want to use them.

'We have to be on the right lines,' Will said. 'Broadstairs has got de Souza to make a drug that probably affects telomeres – and from what I saw in the lab, it looks like it's working. And last night, as Lydia said, they might have got hold of two other techniques.'

Gaia picked up the email. 'Chen told the Viper Club they had two weeks. Those two weeks are up *tomorrow.*'

'So if the drug's working, and Broadstairs has the other techniques, why would he wait?' Lydia asked. 'He'll tell Chen, won't he? He'll try to claim his money?'

Andrew jumped. His smartphone had just bleeped. In his bedroom, he'd set the spyware to sound an alert if Broadstairs received any new emails from Chen, or any other member of the Viper Club.

Now, Andrew's fingers fumbled with the keys – and his eyes widened.

'Broadstairs has new mail,' he said, his throat dry. 'And guess who it's from?'

Thirty thousand feet above the Pacific Ocean, Chen Jianguo stroked his snake.

Across the aisle of the Lockheed Martin QSST private supersonic jet, his secretary, Mei, sipped at a glass of mineral water.

Chen had set Mei a task, and she had gone to work. Three minutes ago, she had given him her report.

There were a number of options. More, in fact, than Chen had thought possible. But three stood out.

Chen had just emailed Frederick Broadstairs instructions in relation to the first two.

The final instalment he would reserve for later.

Broadstairs had to be thoroughly tested. The techniques *had* to work!

When he publicly cursed the Dung Beetle, the Giraffe and the Stick Insect, his enemies would mock.

But when all three died the day before the Meeting of the Tigers – and the deaths *appeared* to be natural – then everyone would say that Chen Jianguo was more powerful than any Voodoo priest.

They might even say he was a god . . .

At last, the decryption was complete. Andrew read the result – and nearly dropped his phone.

His hands trembling, he put it on the table, so the others could see.

The email read:

From: Chen Jianguo
To: Frederick Broadstairs
Subject: The Ex-Prize
Sent: 7 September

In public.
1. Ryan de Bruyn
2. Christopher Collins
You have two hours.
I will advise you of the third name by telephone.
This email will vanish from your system in five minutes.

Andrew was already pulling a pen from his pocket. He grabbed the printout of Chen's first email and started to scribble down the names at the bottom.

It was possible, he knew, for emails to electronically self-destruct. In this case, he had no doubt it would happen. Because this, he'd realized at once, was a *hit list*.

Gaia was staring. 'What does this mean – Chen wants Broadstairs to *kill* these men?'

'They must be trial targets,' Will said quickly. 'Chen

must be asking Broadstairs to prove his techniques work by using them to kill!'

He shook his head. Chen was insane. But if Broadstairs really did have three techniques, and *if* they did work, then right at that moment, Broadstairs was planning to get away with murder.

'If Chen is giving Broadstairs two hours, these men have to be in Sydney, or close by,' Gaia said. 'Lydia, do you have any idea who they are?'

Lydia shook her head. 'I think I might have heard of the second guy – but –'

'We need to find out who they are *now*,' Will said.

Gaia looked at him. 'I think we have to tell Walker. If Broadstairs is planning to kill two men, the police have to know. If the information comes from Walker, they'll have to listen.'

'I can call the police,' Will said. 'We've got the email—'

'Correction,' Andrew interrupted. '*Had.*'

Chen had been as good as his promise. The email had just vanished from his smartphone.

'I agree with Gaia,' Andrew added. 'The police are far more likely to listen if Walker makes the call.'

At last, Will nodded. Telling Walker wouldn't prevent them from acting, he thought. He dialled the number. Heard an irritated whisper:

'*Yeah?*'

The pub stank of stale beer and sweat. Eight men were drinking. Two leaned against a sheet of rusty corrugated iron, schooners of lager in their scabbed hands. The others were slumped on stools at the makeshift wooden bar. Flies buzzed around them.

Walker had been well trained. He still bore scars from his MI6 physical combat courses. But none of these men looked the sort he'd want to take on. Hopefully, he thought, it wouldn't come to that.

Two minutes earlier, Jonathan Simpkin, dressed in jeans and a checked shirt, had got out of a beaten-up ute and walked into this bar.

He and Marshall had been watching from their car. And he'd volunteered to follow, leaving Marshall behind as back-up.

In his newly-stained jeans, dirt-rubbed RM Williams shirt and scuffed boots, Walker decided he *almost* blended in.

He pretended to feel for his wallet, and double-checked one of the men on the stools. It was definitely Simpkin. He was about to stride over when his phone vibrated.

Annoyed, he dug it out. *Will Knight* showed on the screen.

This wasn't exactly a great time for a conversation, Walker thought. But Barrington had told him that if

STORM made contact, he *had* to respond. He was aware that his job probably depended on it. Already, Barrington had developed a reputation for being as irascible as he was brilliant.

Walker hit the answer button. Quietly he said: 'Yeah?'

'It's Will. I need to talk to you.'

'Can it wait?'

A pause. 'No – where are you?'

'The wild west,' Walker murmured. 'A place called Coober Pedy.' He kept his eyes on the dirt floor.

'Listen: we think a British man called Frederick Broadstairs is trying to win a prize for coming up with three new ways of killing someone, and—'

'*What?*'

'Yeah. We think he's developed a new drug that can age someone's cells, and we think—'

Walker's head jerked. Simpkin had just got up.

A blond man rose with him.

They strode towards the exit, their expressions black.

Something was about to happen. Whatever Will had just said, Walker had missed it.

'So will you call the police? You have to get Phoenix House searched and Broadstairs arrested. Walker? *Hello?*'

'Hold on, Will.'

'You'll do it now.'

'*Yeah. I've got to go.*'

Walker flipped his phone shut – and felt himself lifted off the floor.

A thud of air slammed into his chest and sent him sprawling. His ears rang. Pain spiked through his arm.

He blinked and coughed. The air was full of dust. When it cleared, he saw sky.

The back end of the pub was gone. Corrugated iron and wood lay smashed across the ground. The barman was screaming. Blood poured from a thick gash in his head.

Walker wiped a hand across his face. What the hell had just happened?

This was opal territory. Miners carried explosives with them. Sometimes there were accidents. Sometimes those 'accidents' weren't what they seemed. Where was Simpkin? Had that explosion been targeted at him? Or had Simpkin bombed the place?

As Walker staggered up, Marshall raced in through the battered door.

'Go,' Walker hissed. 'I'm all right. *Find him.*'

'So he's going to call them?' Andrew asked.

'He said he would,' Will said. 'But I don't know if he was really listening to me.'

'So now what?' Lydia asked.

Will fixed his gaze on Chen's first email, and on the two names Andrew had written beneath.

Barrington had told them that Walker and Marshall were there to help. Walker was one of MI6's best young officers. Will had explained what they'd discovered. Surely Walker would act.

But Will wasn't about to sit around and hope – or wait to see what happened.

STORM had to do what they could to save these two lives.

But they didn't even know who the men were. And the clock was ticking.

'We could start by doing a web search on the names,' Andrew said.

Will nodded. 'I'll try the police. In case Walker gets tied up.' He glanced at Lydia.

'Triple zero,' she said, guessing what he'd been about to ask.

Will was faintly surprised. Usually it was Gaia who read his mind.

He turned away and dialled the number. After a moment, he heard the emergency services operator. 'Police, fire or ambulance?'

'Police. It's urgent.'

'Is there a crime in progress?'

'No,' he said, '*but there's about to be.*'

20

The late afternoon sun poured through the windows. It made the lounge stuffy.

He could switch on the air con, Andrew thought. But he wanted fresh air.

He strode out on to the deck. Lydia followed. She was working on Christopher Collins, while Andrew searched de Bruyn.

So far, he'd scored about forty-five hits. Most, he decided, he could safely rule out.

There was a 1970s Dutch pop star by the name of Ryan de Bruyn, but according to a fan site, he'd retired to Malta and never left his villa. Then there was a British actor who'd starred in a series of low-budget vampire films between 1944 and 1956. Surely this wasn't *the* Ryan de Bruyn?

Andrew clicked on to a page of an online magazine called *Business Insider* – and saw a long article on a South African businessman, dated only two weeks ago.

As Andrew scanned it, he tensed. This *had* to be the right man.

On the back of Chen's first email, Andrew wrote:

Ryan de B. Born in South Africa. Casino tycoon. CEO of Chips Inc, which has operations in Australia, Hong Kong and Macau. Plans to expand into China . . .

Beside him, Lydia started to talk loudly on the phone. Andrew tried to tune out her voice.

Gaia was right, he thought. If Chen had given Broadstairs only two hours to kill these men, they had to be close. The question was: *where, exactly?*

He clicked through to the Chips homepage. And he saw a map of the world, with golden dollar signs next to the hyperlinked names of several cities. Three were in Australia: one in Melbourne, one in Brisbane and one in Sydney.

Andrew clicked on *Sydney.*

A new webpage opened. Andrew was about to hit the *Contact* button, which he hoped might provide a phone number for the casino, when he noticed a press release scrolling in the body of the page.

De Bruyn in Sydney to Announce New Venture

His pulse rocketing, Andrew read:

Chips CEO Ryan de Bruyn will today announce details of an exciting new casino venture.
The press conference will be held at the Harbour Room of Sydney's Museum of Contemporary Art at 5.30 p.m. To register, please contact –

Andrew stopped reading. He looked up. Lydia was still on the phone. But he couldn't wait!

'Lydia, where's the Museum of Contemporary Art?'

She frowned and cupped a hand across her mouthpiece.

'Where's the Museum of Contemporary Art?'

'Circular Quay. Why?'

'De Bruyn is giving a press conference there in –' Andrew checked his watch – *'twenty minutes.'*

Lydia's eyes widened. Then she listened to the voice on the other end of the line. 'Yeah – OK – thanks heaps.'

Andrew was watching her. 'Collins is an Australian,' she said. 'He owns newspapers and a couple of online auction sites and he wants to expand into China. He's hosting a drinks party in the restaurant in the Opera House. It starts at *quarter to six.'*

'Thirty-two minutes!' Andrew exclaimed. He glanced back through the windows, into the lounge. Will was still on the phone, Gaia beside him. 'We have to update them now!'

As Andrew and Lydia burst into the lounge, Will pushed his phone in his pocket.

He didn't look happy, Andrew thought. But they could hear about Will's conversation with the police afterwards.

Quickly he told them about de Bruyn. Lydia added her findings about Collins.

'Chen has casinos – like de Bruyn,' Andrew said. 'Collins wants to expand into China. Chen must have found out these men are in Sydney, and he's taking the opportunity to test Broadstairs and take out a couple of potential competitors – to kill two birds with one stone!'

'Or, one with an ageing drug, and the other with who knows what,' Will said grimly. 'And there'll be a *third* name.'

Andrew glanced at his watch. 'De Bruyn is up first. In *seventeen minutes*.'

'What are the police going to do?' Lydia asked Will.

'They're going to send someone to knock on the door at Phoenix House.'

'That's *it*?' she said.

'That's all they'll do. I got as far as an inspector, but I think he thought I was making it all up. And he says there's no record of any call from Walker.'

'But when we tell them about all *this* –' Gaia started.

'Yeah, I'll call them back,' Will said, 'but *we* have to act. Seventeen minutes and counting.'

'But what can we do?' Lydia asked. 'We've got two people in two different places – and then the third name. We have no idea who that is. And Chen said he'd phone Broadstairs—'

'Andrew, you and Lydia go to the Opera House,' Will interrupted. Any time they'd had for reviewing what they did and didn't know had run out, he decided. 'Gaia, come with me to the gallery. I'll call Spicer in London and see if we can get access to Broadstairs's phone calls.'

'Who's Spicer?' Lydia said. '*MI6?*'

'Yes,' Andrew said.

After Shute Barrington's promotion, Charlie Spicer had been made head of STASIS. Spicer knew STORM well. And he could tap into Echelon, the international communications surveillance system.

Lydia looked at Andrew. 'But what are we meant to do?' she said. 'How are we supposed to save Collins?'

'You'll think of something,' Will said.

Lydia took a deep breath. She dug in her pocket for her car keys. 'You know it's rush hour. It could take ages to get into the city.'

'Is there a better way?' Will asked.

Lydia racked her brain. 'We could take a water taxi. If there isn't one waiting, we could call one. It'd be quicker than the roads.'

Will nodded. And hesitated. He'd been about to run for the door.

He made a decision.

'Andrew, you and Lydia take a water taxi.'

'Why?' Andrew said, surprised. 'What are you going to do?'

But Will's attention was fixed on Gaia. 'There is another way,' he said quickly. 'It could take the two of us. And it would be faster than a water taxi.'

21

Spicer's new personal assistant was brisk.

She'd arrived at STASIS HQ only the previous week, and Will hadn't met her.

Mr Spicer was in an extremely important meeting, she told him, and on no account could be disturbed. If it became possible, however, she would endeavour to pass on a message.

Will swallowed his anger, and left one.

He ran to his bedroom, tore off his T-shirt, slipped on the vest, and pulled his T-shirt back over the top. He grabbed the last of the Spy Seeds, and a serrated knife from the kitchen.

Gaia was at the dining table, dividing the nanotubes into four transparent freezer bags. She secured each one with a knot.

'Ready?'

She nodded. And she followed Will down the concrete steps, into the garage.

The crate was up against the wall. It was as high as Will and three metres across. Castors were fitted around the base, allowing it to be rolled. Blue plastic straps held the plywood sides together. Taped to the front was a thick packet of paper sealed in plastic.

Will slipped his fingers beneath one of the straps. He closed his fist, and pulled. The crate moved. Slowly.

'Help me get it outside, then we'll push it,' he said.

Gaia took another strap. They hauled it away from the wall, then shoved it across the garage, down the path, and to the esplanade.

The late afternoon air was cool, but sweat dripped from Will's forehead. Partly from the physical effort. Partly from stress. If they didn't get going soon, they'd be late for the press conference.

Quickly he checked the esplanade. An elderly couple sat on a bench at one end. Along the beach, a man wearing earphones walked a labrador. Will was relieved. They were unlikely to ask questions, he decided.

He ripped the plastic packet from the front and thrust it into Gaia's hands. 'Look in there for a manual. Tell me what I need to know.'

She stared at him. 'Don't tell me you haven't actually flown one of these?'

The kitchen knife was in Will's belt. He pulled it out and sliced one of the straps. 'Did you notice them on the school trip?'

At least I noticed you, she thought, but didn't say it. 'Will – *seriously* –'

'*Seriously*, I've flown my Dad's old Cessna. These are for fun. It's going to be a lot easier.' He sliced another strap. 'But if you don't want to come with me, you could take another water taxi.'

Gaia hesitated. Then she tore the plastic open. Inside she found the dispatch notice, a maintenance booklet – and a manual. She flicked it open and scanned the print.

'The 44-litre fuel tank provides a range of 300 kilo-metres,' she said.

Will smiled and moved to the last strap.

'It can fly safely in winds of 20 knots –' and she jumped.

The plywood sides had fallen open.

There in front of them was a microlight.

The two-man cockpit was black. Above it, the purple wings were folded, the Dacron flapping gently in the breeze. Instead of wheels, it had two long black floats, for taking off and landing on water.

Were they *really* going to fly in this thing? Gaia thought.

Will reached up to release the wings. 'Keep going!'

Gaia took a deep breath. 'It's a weight-shift design . . . wingspan 9.97 metres, length 2.74 metres . . . maximum weight per seat 100 kilogrammes . . . 80 horsepower four-stroke, two-cylinder engine . . . carbon fibre pro-peller . . . take-off speed 35 knots . . . 100 metres for take off . . . stall speed 30 knots . . . foot accelerator.'

She looked up. Now the wings were down, the craft looked even less sturdy. It was like a kite attached to a tricycle.

Will grabbed a crossbar. 'Help me get it down to the water.'

'Don't you need to know anything else? *Like how to fly it?*'

'It's a weight-shift design.'

'Yeah –'

'So you turn on the engine and you shift your weight around to steer it. That's it! Simple. Gaia – *come on.*'

'What about *landing*?' she asked, but she took one of the bars that connected the left float to the cockpit.

'It's just a matter of speed and altitude,' Will called.

Gaia shook her head.

Together, they dragged the craft on to the sand, and into the shallows.

The wing caught the breeze. Will dug his heels into the sand. 'Get in.'

She looked at him. Yes, she trusted him. But this wasn't a jet ski. If something went wrong, it would be a lot more dangerous. 'Will – can you really do this?'

'Yes.' He held her gaze. 'Now, please, before it blows away, *get in.*'

Gaia sighed. At least there were crash helmets, she noticed. She picked hers up, slipped it on and clambered into the back. The space was cramped. She twisted her legs to the side and dug around for the seatbelt.

In the front, Will sat down and adjusted his helmet. He activated the in-built radio. 'Are you ready?' he said into the mike.

'If you say so.'

He smiled. And scanned the dashboard.

He saw a key, a START button and two black switches, which had to be for the avionics. So far, so good.

He turned the key. The engine caught, setting the propeller spinning.

Then he flicked both switches, and the digital display burst into life.

There was a speedometer, an altimeter, an air speed indicator, a vertical speed indicator – and more. But so long as he kept an eye on those four, he'd be all right, he thought.

And he looked down. By his right foot was a pedal. Down in the nose, he saw a horizontal peg. The pedal had to be the accelerator. The peg was probably for steering on the water, he guessed. So what was the stick by the right side of his seat? A brake, he decided.

Will hit the START button. Then he wrapped his hands around the control bar.

He knew the theory. The horizontal bar could swing the under-carriage – and so steer the microlight. Pull with your left arm and the machine would veer left. Pull right, and it would turn right.

Simple.

He touched the pedal lightly with his foot.

At once, the microlight jerked. It started to skate across the water.

'Take-off speed 35 knots, right?'

Gaia had the manual in her lap. The cockpit vibrations made it hard to read the text. But she didn't need to. She could remember. '*Yeah*. And you need a hundred metres to do it . . . Did you hear me?'

'I heard you,' Will said.

He steered a slalom course between the buoys and the yachts. As soon as they'd passed the cruiser, he nosed the microlight downwind, and he pushed harder on the accelerator.

Now the machine started to race. The four-stroke engine was smooth.

Will kept one eye on their speed. *Twenty-four knots. Twenty-seven.*

As soon as they hit thirty-three, he pulled on the bar, lifting the nose.

Behind him, Gaia gripped her seat. Suddenly she felt herself thrown backwards.

Will veered towards the left.

Slam. Spray fountained into the air.

Gaia's pulse rocketed. 'Will – *what was that*?'

She wanted to squeeze her eyes shut. But she forced herself to look. They'd just tilted hard, and the left float was ploughing through the water.

'Hold on!' Will yelled.

He eased back on the control bar, and he pulled on the lever. But instead of braking, the microlight shot forward. The nose suddenly dipped, plunging the front section of the floats beneath water.

'*Will!*'

'You didn't tell me the seat lever was another accelerator!'

'*What lever?* You said this was simple!'

Will clenched his fists. The speedometer showed thirty-seven knots, but the drag of the floats was starting to slow them.

Using all his strength, he held the control bar steady. At last, the microlight levelled out.

When they hit thirty-five, he pulled on the bar – and lifted the nose.

This time, Will held his position. Then, using the lever, he increased their speed, and he leaned to the left.

Behind him, Gaia was trying to control her breathing. She could see only sky. And she felt the craft swing. 'Will! We're leaning over!'

'I know! I'm bringing us around. It's all right. We're flying. This is how it's meant to feel!'

'And dragging a float through the water, and nearly rolling over?'

There was a pause. 'That was a mistake. But I know how it works now.'

Gaia took a deep breath. She steeled herself. And she peered over the edge of the cockpit.

She saw beaches and steep white cliffs, and a cemetery, right along the edge. The ocean rippled beneath them. They had to be twenty metres up.

The sun was sinking lower. Pearl-coloured clouds swelled.

Ahead, the harbour spread, inlet after inlet, green and

dark blue, to the jutting white sails of the Opera House. Just beyond, the Harbour Bridge was a graphite silhouette.

Gradually Gaia's fear became exhilaration.

Then Will called: 'Gaia!'

Fear sparked through her. '*What?*'

'Look down, starboard side. Past those yachts. It must be them.' Will banked the microlight slightly and pointed.

Then she saw it. A yellow boat, blistering the water.

Frederick Broadstairs stepped out on to the balcony of his study – and felt uncomfortable.

He was a firm believer in the old adage that if you want something doing properly, you should do it yourself. But this particular *something* was undeniably risky. And he had to be ready for the phone call.

Chen had told him there would be a third name. Chen, the decrepit, dying fool, playing his power for all it was worth.

But could he trust them?

Tench and Hutt would do anything she asked, Eva had assured him. She had taken them in, and she fed their habits. They needed her drugs. They needed her.

So Broadstairs had agreed.

Eva had entrusted Tench with the sports bag and Hutt with a sample from the tin box.

If they failed, Broadstairs had wanted to say, he would hold her personally responsible. But why frighten her?

Instead, he'd stroked her hair and murmured nonsense about the wonderful future they'd have together.

Now his eyes went to his watch. He pulled out his phone and dialled a number. De Bruyn was due to make his appearance at the Museum of Contemporary Art in precisely *nine minutes*.

The rings stopped.

'Tench, where are you?'

There was an agonizing pause. Then he heard: 'It's all right, boss. They believed me. *I'm in.*'

'*Nine minutes*,' Will said.

And Gaia flinched. A sudden shadow had crossed the microlight. The helicopter had come out of nowhere. She ducked. Looked again, and realized it was higher than she'd thought. It whizzed by, the rotors a blur.

'Down there!' Will called. He pointed.

Ahead, to the left, Gaia saw the Botanic Gardens, with its ornamental ponds and lawns. Then the Opera House. At Circular Quay, a blue police boat was pulling out of one of the terminals. But Will was pointing beyond it, to a brown building on the far side.

It was six storeys high. Art deco. Back at Watson's Retreat, Lydia had given them a quick description of the gallery. This had to be it.

'I'm taking us down,' Will said.

He reduced their speed. Then he swung his weight to aim their nose at the water. At once, they began to lose altitude.

When the speedometer showed 45 knots, he looked for a landing path. And they seemed to be in luck. A ferry had just crossed from the quay to Kirribilli. Now there was a good 100 metres of clear water right in front of them.

Forty-two knots.

Will eased up on the accelerator. They were low now – on a level with the tops of the apartment blocks to their right.

'Preparing to land,' he called. 'Hold on.'

And he tensed. Three horn blasts had just filled the air.

'*Ferry!*' Gaia cried.

Will glanced over his shoulder. A Freshwater-class ferry was backing out of a terminal. But if he aborted the landing now, he'd have to come around again and they'd waste valuable time.

Thirty-eight knots. Will took his hands off the controls. They were at trim speed, and right on course.

Thirty-six knots. Will lifted the nose.

And he felt a gentle thud as the two floats hit the water.

A perfect landing.

'Will – *the ferry*!'

He shifted his feet to the peg and he pushed with his left foot. They veered away sharply.

The microlight lurched. And the ferry swept past, with barely two metres of water between them. A second later, the wake hit. It set them see-sawing.

'Will!' Gaia yelled. 'Didn't you see it?'

'Did we crash?'

'It was *close*!'

'Close is OK,' Will said, as he steered through the wash. 'This is the middle of Sydney. If we'd waited for totally clear water we'd have been here for hours! De Bruyn would be dead!'

His gaze shot to a jetty on their right. Beside it was a ladder that ran down into the water. At the top, only an esplanade separated them from the MCA. But it was thronged with people. Some were standing in groups between buskers, watching the microlight. Two even had their cameras out. In the back, Gaia scowled at them.

Will aimed right at the ladder. As soon as they were close enough, he grabbed a rung.

A man in a baseball cap took a few steps towards them. He cupped a hand around his mouth. 'What were you kids thinking?' he shouted over the noise of steel drums. 'That ferry would have run right through you!'

Will flicked off the avionics and cut the engine, ignoring him. Gaia pulled off her helmet.

'It looks like you're still in one piece,' he said.

'Just,' she said. And she paused. They were down. And de Bruyn's life was on the line. 'But *just* is OK.'

Will smiled.

He slipped the mooring rope around the rung and knotted it. Then he zipped the key into his jacket pocket and he climbed out of the cockpit and up. Gaia followed him.

When she got to the top, the man in the baseball cap shouted: 'You're not going to leave that thing there?'

'Yeah,' Will said. 'We are.'

And he turned away.

People milled everywhere, picking at fish and chips, drinking coffee. He fixed his eyes on the gallery. And he pulled out his toothphone keypad, and hit the black button. 'Andrew, Lydia, we're here. We're heading in.'

Gaia checked her watch. *'Three and a half minutes,'* she said.

22

It was breezy on the roof-top Harbour Terrace, and Ryan de Bruyn's tie flapped all over the place. But the views more than made up for the chill.

Behind him, the clouds glowed peach-gold. As the sun sank even lower, the Opera House and the glitter of the harbour would provide a suitable backdrop for his announcement.

Chips Inc had just secured licences to open three new casinos, one in Melbourne, one in Shanghai and one in Beijing. They would be the most luxurious the world had ever seen. The Las Vegas Strip could eat its tacky heart out.

'Two minutes, Mr de Bruyn!'

A small woman with a frizz of curly hair was heading towards him. Jackie, his media director.

She had already ushered most of the fifty or so journalists out of the indoor reception room. Now they stood in a semi-circle around the platform, chatting and drinking champagne.

De Bruyn's gaze flickered over them. None looked familiar. An anxious-faced young man with a goatee beard was trade press, he guessed. A loud, attractive blonde woman in a rainbow-coloured dress had to be from a local tabloid.

What about the stocky, red-haired man, standing alone at the side? He was sweating. Instead of champagne, he held a black briefcase.

Jackie jumped up to the lectern and clapped her hands. 'Good evening, everyone, it's great to see you all here. Let me present Mr Ryan de Bruyn!'

Will ran. Gaia was right behind him.

They dodged seagulls and tourists and veered right, up three sets of shallow steps and into a marble foyer.

A staircase rose in front of them. Beside it, a sign indicated the main entrance to the galleries was to the right. Gaia started for the stairs.

'Hold on,' Will said. 'We need to know exactly where the Harbour Terrace is.'

He headed past the sign, hoping they'd find a better map. But then he noticed two metal doors to the left. *Lifts.*

Pinned between them was a listing of the gallery's rooms and exhibitions.

'There!' Gaia said. 'Level Six.'

Will pounded the call button once with his fist, and glanced back. The foyer was quiet. There was no one else around. They were all upstairs, he thought. The press conference would be getting under way.

'*Come on,*' he urged, under his breath.

Gaia bit her lip. 'He's starting *now*.'

Now meant they might be too late, Will thought. Perhaps they should run for the stairs.

Then the right-hand set of doors pinged open. They dashed in.

The lift was slow.

It seemed to take forever to get to *2*. After an age, a *3* lit up on the chrome panel.

Will's hand tapped impatiently against his leg.

At last, they reached *6*.

To their left was a rectangular room. Tables pushed up against the white walls were littered with used napkins and wine glasses. Beyond them, Will saw a glass door. It was standing open. Through it, he glimpsed sky.

Gaia had seen it too. 'Out there!' she said.

They hurried past the tables – and outside, into dusk.

The terrace was crammed. Between the reporters' backs, they made out fairy lights strung around the perimeter of a platform. And they heard a South African man. His softly accented voice boomed:

'So, the first stage of construction will begin in approximately two months, giving ample time for lavish coverage of our plans.'

De Bruyn. Surely. They weren't too late!

Will began to skirt the crowd, looking for a gap big enough for them to look through. Behind him, Gaia kept her eyes peeled for Broadstairs. De Bruyn began to talk about silk quality, and a firm of interior decorators from Paris.

They reached the wall, and stopped. Will peered around a man in a black suit – and he saw de Bruyn, smiling at the lectern. He was tall, with freckled skin. A small woman with frizzy hair stood beside him.

Will scanned the reporters' faces. He saw blond hair, a goatee beard, a grey comb-over. But *where was Broadstairs*?

'Can you see Broadstairs anywhere?' he whispered.

The man in the suit turned to look at him. Will avoided his eyes.

'Not yet,' Gaia said.

Suddenly Will tensed.

On his own by the far wall was a red-haired man. He was standing side-on to them, cradling a black brief-case.

'Over there!' Will whispered and pointed. 'He looks like the guard that chased Lydia – the one I saw going down to the labs.'

'Are you sure?'

From this angle, it was difficult to be positive. 'Pretty sure,' he said.

'So what do you want to do?'

Will pulled Sam from his pocket.

Gaia raised an eyebrow. 'You're going to stun him?'

He nodded. 'You start off towards him. I'll hit him hard. He'll stumble. You take the briefcase.'

Her eyes widened.

'He won't know what's happened,' Will whispered. 'And we need that briefcase. *Gaia.*'

'All right!'

As she crept back around the terrace, a couple of reporters noticed her. They flashed her surprised glances. Gaia ignored them. They could think what they liked. But they were too busy listening to de Bruyn to ask her questions. He was still talking about interior decor.

'The marble will come from Carrera. The gold will follow. The order has been sent to Dubai. Twenty-four carat, and as much as they can send me. If necessary, I will melt the camels from the palace itself!'

The reporters' heads bent over their notebooks as they jotted down the quote.

And Gaia reached the entrance to the reception room. Here, the crowd was at its thickest. She couldn't see the guard any more. He was hidden behind three young female reporters in short dresses and high heels.

'Where are you?' Will whispered hard. 'He's just backed up. I can't see him any more!'

'Almost there,' Gaia breathed.

She was about to slip behind the women – and she stopped.

One had just gasped.

Suddenly Gaia realized de Bruyn wasn't talking any more. *No one* was talking.

'Will!' she whispered. And heard a groan. Then a thud.

A woman cried out: 'Mr de Bruyn? *Mr de Bruyn?*'

'Will!' Gaia hissed. 'What's happening?'

'De Bruyn's *down*!'

'Is there a doctor here?' the woman called. 'Does anyone have medical training?' Her voice was raw.

Gaia pushed between two of the reporters and saw her. Her frizzy head was bent over de Bruyn, who was kneeling, clutching at his chest. He took two quick shallow breaths.

A white-haired man bounded on to the platform. He put his champagne on the ground, and felt for de Bruyn's pulse. After a few moments, he called: 'Ring for an ambulance. He's gone into cardiac arrest!'

De Bruyn's face was grey. Sweat poured from his forehead. His eyes were closing.

This wasn't coincidence, Gaia thought. It couldn't be!

The reporters had pushed forward around her. Now she slipped back through them.

'*Can you see the guard?*' Will hissed in her ear.

Gaia was at the back of the terrace. She stood on tiptoe, her gaze darting across the faces. *Where was he?*

'*Gaia?*'

'I can't see him!'

'*What?*'

Where was the guard?

Suddenly she heard Will curse.

'*Will*,' she said.

'It's nothing,' Will said. 'I'm *no one*.' There was a

pause. Then: 'Gaia, someone's just seen Sam. They're asking questions. I'm coming over to you.'

And a woman shouted: 'Who's that boy? Why's he running?'

'Gaia, if he's gone, we have to follow him. There's only one way out. I'm right behind you!'

Gaia ran back to the reception room. Something caught her eye. Movement. In the corridor.

'Will, I think he just got into a lift.'

'I'm coming!'

Gaia dashed across the floor. From behind, she heard shouts. She glanced over her shoulder, and saw Will. He was running.

Gaia skidded to a stop by the lifts. She was about to press the call button when she saw *both* were in motion. One was going up, the other down.

Will reached her. He glanced at the display panel. 'He must have sent one up before he took the other down. The stairs. Let's go!'

'*Andrew, can you hear me?*'

Gaia's trainers squeaked on the marble.

In front of her, Will jumped three steps and rounded the corner, to the next flight down.

Level Two.

De Bruyn's face was pulsing in Gaia's head.

The guard had hit him, there was no doubt about that. But with what?

The briefcase had to be the one Broadstairs collected from the cruise boat.

Inside, Lydia had seen a device shaped like a hairdryer, and a microwave warning.

Microwaves could mess with electrical equipment. STORM had seen that first hand in Switzerland. And heartbeats were also controlled by electrical signals.

Chen had said he'd wanted weapons that could be used to murder without suspicion.

De Bruyn had gone into cardiac arrest. For all they knew, he was already dead.

What if the guard really had used a gun to trigger a heart attack, but at a frequency that wouldn't leave a burn?

Gaia's trainers thudded on to the floor.

Level One.

Below, she could see the lights of the foyer. And something else: a man in a dark blue uniform, with a radio in his hand.

Andrew's voice burst into her ear: 'Will, Gaia, we are still trying to negotiate access to the location. I've just checked your contact lens feeds. I can't really make out what you're seeing.'

The security guard looked up. Frowned at them.

'*Will –*'

'I'm on him,' he hissed.

Gaia saw a silver flash as Will aimed Sam.

He hit FIRE.

Instantly the man dropped his radio. His hands flew to his ears.

'Will, Gaia,' Andrew said, 'check in!'

Gaia jumped off the last of the steps. Will had already darted towards the lifts. The guard was stumbling towards the wall. He groaned and reached out.

'Will, Gaia, what is your status?'

'Our *status*,' Gaia hissed, 'is that de Bruyn has just apparently had a *heart attack*!'

'Broadstairs *got him*?' Andrew's voice was loaded with disbelief.

'No, the guard from Phoenix House – the one that chased Lydia.' And Gaia stopped. Will had about-turned.

'The lifts are empty,' he called to her. 'He's gone!'

The security guard took his hands from the wall. He grimaced in pain. And he noticed Gaia.

Quickly she followed Will on to the esplanade.

The outside world hit her. People and noise.

The sky was dim. Tourists grinned and laughed at the buskers. A gold-painted Statue of Liberty looked grue-some in the half-light. He shot out an arm, making a girl squeal.

Where was the red-haired guard?

Suddenly Will darted off to the right.

Gaia squinted. What had he seen?

'Andrew, what's going on?' she said, as she followed Will. 'Why aren't you in?'

No answer. Will broke into a run.

Then she heard: 'Gaia, sorry, I just had to talk to Lydia. What did you say?'

Gaia didn't reply. Will was halfway along the

esplanade. Beyond him, just past the railway bridge, a taxi had stopped. A man was jumping inside.

He was stocky. Red-haired.

Gaia veered around a family, accidentally knocking a small boy. Ice cream fell to the pavement. His mother screamed after her.

At last, she caught up with Will. Just in time to see the taxi door slam. And the car streak away.

Will's hands were at his head.

Gaia's chest was heaving.

Will let his hands drop. He looked at her.

The stunned expression on her face echoed what he was thinking: de Bruyn was dead, or close to it.

His assassin had escaped.

For the first time, STORM had failed in a mission.

After a moment, though, disbelief became anger. Thinking that way would get them *nowhere*.

Even if they couldn't prove it, they knew who'd attacked de Bruyn. And they knew why.

Will had given the police inspector the two names on Chen's hit list. Now de Bruyn was down, they'd have to take him seriously.

But STORM needed that third name. He'd have to try Spicer again, Will thought. And they *had* to save Collins. His gaze shot to the Opera House, at the far end of the quay.

Then back to the gallery.

The security guard was on the steps: 'Hey you! Stop! Yeah – you!'

23

'What is that woman *doing*?' Lydia asked.

Andrew slipped his contact lens screen back into his pocket and shook his head in exasperation.

They were standing behind a brass chain. On the other side was a staircase that led down into the beige-and-brown dining room of the restaurant.

Christopher Collins was at the back, talking to two men in suits. He was tall and slim, with thick dark hair and a red tie knotted tightly.

To Collins's left, waiters were polishing glasses and arranging platters of canapés on a table. Stationed in the far right corner, and at each side of the foot of the staircase, were bodyguards. Wires crept from their earpieces into their collars. One held a radio. He glanced blankly at Andrew. Who shuffled anxiously.

Three minutes and twenty seconds ago, Andrew and Lydia had hurried in through the glass door behind them. They'd spotted Collins almost at once. But at the chain, they'd been intercepted by a Singaporean woman in a trouser suit, who'd asked what they wanted.

If he started telling this woman about assassins and

death threats, there was a good chance they'd be immediately escorted from the premises, Andrew thought. They *had* to tell their story to Collins.

'My name's Andrew Minkel,' he said. 'I'm in town for a few days, and I'd just like a few minutes of Mr Collins's time before the party starts. My readers would really appreciate it.'

The woman looked taken aback. 'Your readers?'

'All 7.9 million of them.' Andrew smiled smugly.

'Exactly what newspaper –'

'A blog. A *web log*. I run an e-business gossip blog. *Who's In, Who's Out*. It's very influential.'

The woman had pursed her lips. She'd told them to wait, unhooked the chain, slipped through, re-hooked it, headed down the stairs, and vanished, without going anywhere near Collins.

The hands of Andrew's gold watch ticked.

Three vital minutes and twenty-five seconds had passed.

Collins was still talking to the two men in suits. The bodyguards were fingering their earpieces. Behind Andrew and Lydia, guests were starting to congregate in the bar.

Perhaps they should call out to Collins, to warn him, Andrew thought. But he seemed safe for the moment. The danger would come with the influx of guests.

'Do you think she's looking you up online?' Lydia whispered now.

'Probably.'

'Then she'll see there's no such thing as *Who's In, Who's Out.*'

'Actually, there is.'

'It's *real?*'

'Of course,' Andrew said quietly. 'But obviously I don't run it.'

'Who does?'

'I have no idea.' Before Lyda could protest, he added: 'But neither does anyone else. It's anonymous.'

Lydia raised an eyebrow. 'Good thinking.'

Andrew coloured, and he checked his watch again, to try to conceal his pleasure. Lydia nudged him.

At last.

The woman had reappeared and was heading for Collins.

He'd strolled away from the two men, towards the table. As the woman tapped him on the shoulder, a waiter proffered his plate. Collins grabbed something and chewed while he listened.

Then his gaze flashed towards Andrew and Lydia. Andrew stiffened. Behind them, the bar was packed with waiting guests. Was Broadstairs back there? Collins had to talk to them *now.*

Then the woman started up the stairs. After a moment, Collins followed. He was coming over!

'Let me do the talking,' Andrew whispered.

'But –'

'Lydia, only one of us –'

'Then let me this time,' Lydia said.

Her jet eyes were shining. Andrew's stomach twitched. He nodded quickly.

The woman stopped at the chain. She smiled. It was fake. But Andrew didn't care. 'Mr Collins has agreed to talk to you. But the party is due to start, so if you could keep it brief, that would be much appreciated.'

'No problem,' Lydia said, glancing past her at Collins, who looked irritated.

Andrew was watching Lydia.

And he saw her expression freeze.

A split second later, her mouth fell open.

Gaia led the way. She ran with her head down, swerving around strolling tourists, past an oyster bar and on – to the open concourse of the Opera House.

From a distance it looked like a single building. Now it dissolved into three arched shells connected by a broad flight of shallow steps. The two performance halls were at the back. At the front was the restaurant.

Gaia ran to it, panting. Through the glass wall they saw a long table set with candles, glasses and platters, and beyond, a staircase. At the top was a huddle of people.

Will checked his watch. '*Five fifty-two*. The party should have started. Come on.'

They ran on up the steps, until they found the way in. The door was also glass. Through it, they watched a hefty man in a black suit jog towards them. Will got the door half-open. The man reached out, and held it. In his other hand was a radio.

'The restaurant's closed.'

'We're on the guest list,' Will said. 'Mr Collins is expecting us.' He tried to peer around the man's shoulder.

The radio crackled into life.

'Five-zero,' a voice said. 'The ambulance is on its way.'

And Will's blood ran cold. An *ambulance*. Were they too late? Where were Andrew and Lydia?

'Five-zero, roger,' the man replied. He started to close the door.

'What ambulance?' Gaia asked quickly. 'What's happened?'

The man only shook his head. 'Sorry, kids.'

'Christopher Collins—' Will started.

'Has been taken ill. The party is *cancelled*.' The man shoved the door shut.

Will wheeled. His pulse hammered hard in his neck.

'He got him!' Gaia whispered. 'Broadstairs got him!'

Will hit the black button on his keypad. 'Andrew, we're at the entrance to the restaurant. Where are you? *What's happened?*'

After a moment, Andrew's voice came through the toothphones – and the air.

He and Lydia had been at the other side of the restaurant. Now they hurried round. Andrew's blue eyes looked stricken. One hand was at his glasses. The other held his phone.

'*What happened?*' Gaia demanded.

'Collins has been hit,' Andrew said. 'Everyone, apart from Collins's people, was ordered to leave. I just called the police, and they've put me on *hold*.'

Will stared at him. 'Is Collins *dead*? How did Broad-stairs do it?'

Andrew took a deep breath. 'He's still alive. Or he was.' But when it came to how Broadstairs did it, they had no idea. 'The party hadn't even started . . .'

And he reviewed what they'd seen.

Collins had seemed fine while he talked to the two men. Then what? The Singaporean woman had tapped him on the shoulder. Collins had followed her to the steps . . .

What was he missing?

'The waiter!' he exclaimed to Lydia. 'A waiter offered him his plate, remember? Collins took something. He ate it.'

'*Poison?*' she said. 'Could it have been the *drug*?'

'You saw the waiter?' Will said quickly. 'Was it Broad-stairs?'

Andrew shook his head. 'He was tall but he was blond. And his shoulders were narrow. It wasn't him.' Perhaps the waiter was innocent, he thought. But they had nothing else to go on.

'But what happened to Collins?' Will asked. 'What *exactly*?'

'He was on the stairs,' Andrew said. 'He was about to talk to us. Then he stumbled. He went pale. He made it back down the steps and collapsed on to a chair.' He looked at Lydia for confirmation.

'Then the bodyguards were all over him,' she said, 'and after a minute, one of them called out that the party was cancelled and everyone had to leave. We were pushed out before we could get anyone to seal the restaurant.'

'How could they be so *stupid*?' Gaia cried. 'They let the attacker go!'

'But they aren't suspecting an attack,' Lydia said. 'They think Collins is just ill!' And her head snapped round.

The bodyguard with the radio had just stepped out of the door, his back to them. From the bar, they heard shouts. A woman was crying. In the distance, a siren blared.

One hand cupped over his ear against the noise, the man said: 'Roger, four-zero. Confirmed. Collins is deceased. Repeat: Collins is deceased.'

Lydia's black eyes shot back to Andrew. All the colour had drained from her face.

The guard's voice echoed through Will's brain. *Deceased. Collins is deceased.*

He pulled his phone from his pocket. His blood rushing, he dialled the police inspector he'd talked to from Watson's Retreat.

Collins was dead.

Collins *and* de Bruyn. STORM had failed *twice.*

A woman answered the phone.

'I thought I'd called Detective Inspector Portofino,' Will said.

'You've been forwarded to the front desk. DI Portofino's off duty. He must have his phone switched off. Can I help?'

Will cursed. 'Is there some way you can contact him? It's urgent. Tell him it's Will Knight. I talked to him earlier. He *has* to call me.'

'On this mobile number?'

'*Yes!*'

'Right, sir.'

Will flipped his phone shut.

'What do we do now?' Andrew asked.

Will ran a hand across his face. His head felt hot. He *had* to think.

'Two down,' he said, the words sticking in his throat. 'But there's still one to go. I'll give Spicer another go. *We need that third name.*'

The Lockheed Martin QSST jet rolled to a halt.

Mei carefully coiled the viper inside the false lining of her handbag. Then she led the way out into the cool breeze, and to a waiting limousine.

Chen Jianguo did not walk down the steps. He glided to the ground on a silk-cushioned chair-lift. The air smelt strange, he thought. He sniffed, and the stench of aviation fuel mixed with sweet eucalyptus made him sneeze. He spat, splattering blood on to the tarmac.

As Mei opened the door for him, Chen noticed two men striding towards them.

'Immigration and quarantine,' Mei said. 'I will deal with them.'

Chen smiled faintly.

The false lining of Mei's bag contained not only his viper but the dismantled components of a lightweight ceramic pistol.

In his own pocket, Chen carried one of his favourites from his collection: an eighteenth century English silver scorpion.

The mechanism was simple. Flick the gleaming tail and the mouth would fire a silver dart impregnated with venom from the Indian red scorpion, *Mesobuthus tamulus*.

Chen clambered into the car and settled back on to the soft leather. A black screen concealed the driver. But whoever he was, Chen knew the man was trustworthy. He paid a hefty monthly subscription to the international limousine agency, which dispatched only the best and most dependable drivers to work wherever they were required.

Movement through his window caught his attention. The immigration officer was glancing in, checking Chen's face against his passport photo. He seemed satisfied. The two men strolled off. And Chen felt his pocket vibrate.

He pulled out his phone: 'Yes?'

'Mr Chen. The jobs are done. What next?'

Chen looked up. Mei was getting into the car.

He had instructed her to monitor police and ambulance frequencies, as well as wire agency reports. He already knew that Ryan de Bruyn had died of cardiac arrest, and that the death was being treated as natural.

Chen covered the mouthpiece of his phone. 'It is Broadstairs. He says both jobs are done.'

'I will check on Mr Collins right away,' Mei replied.

Chen nodded. He would have to withhold judgement on the success or otherwise of Collins's assassination until Mei had confirmed Broadstairs's report. But he had to hand it to Broadstairs – de Bruyn's murder appeared to have gone perfectly.

So now for challenge number three!

Both de Bruyn and Collins had businesses that impinged on Chen's own. He was glad to have them out of the way. But they weren't, strictly speaking, enemies.

But the third . . .

Yes, there were at least a dozen men back in Shanghai that Chen would wish dead before him. But they weren't in Shanghai. So it was a stroke of luck that this man was *here*. The 'do-gooder'. The 'champion of the poor'. The man who had tried to put Chen Jianguo behind bars!

Chen cleared his throat. Anticipation made his breath rattle.

He rasped: '*Yu Jichei. Government House.*'

Will paced, his mobile clamped to his ear. Andrew, Lydia and Gaia were watching him.

Two down, he thought again. *One to go.* But *who*?

To have even a chance of answering the question, they needed Spicer. Will had called his personal mobile. His assistant had answered, and asked him to hold.

'Mr Knight –'

'Please, can you just get him –'

'Mr Spicer is with the *Prime Minister*,' she interrupted. 'But he did receive your message, and he asked me to help if I could. I've been very busy, but I was about to check for you.'

Will heard keys being tapped. He waited impatiently. And he hit speakerphone, so the others could hear.

'Mr Chen has received a number of calls to his mobile today. The last one was two minutes ago. It lasted fifty-three seconds.'

'What did he say?' Will demanded. 'Who was he talking to?'

'One moment.'

There was another pause, longer this time.

'The caller had a British accent. I can't identify him from the number. He said, *The jobs are done, what next?* After a pause, Chen replied: *Yu Jichei, Government House.*'

Will's heart pounded. The man with the British accent had to be Broadstairs.

'*Yu Jichei?*'

'That's what I said.'

They had the third name!

'I *need* to talk to Spicer.'

'I'm sure that will be possible, *when* his meeting finishes.'

'When will that be?'

'It's scheduled to run for another two hours.'

'*Two hours!*'

'Mr Spicer and Mr Barrington are briefing the Prime Minister –'

'Barrington's in there too?'

'*Mr* Barrington is in the meeting, yes.'

Will shook his head. The only people who could really help them – Charlie Spicer and Shute Barrington – were tied up. They could go to their embassy contact. But Marjorie Blaxted was a headmistress type. She'd be more likely to tick them off than to help them. Spicer's assistant cleared her throat. 'Is that all?'

'Yeah.' Will forced himself to add: 'Thanks.' He pocketed his phone, and looked round.

The sky had turned mauve. Two women in evening dresses were climbing unsteadily up the steps. A man in a suit was munching on a sandwich, gazing at the view across the water to the east.

Will barely noticed them.

Beside him, Lydia was talking on her mobile. Andrew

and Gaia were reading something on the screen of his smartphone. Andrew's blue eyes were shining. Now his head shot up.

'Will, a Yu Jichei was profiled by the *Economist* just last week,' he said. 'He's based in Shanghai. Until last year he was a lawyer, and he prosecuted all sorts of companies for corruption and environmental pollution and that sort of thing, including Sino Enterprises.

'Now he's a rising star in Chinese politics. He wants open government, an end to bribery, a taskforce for organized crime. He'd be just the sort of person Chen would want to get rid of. He'd be a perfect target for Broadstairs!'

Will took this in. 'Lydia, what do you know about Government House? Is it in Sydney?'

She looked at him, but she was still on the phone. She held up a hand to tell him to wait. '. . . OK. Yeah. Thanks very much.' And she ended the call.

'What's Government House?' Will said again. 'Where is it?'

'It's where the New South Wales governors used to live,' she said quickly. 'Now it's used for things like receptions. I just talked to the press officer and there's a dinner tonight. It's some kind of business event. The mayor's holding it, and Yu Jichei is the guest of honour. They're sitting down at seven. But they're meant to be there by half past six.'

Will checked his watch. 'It's ten past six! *So where is it?*'

Lydia pointed down over the Opera House steps, past a set of gates and black railings, into the Botanic Gardens. 'You see those turrets. That's it.'

Will nodded. He could just make out the tops of the towers. They were half-concealed by the trees.

So, he thought, they had the name, and they had the location. Spicer and Barrington were tied up. The police weren't taking them seriously.

'We have to get to Yu,' he said.

He started down the steps. Gaia and Andrew followed – and Andrew glanced back. Lydia hadn't moved.

'For an event like this, security will be really tight,' she said.

'We've done this sort of thing before,' Will called back. 'We'll find a way in.'

'Not through those gates, you won't.'

Will stopped.

'They're locked at dusk.'

'Is there another way in?' Andrew said, before Will could ask the same question, only less patiently.

'The only gates that might be open are the main ones.'

'Which are *where*?' Will demanded.

'Macquarie Street,' Lydia said, and added, before Will could explode, '*Follow me.*'

24

Macquarie Street was almost deserted.

Through the railings on the left, the gardens were dim and shadowy. Two taxis hurtled past in the opposite direction, heading for the Opera House.

Lydia had taken the lead. Now she stopped. Beside her, a plaque was attached to an open gate. It read *Old Government House*. A black arrow pointed along a path that wound through the trees.

'This is the main entrance?' Andrew said doubtfully.

'It's further on. But this path meets up with the driveway. There'll be a gate to climb to get to it, but at this time there might not be anyone around. The security should all be at the main gate at the end of the drive.'

Andrew still looked uncertain.

'I know exactly what the gate looks like,' Lydia said. 'It's not high. You'll be OK.'

And he stiffened. He hadn't meant *that*. Clearly if Gaia had talked him up, the talk hadn't touched on sporting ability. Which perhaps was as well. Lydia could probably see for herself that his talents lay elsewhere.

Lydia was already heading up the path. Will and Gaia were right behind her.

Gaia glanced round. 'Andrew,' she whispered.

'I'm coming!'

Before long they came to an iron gate set into a wall. It was locked, but low, with two horizontal cross-bars and worn spikes.

Lydia was first over. Then Andrew threw himself at it. To his astonishment, he didn't immediately lose his footing. He scrambled to the second bar, and climbed over. As he dropped down on to the grass his right ankle kinked. He did his best to hide his grimace.

Lydia had run on, and was kneeling in the shadows of a fig tree. 'Over here,' she hissed.

Andrew jogged over.

'See,' she said. 'Easy.'

'Easy,' he echoed, and had to rub his ankle. He really didn't want it to swell.

'You OK?' Lydia whispered.

'Fine. Just a bit rusty when it comes to jumping over gates.'

'Maybe we should have left you in Phoenix House long enough for de Souza to give you a dose of the drug.'

'I'm just rusty,' Andrew said. 'Not *old*.'

'Yeah, I bet that's what Neil Murray and Sheila Barlow said too.' Lydia smiled slightly. And she looked past Andrew.

Gaia was running over. She dropped to her knees in the leaves. Will followed.

'This way,' Lydia whispered. She edged around the tree and pointed.

Will tensed. The driveway was to their left. It was only about fifteen metres away. A short distance along it was a red-brick guard's house with another gate. A man in a black uniform stood outside, his back to the wall. Beyond him, in a clearing, was Government House.

In the moonlight, it wouldn't have looked out of place in a horror movie, Will thought. It was Gothic-style, with turrets, an arched portico and leaded windows.

Spotlights illuminated the front. But the left side was poorly lit, Will noticed. He could just make out a footpath that ran alongside the sandstone wall. Perhaps they could use it to search for a back way in. First, though, they'd have to make it through security.

Four guards had just walked out of the portico. They strode over to a colleague at the gate. One lit a cigarette. Another grabbed a stool from inside the guard's house.

'They look like they're settling in!' Andrew whispered. 'There's no way we can get past.'

'No,' Will said bitterly. And something struck him. If guards were coming outside, did that mean the guests had all arrived?

His watch showed 6.22 p.m.

'Yu and Broadstairs are probably already in there,' Will said. 'Lydia, is there any other way in?'

She frowned, thinking. And her expression changed.

'Lydia?' Andrew asked.

'There might be,' she said. 'But when I say *might*, I mean it. I don't even know if it's still useable.'

'*What*'s still useable?' Will asked.

'And even if it is, it would be dangerous. I don't know –'

'*Lydia!*'

'I saw it on a school trip.'

Lydia led them downhill through the gardens, away from Government House. There were few lights, and she stuck to the shadows.

'It's sealed up now but convicts built it from somewhere in Government House – from near the kitchen, I think – to the gardens. It was meant to be an escape route.'

'A tunnel!' Andrew exclaimed. His eyes lit up. 'So we can use it to get in!'

'*Maybe.*' Lydia headed on to a narrow path that cut across the lawns. The grass glowed in the moonlight. 'But like I said, it's sealed up – and it's probably flooded. It wouldn't have been used for years. If it ever was.'

'Sealed up how?' Gaia asked.

'There's a metal grate over it. Maybe we could lever it open.'

'Or if there's no one around, I could blast it,' Gaia said to her. 'I've got some nanotubes with me.'

Lydia nodded. 'OK. But if it's flooded?'

'There's an old saying,' Andrew said. 'Don't worry about something until it happens.'

Lydia looked unconvinced. 'If you say so,' she said.

The path got steeper. Ahead was a stand of palms, and then towering figs. They were black in the darkness.

And Andrew stared. A dark object with scalloped wings had just screeched and swooped down to one of the branches. As they approached the trees, the screeches got louder. And he noticed what looked like large seed pods hanging from the branches. *Hundreds* of them.

'Lydia –' he said nervously.

She glanced back. He pointed up.

'Bats,' she whispered.

'They're very large bats.'

'Don't worry, they only eat fruit.' And she paused. 'I think.' Then she jogged on, leading them in among the trees.

Andrew screwed up his nose. The path was covered with bitter-smelling guano. Around them, the canopies were alive, the bats squabbling, fighting for space. *Fruit,* he told himself. *Only fruit.*

He gazed up, and he caught a glimpse of hooked claws and a leathery wing. He shuddered.

When he looked back down, he saw that they'd reached a cafe. The shutters were closed. White plastic chairs were stacked outside.

Lydia hesitated. 'It was over here somewhere. The ranger showed it to us.'

Suddenly she started down a path to the right. And she broke into a run. A moment later, she stopped and waved them on. Then she vanished among spiky-looking bushes.

Branches snapped as Lydia moved around in the undergrowth. Andrew glanced around. But apart from them and the bats – and shadows on the trunks that he thought might be possums – the gardens seemed deserted.

Then Lydia whistled. 'Over here!'

They pushed their way through the bushes and found her looking at a square iron grille, about a metre by a metre. It was set into the slope of the hill.

Gaia couldn't help feeling dubious. 'It looks like a drain. Are you sure this is the tunnel?'

'That's what they told us,' Lydia said. 'But they'd hardly put a plaque on it, would they?'

Gaia frowned, but Lydia didn't see her. She was gripping two of the metal bars. She heaved. Nothing happened.

Will crouched beside her. He ran his fingers around the edges of the grille. 'I can't feel a latch or a lock.'

Gaia knelt.

'Did you bring the torch?' Will asked.

'No. I remembered about Sam. How strong's his beam – six watts? It'll be more than enough.' She pulled the bags from her jacket pocket. And she tied the free ends around the base of two bars.

Will, Lydia and Andrew had backed up as far as they

could. Now Will had Sam and the control screen ready. He activated the robot. Its metal head twitched.

Gaia joined them. And Will switched on the torch.

The beam shot out.

It struck the first bag. Then the second.

They erupted one after the other, snapping like fireworks.

After the light came smoke.

One hand over her mouth, Gaia went back to the grate. She pulled at a bar. This time the grille flopped backwards on to the grass.

Will dropped to his knees beside her. He aimed Sam's torch into the darkness.

'What can you see?' Andrew asked.

Will and Gaia blinked. As the smoke cleared, Will panned the beam. On either side of the entrance they saw large sandstone blocks, criss-crossed with blackened cuts.

Lydia pushed Will's shoulder out of the way. 'Look at those chisel marks,' she said. 'This is definitely it!'

'How do you know?' Will asked.

'That's exactly what convict sandstone looks like. There's still loads of it around the city.'

Will lowered the beam. The bare rock floor was dark with damp, but not wet. Then he checked the roof. For the first ten metres or so it seemed low. They'd have to crawl.

And he reached for his phone.

'What are you doing?' Lydia whispered.

'There'll be no reception in there,' he said quietly. 'And the police should have heard about de Bruyn and Collins by now. They'll have to act.'

He dialled Portofino. Got through to the same duty constable.

She apologized. She'd paged Portofino, but he had to be tied up.

'Just tell him: *Yu Jichei, Government House*,' Will said. 'I don't care if he doesn't want to talk to me. But make sure he gets the message. Tell him: *that's the third name.*'

Broadstairs fixed his gaze on a portrait of a portly old man with a handlebar moustache and an official-looking medal, and smiled to himself.

Here they were, inside Government House.

The mayor herself had apologized for the inconceivable mistake. If invitations had been accepted, of course their names should be on the guest list. Thankfully there had been three cancellations, so there would certainly be room for de Souza and her *partner*. Broadstairs had smiled as graciously as was possible through tightly clenched teeth.

The dinner was due to start at seven, she told them, but guests would be seated for speeches shortly beforehand. At that moment, champagne was flowing in the Green Room. Why didn't they go right on in?

So now, here they were, in a stuffy oblong room packed with about thirty 'leading business thinkers'.

They looked even duller than the men in the portraits, Broadstairs thought.

So far, there was no sign of Yu. Broadstairs had heard of him. He knew Yu was considered by progressive types to be a necessary breath of fresh air in Chinese politics.

And Broadstairs couldn't help wishing Chen had come up with someone else. Not because he cared about the future of China. But because a man like Yu was bound to have well-trained bodyguards.

Still, he reflected, if all went to plan, one hundred bodyguards wouldn't be able to stop him.

Broadstairs's gaze slid to de Souza. She was collecting a glass of champagne from a waiter. She looked suitably stunning, he thought. Her scarlet silk dress clung to her curves.

Together, they had devised three methods for transferring the drug.

The first – and the most inventive – would depend on de Souza getting very close indeed to Mr Yu.

If that proved impossible, a perfume bottle in her ruby purse also contained a generous dose. Method B.

If the spray also failed, there was a final solution. It was inelegant, but more reliable.

According to a label stuck to the side, the self-injecting syringe contained insulin. Of course, it did no such thing. This was Method C.

Broadstairs stiffened. There was a commotion behind

him. The mayor gushed: 'Mr Yu, a very warm welcome to Government House!'

'He's here,' de Souza whispered suddenly in Broadstairs's ear.

'Yes, I can hear,' he hissed. 'Make sure he sees you!'

Broadstairs inched further along the line of portraits, and glanced back.

Yu Jichei was tall and broad. He had a round face and glossy black hair, neatly parted. Two men, even taller and broader, were right behind him. *Only two*, Broadstairs noted.

While Yu was smiling pleasantly, the bodyguards looked grim. They'd be looking grimmer still by the end of the evening, Broadstairs thought – when their boss was lying dead, and they had no idea what had happened!

His gaze twitched.

De Souza was on the move. She was crossing the room. Her scarlet heels clicked on the polished floorboards. Her bare back swayed.

Everyone watched her.

Everyone, Broadstairs noted. Including Yu.

Good, he thought. His honey-eyed trap was set.

25

For the past six minutes the tunnel had climbed steadily.

The roof had opened out, so they could walk upright. While the air smelt stale, it was breathable.

Gaia stumbled. She was at the back, and Sam's light was faint.

Andrew reached behind him. 'Hold on to me,' he said.

'If I do that, when I fall, I'll pull you over.'

'Oh, I don't think so,' Andrew said as boldly as possible, for Lydia's benefit.

Gaia took his hand. And instantly bumped into him.

'What's wrong?' Andrew called softly. He tried to see past Lydia to Will. 'Will, why have you stopped?'

'We're starting to head away from Government House,' Will said. And frowned.

They'd been heading right for it. But now the tunnel was curving to the north.

For a moment, no one spoke.

What if this isn't the tunnel? Gaia thought, and held her tongue.

'Maybe they hit a bit of really solid rock and they had to take a detour,' Lydia suggested.

'Yeah,' Will said. 'Maybe.'

He pressed on. After fifty more metres, though, the tunnel started to slope downward, instead of upward. The slope got steeper.

'This doesn't feel right,' Gaia whispered.

'But this *is* the tunnel,' Lydia said.

After another twenty paces, Will had to bend his neck. The roof was getting lower. And he could smell something. *Damp.*

He ran Sam's beam around the walls – and saw dark patches. The air got cooler. He had to hunch his shoulders to stop his head hitting rock.

Suddenly Will stopped.

Right in front of him was a puddle of black water. Ahead, there was *worse*.

'What?' Lydia whispered.

'Will?' Andrew called. 'What's wrong?'

'It's flooded,' Will said, his voice flat.

'How flooded?' Gaia asked.

Will squeezed up to the wall so Lydia and Andrew could see past him. Gaia rested her hands on Andrew's back and looked over his shoulder. Disappointment welled through her.

The floor descended into grimy water. Sam's beam showed the roof approaching the surface. From here, though, it was hard to tell if the tunnel became completely flooded.

'We'll have to wade,' Gaia said quietly.

'Until our heads hit the rock?' Andrew asked.

'It might not come to that,' Will said.

'Our only choices,' Lydia said, 'are to try, or to go back.'

Andrew swallowed. 'I know. We can't go back now.'

Will checked his watch. 6.40 p.m. Both Yu and Broadstairs had to be inside Government House by now. Time was running out. If it hadn't already. But they couldn't let Yu die.

Will stepped into the water – and his trainers disappeared. Cold lapped around his ankles.

As Gaia followed Andrew, she touched the wall. Her hand came away dripping. She wiped it on her jeans. It still felt clammy. She shivered.

Will moved as fast as he could. But the water quickly rose up to his knees. After three more steps, it was at his thighs.

Behind him, Lydia staggered. She reached for the wall to steady herself.

No one spoke.

Will waded on. As the water rose higher, the cold clutched his flesh. And still, the roof got lower.

Suddenly Andrew gasped hard.

'Andrew?' Will jerked Sam, catching Lydia full in the face with the beam. She flinched.

Then the torch hit Andrew.

The water was at his chest. He was blinking wildly, his heart racing. 'Did you feel it?' he demanded.

'Feel *what*?' Gaia said sharply.

'I felt something! It brushed my leg.' Andrew stared at the black water, and trembled.

'Did anyone else feel anything?' Will asked. He did his best to keep his voice steady.

'The worst it could be is frogs,' Lydia said quietly. 'Or maybe rats. Or eels.'

Eels. Gaia dug her nails into her palms. 'It's all right,' she said, more for her own benefit than anyone else's.

But Andrew's heart was pounding. Recently he'd read an article about moray eels. Scientists had only just discovered they had a second set of jaws, hidden inside their throat. When they caught prey, that second set shot out –

But moray eels lived on reefs. They were inside a tunnel. And Will was talking.

His voice was quiet.

'Will,' Andrew called, 'I can't hear you.'

No answer.

'*Will?*' Gaia said. 'What did you say?'

At last, Will turned. '*The water hits the roof,* I said.' And he shook his head. He'd got used to success. Now STORM was failing. First with de Bruyn. Then with Collins. *Now this.*

They had to be close, but their way was blocked. Frustration burned through his veins.

'It's *totally flooded*?' Andrew asked.

'*Yes,*' Will said. He turned to Lydia. 'Hold Sam for a minute.'

She took the robot. 'What are you doing?'

'I'm wearing the vest.'

Will took off his T-shirt and pulled the mouthpiece from its pocket.

'You're going to swim in on your own?' Gaia asked.

'Government House is that way,' Will said, pointing slightly to the left and up. 'If this is the right tunnel, it has to start climbing again soon. Maybe only a bit of it's flooded. I'll check it out.'

'But how will you see?' Lydia asked.

The answer was obvious, Will thought. 'I'll have to take Sam.'

'Right,' she whispered, as she realized what that meant. They'd be left in absolute blackness.

Will faced the water. Apprehension gripped his stomach. Swimming underwater in the ocean wasn't a problem. This tunnel was a totally different prospect. He had no idea what lay ahead – or what had hit Andrew's leg. Even the dungeons in Venice would have been better. But the clock was ticking. *Yu's life* was at stake.

Will took a breath. Air rushed into his lungs. The vest was working.

He wedged Sam into the pocket, his torch aiming out. And he dived.

In the murky water, it was difficult to see.

Will caught blurred glimpses of blackened sandstone. Debris on the floor. *Motion* – a tail.

An *eel*?

His breathing was loud, his muscles clenched. His pulse throbbed.

Will kicked harder, his eyes straining. He distracted himself by counting seconds. One minute and seven.

And eight.

And nine.

He was still swimming in a straight line . . . Or was he?

Sam's beam bounced off the wall. Will looked up. But was it really *up*? Or was his brain playing tricks. He saw rough rock. It could be the roof. Or the floor. Fear suddenly needled his spine. They should have turned back.

What was that?

Something had hit his knee. Will jerked it up. He took a deep breath. But his lungs wouldn't fill. *Oxygen*. He needed more oxygen!

Again, something touched his leg.

Hooks of fear snarled through his spine. He couldn't panic. He *would not* panic.

He tried to concentrate on what he could see. And made out coarse stone. Then something else. *Ripples.*

Ripples could mean only one thing!

Will reached down. Felt rock. He scrambled for a footing, and pulled Sam from his vest. The robot clamped in his fist, he *stood up*.

Water poured from his vest. He was almost upright, and the water wasn't even at his waist. The tunnel must have started to slope upwards without him realizing.

Will spat out the mouthpiece. Panting hard, he tried to hold Sam's beam steady.

And he saw a wooden door, studded with nails.

Then he noticed something else. The ground was *moving*.

The limousine turned a corner, and Mei glanced up from her smartphone.

'Mr Chen,' she said. 'Collins's death is confirmed. Heart failure.'

'The cause of the heart failure?'

'Unknown.'

'Ha!' Chen's eyes glinted. So far, Broadstairs had been as good as his word.

What would it be for the Dung Beetle, he wondered. Cardiac arrest or heart failure? Or the method of Death Number Three? Would Yu experience a great deal of pain? Chen hoped so.

'As he made me suffer,' he breathed to his viper. She was draped across the seat beside him, her golden muzzle glimmering.

Suddenly the car stopped. The driver's voice came through a speaker in Chen's armrest: 'Sir, we are here.'

Through the window, Chen saw a pavement, black railings, and trees.

Mei checked her phone. The GPS map showed Government House inside the gardens. 'Confirmed,' she said.

Chen rubbed his hands together. His skin crackled like paper.

'Go,' he ordered. 'And stay in close contact. I want to know *exactly* what takes place.'

Mei nodded. She picked up her handbag and got out.

Chen pressed the green button in his armrest. 'We stay here,' he barked.

'Yes, sir,' the driver replied.

A communications headset was on the seat beside Chen. He fitted it in place. And he waited.

After a few minutes, he heard: 'Mr Chen, I can see Government House. When I locate Broadstairs, I will check in.'

'Good,' Chen said, 'and remember: you must be clear. My future is at stake! There must be *no tricks* from Broadstairs.'

'Quite so, Mr Chen.'

26

They weren't eels.

They were *rats*.

Dozens of them.

In the light from Sam's torch, Will saw flashes of dirty teeth and tails. Wet brown bodies scurried over each other. Then he noticed something else: in between the rats, insects scuttled. Antennae waved. Cockroaches.

Rats and *cockroaches*.

Will owned a rat. In London and in Switzerland, he'd used cyborg cockroaches. *This* was different.

The air stank of decay and faeces. Disgust rose in his throat. And he jumped as a rat slithered past his leg.

Breathing through his mouth, Will trained the torch at the door. The planks looked solid. A round iron handle was attached with nails. It could easily be Victorian. And it *had* to lead into Government House, Will thought.

He swung Sam's beam to his watch. The swim had taken more than a minute and a half. Too long to make unaided, underground.

Will took a deep breath – and regretted it. The foul

air made him retch. He spat. 'Can you hear me?' he whispered.

'*Will!*' He heard the relief in Gaia's voice. 'Where are you?'

'I'm through. The tunnel does slope up after a bit. And I'm at the end.'

'What can you see?' Andrew asked.

'A wooden door.' There was no point telling them about the rats and the roaches. Not yet.

'Hold on, I've got a contact lens screen here,' Andrew said.

Will backed up a few steps. He held Sam's beam steady.

'Yes!' Lydia said. 'That has to be the way in.'

'But how are we going to get to you?' Andrew asked.

Will had been wondering the same thing. One idea had occurred to him.

He undid the first of the Velcro straps that held his vest in place. 'I'm going to send Sam back to you with the vest. You'll have to use it to come through one at a time.'

Silence.

And Will leaped sideways. He'd felt *feet* through his jeans. A rat was climbing up his leg. He jabbed Sam at the animal's head. Missed. It ran around his thigh, to his back.

'*Hello?*' Will hissed, as he activated Sam's sonar weapon. 'Did you hear me?'

'Yeah . . .' Lydia said.

On their side of the flood, the only light was from Andrew's contact lens screen. He couldn't see Lydia's face. But he could guess what she was thinking. She really didn't want to make the swim alone. But neither did she want to hang around any longer in stinking water, with unknown animal life for company.

'Will, roger,' Andrew said quietly.

And he frowned.

On the screen something had moved. Now he glimpsed a flash of an eye – and *teeth*.

DI Steve Portofino hoisted his gym bag to his shoulder.

It had been a long day. One arrest, two wild goose chases and three crank calls, followed by five kilometres on the treadmill and a game of touch rugby with some of the constables.

As he left the changing room, he glimpsed himself in the mirror. Saw receding black hair and a red face. But at least his stomach was tight. For forty-two, he decided, he wasn't doing too badly.

He headed outside, and in the direction of the Royal Hotel, where most of his colleagues hung out when they were off-duty. As he walked, he checked his messages. There were two.

The first told him the British kid responsible for his second crank call of the day had rung back and asked to talk to him. In the second, he heard:

'I just had the British kid again. He said to tell you:

Yu Jichei, Government House. Then he said: that's the third name.'

Portofino was surprised. Usually the kid cranks were satisfied with a single call. This one was unusually persistent.

He pushed through a swing door into the bar. It was packed. At last, he found a free stool beside a couple of the PCs from the rugby match, and he ordered a beer.

Yu Jichei. The name sounded vaguely familiar . . .

The TV on the wall was on. Portofino tried to tune into the news bulletin. A judge was being charged with perjury. Storms were lashing the Queensland coast. Employment reforms were being challenged by –

His spine snapped taut. A breaking-news ticker was scrolling along the bottom of the screen. It read: *Casino tycoon Ryan de Bruyn has died of a heart attack while giving a press conference in Sydney. More soon.*

Ryan de Bruyn. The British kid had talked about de Bruyn. What had he said? He was the *first name*, and he was going to be killed that evening.

Was the heart attack a coincidence?

There had been a second name. Portofino racked his memory. Christopher Collins, that was it.

Portofino dialled the duty constable. He asked whether there had been any reports that night involving Collins.

At last, she said: 'Sir, there was an ambulance report. Collins was taken to St Vincent's at 17.54. He was pronounced dead at the scene five minutes earlier. Heart failure.'

Portofino's pulse rocketed. The call had *sounded* like a hoax. The station got at least a dozen a week. Kids did it all the time. Only this time, both de Bruyn and Collins were *dead*.

'When did the kid last call?' he demanded.

'About fifteen minutes ago, sir.'

'This Yu Jichei. Check all the assignments for tonight. I want to know if there's any record of anything happening to this guy. Now!'

After a few moments, the constable came back on the line. 'Nothing, sir, but there is something in the system from the mayor's office. She'd requested a couple of uniforms for a dinner for Yu at Government House tonight.'

'And those uniforms?'

'We had to ask them to use their own security, sir. With the overtime used up and—'

Portofino stopped listening. He ended the call. Then he flicked through his notebook for the kid's mobile number. Dialled it. Heard:

'This is Will. Leave a message.'

'This is DI Steve Portofino. *Call me back!*'

Andrew crouched in the darkness.

Feet scurried, antennae brushed the walls – and his skin crawled.

It didn't help that his clothes were soaked. Water trickled down his body, feeling exactly like *roaches*.

Behind him, Gaia cried out. Then he heard a batting sound. She and Will were by the door. Lydia was still in the water.

She'd insisted on being the last to make the swim. Because of bravery – or bravado? Andrew wasn't sure. And wished he'd persuaded her to go before him.

It had been the most unpleasant experience of his life, he decided. He'd felt the rats before he'd seen them. The rock walls had seemed to close in around him. It had felt like a watery catacomb. Like an underground tomb.

Twice, he'd come close to panicking. He'd had to swallow the fear down. Now it boiled in his stomach.

'Ugh!' Gaia swiped at her neck. She stamped hard. Rats squeaked as they shot away.

Andrew used the light from his contact lens screen to check his watch.

One minute and thirty-five seconds. Gaia had done the swim in one minute and fifty-five.

It had taken him one minute and forty-four. Lydia was a girl. But there was a definite chance she was stronger than him.

'Shouldn't she be here by now?' Andrew whispered.

'How long's she been?' Will asked

'One minute and –' he paused, 'fifty-three.'

'She'll be here any second,' Will said. And tried to keep a check on his impatience. He was desperate to find out what was on the other side of that door.

Yu's life was on the line. They *had* to stop Broadstairs. He felt for the handle.

'What are you doing?' Gaia whispered.

'*Two minutes!*' Andrew called.

Will's fingers touched iron.

'Something's wrong,' Andrew said. He stood up.

Where was she? But he could only guess. The tooth-phones didn't work through water.

'She'll be all right,' Gaia said. 'She's just going slowly.'

'Not this slowly.' Andrew flinched as a rat ran across his soaking trainer. 'Why would she? She'd want to get to us.' His watch showed 6.46. 'Two minutes twenty-three. Something's definitely wrong.'

Will let go of the handle. Two minutes twenty-three *was* slow. In the darkness, he could just see Andrew's outline. He was crouching right at the edge of the water. He took a step forward.

'*I* almost panicked . . .' Andrew whispered, half to himself.

He adjusted his glasses and blinked. He still couldn't see anything. But if she didn't appear in the next five seconds, he'd have to swim back as far as he could to look for her. He stepped into the water.

Will heard the sloshing sound. 'Andrew?' Will's eyes strained.

Then Andrew exclaimed: '*Lydia!*'

Lydia spat out the mouthpiece. She gasped three deep breaths.

Andrew grabbed her arm. 'Are you all right?' He took Sam from her hand and aimed the beam at her face. It was pink. Her eyes were squeezed shut. 'Lydia – *are you all right*?'

At last, she nodded. She swiped water from her eyes. And she stared. 'What is *that*?' She grimaced. '*Rats*.'

'And cockroaches, I'm afraid,' Andrew said quietly. He turned, and hit Will with Sam's beam.

'Pass Sam to me,' Will said. 'Lydia, if you're all right, we have to get going.'

'I'm all right,' she said.

Andrew gave the robot to Gaia, who handed it to Will.

Lydia coughed. She looked at Andrew. He was watching her. He looked concerned. 'That wasn't much fun,' she whispered.

Andrew shook his head. 'I was worried –' he started. 'I thought you might have got into trouble.'

'Only a bit,' she said.

'Only a *bit*?'

Lydia swallowed. 'I couldn't get enough air. But I was breathing too fast. And I thought of Collins –' She stopped.

'You were worried you'd *die*?'

'No, I mean, I thought of Collins, and I didn't want to die, so I told myself to get a grip.'

Andrew smiled slightly. 'I have to tell myself that a lot.'

In the darkness, Lydia smiled back. And suddenly squinted.

Faint light was drifting down from the end of the tunnel. Will had opened the door. He was peering through the crack.

'What can you see?' Gaia whispered.

'Boxes,' he replied.

Cardboard boxes were stacked against the door, four high. Will knelt and pushed. The tower wobbled, but it didn't collapse. He inched it away, to make a gap big enough to slip through.

And he found himself in a small room. There was a door in the opposite wall. The others were lined with shelves piled with cans of food. 'It's a store,' he whispered. 'Come on.'

Gaia crept out next, then Andrew and Lydia. They pushed the boxes back into place. But the floor was covered in water. If anyone came in, perhaps they'd think it was a leak, Andrew thought hopefully.

'Will,' he whispered, 'what exactly is our plan?'

'First, we try to get to Yu or his bodyguards,' Will said quietly. 'Lydia, do you know where the dining room is?'

She shook her head and shivered. 'I've never been in here.'

'Then we need to split up, and spread out. Keep your toothphones on the open channel, and use the contact lens displays. And remember, Broadstairs could be here, or he might have sent someone else.'

Will opened the second door. He saw a wood-panelled passage. Ahead was a steep flight of wooden stairs. 'Lydia, there are stairs going up,' he whispered. 'You take them. Andrew, you head left. Gaia, you go right.'

'What are you going to do?' Gaia asked.

'I'll start out with you,' Will said to her. He checked the time. 'It's *ten to seven*. Our priority is to locate Yu. *If* he's still alive, he won't be for long.'

Portofino jumped down from his stool.

Impatient, he'd just re-tried the kid's number – and got voicemail.

If de Bruyn and Collins had died natural deaths, they were the two biggest coincidences of his career, he thought. The constable had told him Yu was attending the mayor's dinner. The least he could do was pay a visit.

He *could* go alone, but it was always better to have back-up. There was, however, the small matter of over-time.

'Taylor,' he said.

The fresh-faced PC beside him turned.

'How much have you had to drink?'

'This is my first schooner, sir.'

It was still half full. Portofino scoured the young man's face. He looked sober enough.

Portofino knew Taylor wanted to become a detective. And Taylor knew that he knew the station's short-list for selection would be drawn up that week.

'I know there's no more overtime,' Portofino said. 'But

I need some back-up. You support me, I'll support you.'
He winked.

Taylor's eyes lit up. He put his glass on the bar. 'You're on, sir.'

Andrew's wicking trousers were almost dry. Which was more than he could say for Lydia's jacket. It was dripping on the wooden floorboards, leaving a trail.

He couldn't help wishing Lydia was with him. Of course, Will was right: the fastest way to locate Yu was to split up. But then Will had gone with Gaia. Andrew sighed. And paused.

He'd reached a corner. Ahead was a door. The passage continued to the right, but it was narrower. It looked like a dead end. He was about to try the door when he heard a woman's voice. It seemed to be coming from along the passage.

Surprised, Andrew took another look. And he noticed something. About halfway along, just above the skirting board, was a brass grate. Light drifting through it speckled the floorboards. It was a ventilation panel. His own house had them.

Could the voice be coming from the same place as the light?

Andrew crept around the corner and on, as quickly as he dared. Then he dropped to his stomach and pressed his right eye to the grate.

His heart jumped.

He was peering into the dining room, no doubt about it!

It was lavishly decorated. Beneath a grand ceiling rose and a glittering chandelier were two oblong tables set with white cloths and crystal.

The diners sipped at their wine. They were watching a woman on a platform at the far side of the room, who was gesticulating wildly as she talked.

'Cross-cultural dialogues are just so important to us *all.*'

The mayor. Andrew recognized her from the photograph in *Sydney Sauce*.

To her left was a series of French doors hung with plum damask curtains, tied back. Andrew could see only reflections in the glass, but they had to lead outside, he thought.

But Yu. Where was *Yu*?

Andrew's eyes skidded over a large woman in green silk and pearls, a man with glasses and grey hair, another man with glasses and grey hair, yet *another* man, ditto – and stuck.

He was looking at a stunning, dusky-skinned woman in a scarlet dress. The man beside her had slick black hair and gunmetal eyes.

De Souza *and* Broadstairs. Andrew swallowed. They were both here. Could that mean they were planning on giving Yu the new drug?

His gaze raced over the other guests. At last, he spotted a broad-shouldered Chinese man. Two goons in black stood behind him. *Yu!* He was alive. They weren't too late!

'Will, Gaia, Lydia, I have located the dining room! I have visual contact with Yu, Broadstairs *and* de Souza. Yu is alive and well! Over.'

At once, he heard Will's voice: 'Andrew, where are you? What *exactly* can you see?'

Andrew told him. And Will and Gaia exchanged glances.

They were in a corridor, hiding behind a glass-fronted bookcase. Across to their left was a pair of wooden doors. A few moments ago, two waitresses carrying empty wine bottles had slipped out through them. They'd guessed the women had been leaving the dining room. Now they were sure.

And Yu was inside. He was *alive*. This time, Broadstairs would not win.

'Andrew, we're close to the entrance,' Will breathed. 'Lydia, where are you?'

'I must be right above the dining room,' she whispered.

Two minutes earlier, Lydia had tried a handle and found herself in a dark office. She'd crossed to the window, to try to get her bearings.

Directly below her was the stone roof of a verandah. It ran almost the entire length of the house. Beyond were lawns and rose bushes, and two security guards in black uniforms. Then railings, a pathway through the Botanic Gardens, and the harbour.

She explained what she could see. 'Andrew, your French doors must open on to the verandah.'

'Right,' Will whispered. 'Andrew, scan the room slowly. I'll check your contact lens feed. I want to know exactly where Yu and de Souza and Broadstairs are sitting.'

Will held the screen close to his chest. And he made out grainy images of two tables. A woman with dark spiky hair was standing in a corner behind them. The mayor. Still speaking.

Broadstairs and de Souza were on the right-hand table, at the far side, close to the French doors. Yu was at the head of the other table. To get to him or his men, they'd have to make it past at least eight people.

'Andrew, I can't see any security, apart from Yu's bodyguards,' Will whispered. 'Can you?'

'No. Perhaps now everyone's sitting down ready for dinner, they're all outside?'

'I saw one guy up here,' Lydia whispered. 'I hid. He didn't see me.'

And Will frowned, thinking. 'All I can think of is to try to get Sam in and hit a bodyguard with the sonar. If he felt dizzy, he might come out, and I could talk to him.'

'You think he'd leave his boss?' Lydia asked.

'The other guard would still be there,' Gaia said. 'He *might.*'

It wasn't a brilliant plan, Will thought. For a start, they'd have to wait for someone to go in or out, and then try to slip Sam through. There was a good chance the robot would be spotted.

Alternatively, he could run in, get grabbed by Yu's men, and try to talk to them. That was even less promising.

'I'm going to wait for a chance to send in Sam,' Will said. 'But Andrew, keep your eyes on Yu. If Broadstairs or de Souza go anywhere near him, I want to know.'

'Roger,' Andrew said.

'Lydia, if you think you're safe, stay where you are. If Gaia and I get caught, it'll be up to you two to save Yu and get Broadstairs and de Souza arrested. OK?'

'Roger,' Lydia said.

Roger. Andrew smiled.

Andrew did his best to keep Yu in his sights. But it wasn't easy.

The mayor had just sat down. In the corner now was a smartly dressed man. He was giving a speech about China's economic future. Yu was watching him closely and nodding, apparently in agreement.

Broadstairs –

Andrew couldn't stop himself. He snatched a glance at Broadstairs, whose face was blank. In other circumstances, Andrew would have assumed he was bored. But he could hardly be that!

Then he remembered the psychiatrist's report on Parramore. For him, murder was non-emotive. Was there a chance Broadstairs and Parramore were the same man? Now really wasn't the time for speculation, Andrew told himself. He was meant to be focusing on Yu.

But he noticed something moving. De Souza's fingers. They were fiddling with a red purse. She wouldn't leave it alone.

She was a psychologist, and yet she seemed oblivious to her body language, he thought. To anyone who could read it, it was obvious she was nervous. She kept picking up the purse, adjusting its position.

This wasn't *abstract* nervous behaviour, Andrew realized.

It was focused on that purse.

Why? Was the ageing drug inside?

'Will,' Andrew whispered. 'I am keeping an eye on Yu, but de Souza is playing with her purse. I think the drug might be inside.'

Gaia was half-watching the screen while Will kept an eye on the corridor. She squinted at the image. 'If it is, how might they be planning on getting it into Yu?' she whispered.

'They got something nasty into Collins's food,' Lydia said.

'But the waiter must have been an accomplice,' Gaia said. 'And with the two bodyguards in there, and a room full of people –'

She stopped. The guests had begun to clap. Applause drifted through the wooden doors. The speech must have finished. Perhaps now the entrées would be delivered, she thought, and they'd be able to send Sam in.

But suddenly Andrew's voice burst through their toothphones: '*De Souza's on the move!*'

She had just got up! Now she was walking towards the end of her table. To the exit? To the toilets? Adrenalin made Andrew's blood rush. And he noticed two things:

The ruby purse was still on the table.

Broadstairs was taking a sip of his drink – but his gunmetal eyes were glued to her.

De Souza was about to do something! But *what?*

She rounded her table, her back swaying, and continued on, towards Yu's.

'She's heading for Yu!' Andrew hissed. 'Repeat: *de Souza is heading for Yu!*'

Now they had no choice, Will thought. He had to burst in!

But who should he go for – Yu? Or de Souza? Which could be extremely risky if she was carrying a deadly drug.

'Andrew, talk to me,' he hissed. 'Where's the drug?'

Andrew was wondering the same thing. He scoured de Souza. Her dress looked moulded to her body. Her arms were by her sides, her hands open. Her hair was loose.

Around her, the guests were chatting. One or two looked up, watching her.

'I can't see *anything*,' Andrew whispered back

But she *had* to have the drug! Where was it?

Andrew's gaze shot to Yu. De Souza was no more than *six strides* away. And Andrew saw Yu's brown eyes widen with pleasure. The beautiful Brazilian was heading right for him.

Four strides.

'Will! Gaia! You have to get in there!'

But *what was de Souza going to do*?

Then Andrew noticed something. Or rather, something he'd noticed earlier but dismissed as irrelevant suddenly exploded through his brain.

Was it *possible*?

Why not?

DI Steve Portofino hit the brakes.

Three security guards were hanging around the gate. One sauntered over. Portofino wound down his window and flashed his badge.

The man stiffened. 'Any trouble I should know about?'

'Nothing like that,' Portofino said. 'We just finished our shift and thought we'd drop in and show our faces. The mayor's on our back for not sending any uniforms.'

The guard relaxed. He hit a button on a remote in his pocket and the gate swung open.

Portofino sent the car screeching to the portico.

'What now, sir?' Taylor asked, as they got out. So far, Portofino had said only that there might be a threat to the life of a Chinese guest.

'We both go in,' Portofino said. 'You stay in the background. I'll send in a waiter to get Mr Yu out to talk to me. I'll have a quick chat with him, and we'll see if he feels like leaving early. That's all there'll be to it.'

Taylor nodded. 'Too easy,' he said.

28

In her office at Phoenix House, Andrew hadn't exactly scrutinized de Souza's face. But he had noticed her mouth, only because it was slightly out of proportion. She had a long nose, doe-like eyes, a broad forehead and a perfectly attractive but *normal-sized* mouth.

But here, in the dining hall of Government House, her lips looked very full. Of course, she might have injected them with collagen, Andrew thought. But it was possible there was another explanation.

Because he'd remembered something else: the nicotine patches and the translucent rubbery substance he'd found in her desk.

Patches were usually designed to release a drug slowly and steadily. But surely it didn't have to be that way, he thought.

'Her *mouth*,' he said now.

'What about her mouth?' Gaia asked.

'I think she's wearing a lip prosthetic coated or infused with the drug!'

'A *lip prosthetic*?' Lydia sounded incredulous. 'She's planning on *kissing* him? That's insane.'

'Andrew, are you sure?' Gaia asked. And, as she and Will watched the image on the screen, her eyes widened.

De Souza was advancing rapidly on Yu. She was smiling, and extending her hand. But she *was* South American, Gaia thought. If she also kissed someone's cheek on meeting, would anyone think it strange?

'I think she's going to do it!' Will said.

He jumped up, Sam in his hand. Gaia behind him, he ran for the doors and shoved them open.

In the split second it had taken for them to run in, Yu had risen to greet de Souza. She was taking his hand. She was leaning in.

'*Stop!*' Will shouted.

The reaction was instant.

All eyes swivelled to him. Including de Souza's.

Will didn't waste any more time. He focused on Yu. 'Yu Jichei, you have to get away from that woman. She's trying to kill you.'

There was a stunned silence.

De Souza broke it. She spluttered: '*What?*'

A woman called out: 'Who are *you*?'

Will didn't answer. He was watching Yu's body-guards. One was taking his boss's arm. The other was already on the move. He was heading towards them. Yu looked astonished.

'*Broadstairs,*' Gaia whispered.

Will turned, and saw an empty seat.

Broadstairs – and the ruby purse – were *gone*. One

of the French doors was ajar. Frustration surged through him. Broadstairs couldn't escape!

He spun round. Yu was in the corner. *Safe.* The bodyguard was striding faster now. A few of the guests had risen. The others were rooted to their chairs, staring. And Will noticed the mayor, talking into a radio. Summoning security, he guessed.

He hissed into his toothphone: 'Andrew, Broadstairs has run. We're going after him. Come in here and explain!'

Then he felt Gaia's hand, tugging at his arm.

Will followed her. They skidded around Broadstairs's table. The open window was right in front of them –

And a man with a thick accent called: 'You! Stand still!'

Will glanced back.

Yu's bodyguard. In his right hand, he held a black object. It sparked. A Taser.

'*Will!*' Gaia said.

'Go,' he hissed. 'I'm right behind you!'

The man raised the Taser.

Will reached into his pocket. He *had* to get Broadstairs. He touched a Spy Seed. Pulled it out. Aimed. *Fired.*

The tiny robot pierced the air. It struck the bodyguard in the cheek. Blood spurted from the wound. He clamped a hand to his face. A woman screamed.

And Will spun. Gaia was already outside. He sprinted after her.

'Will!'

She'd darted down behind a rose bush. Across the lawn, five security guards were jogging towards the house, hands at their holsters. His heart thumping, Will joined her. He scanned the gardens.

Where was Broadstairs?

And he glanced back. There was no sign of Yu's bodyguard.

'Lydia,' Gaia hissed, 'can you see Broadstairs?'

'I had him!' she whispered. 'Hold on – yeah! He's past the big fountain. It's just down from you. There are railings. He's climbing over them. *Go!*'

*Who was the boy? What did he know? How did he know **anything**?*

Broadstairs's brain burned as he ran.

The boy had burst into the dining room with the girl. And he hadn't hesitated. He'd accused de Souza of trying to kill Yu. They were the *facts*.

In twenty-five years of business, nothing like that had happened to Broadstairs before. He'd had major – and hugely expensive – setbacks. Anyone who took the risks he did had to expect them. And anyone who'd experienced his level of success understood something else: when the cards turn against you, *quit*.

Whatever the boy knew exactly, and however he knew it, were, at that very moment, irrelevant.

So too was the $100 million.

Broadstairs's decision had ultimately been simple: stay in Government House to watch de Souza crumble, and risk being exposed, and even arrested. Or run.

He'd made the only choice possible.

But that didn't mean he liked it.

He'd phone Tench. He'd give him the over-ride code for the safe. He'd order him and Hutt to take the brief-case and the kernels to a safe location, and he'd meet them there. Then he'd kill them.

When he was out of all this – when he'd got the three techniques back together, when he'd spoken to Chen, when he had his hands on that money – he'd find out who that boy was, and he'd kill him too. That was another *fact*.

'Detective Inspector Portofino!'

Portofino burst into the dining room, Taylor behind him.

They'd been striding along the corridor – and they'd heard a woman scream.

Now, Portofino scanned the scene. Two chairs were toppled. Guests were standing in huddles, talking loudly. A large Chinese man was pressing a napkin to a bleeding cheek.

'*Yu?*' Portofino called.

The man looked round – and Portofino spotted another, smaller, Chinese man behind him. 'Yu?' he said again. '*Yu Jichei?*'

The smaller man nodded.

Portofino exhaled hard. The third name was still alive.

But what was going on here?

He saw the mayor, who was trying to weave her way towards him. And a security guard. He was talking to Taylor.

'Guv!' Taylor waved him over. He repeated what the guard had told him.

Portofino's gaze shot to a beautiful woman in a scarlet dress. Another Chinese man – a second bodyguard, Portofino guessed – was holding her arm. She was trying to peel his fingers from her. Her golden eyes were shining.

'The boy said *she* was trying to kill Yu?' Portofino said.

The security guard nodded.

And the woman looked round. She fixed her eyes on him.

'You are police?' she cried. 'Then tell him to let me go! Why would I want to hurt Mr Yu? I am a businesswoman. Look at me. Do I look like a killer?'

Portofino frowned.

The woman's eyes shot down to her shimmering dress and her ruby shoes.

Suddenly no one was talking.

Then, from behind Portofino, someone coughed.

'The most dangerous animals are often the most brightly coloured. At least, that's, um, what I've read.'

Portofino spun.

And de Souza felt sick.

There in the room was a skinny boy in wet clothes. He raised a hand to adjust his glasses.

Jason Argo.

A whirlpool was sucking de Souza's brain inside out. It was difficult enough to comprehend that the first boy had somehow known she'd been planning to kill Yu. Then she'd seen Broadstairs flee. But he'd taken the purse – and, with it, the only obvious evidence. She'd be all right, she told herself. She'd get out of this.

Now what was going on?

But before she or Portofino could say anything, another two security guards entered the room. They were dragging a sturdy olive-skinned girl, who kicked at their legs.

Again, Portofino raised his badge. He jabbed a finger at the man holding de Souza. 'Let go of her,' he ordered. Then he turned to the guards. 'Explain.'

'We found her upstairs,' one said, and winced as Lydia bit his arm. He shook her. 'Listen here, a little more respect wouldn't go astray. I'm a security officer for the mayor –'

'Oh, get over yourself!' Lydia cried.

Portofino's expression had been getting darker by the second. Now the thunderstorm broke. *'Enough!* Can somebody tell me what is going on here?'

'I think I can.'

The boy. Portofino ran a hand through his hair. 'Are you Will Knight?'

Andrew looked surprised. 'Are you DI Portofino?'

'*Yes!* Now are you –'

So the police had listened! 'Will and I work together,' Andrew said quickly. 'My name's Andrew Minkel.'

Across the room, de Souza's blood chilled. This boy had been inside Phoenix House. A boy who had given a false name. Who'd been left alone in her office.

'Can you ask those men to let go of Lydia?' Andrew went on. 'She works with us too.'

Portofino waved a hand at the two security guards. They obeyed.

'Now,' Portofino said to Andrew, 'for the last time – what is going on here – Yu was the third target Will Knight talked about?'

The third target. De Souza could only stare helplessly. How much did these kids know?

Andrew turned to her

Stand your ground, she told herself. *No matter what they think they know, stand your ground.*

And Andrew took a deep breath. He hadn't expected to share their knowledge with a room full of people. But Portofino had asked him.

'A man called Frederick Broadstairs is behind it all,' Andrew said. 'But this woman was going to kill Mr Yu for him. Her name's Evangeline de Souza.'

The room fell so quiet, Andrew's head seemed to echo.

De Souza whispered: 'Me? But *why* would *I* want to kill Mr Yu?'

Andrew sought out Yu. He spotted him, still in the corner.

'Mr Yu, does the name Chen Jianguo mean anything to you? He belongs to something called the Viper Club – as does Frederick Broadstairs.'

'Go on,' Portofino said.

Andrew explained about the prize, and the three targets. 'The first two are already dead,' he said to Yu. 'You were meant to be the third.'

'A *prize*?' Portofino said. 'Why would someone come up with a prize like that?'

'You'd have to ask Chen,' Lydia said. 'But why would we make it up?' And she looked at de Souza, who'd stumbled backwards.

De Souza pressed her back hard against the wall. Somehow these children knew *everything*. And the only other two people who knew as much were her and Broadstairs. *Broadstairs* must have betrayed her. But *why*? She swallowed. She could think about that later. Right now, her only hope was to bluff.

'But how,' she said as wearily as she could manage, 'was I going to kill Mr Yu? Look at me. Where am I concealing my dangerous weapon?'

Portofino turned to Andrew.

'On her lips,' he said. 'I think.'

'Her *lips*?'

'Tell her to kiss her arm, or something,' Lydia called. 'See what she says.'

'Good idea,' Andrew whispered.

But, he decided, there was no need.

He was watching de Souza closely. And she'd started to tremble. Suddenly her skin looked bleached, her face hollow. This particular body language was a clear confession, he thought. And he couldn't help feeling relieved that he'd been right.

Very slowly now, de Souza raised a shaking hand to her mouth. She pulled a thin film from her lower lip. Then another, from the upper lip.

She dropped the prosthetics on the table beside her.

Her stricken eyes rested on Andrew. In a hoarse whisper, she said: 'How did you know?'

Portofino jabbed a finger at Taylor. The constable crossed to de Souza. He started to talk quietly. Reading her her rights, Andrew guessed. And he noticed the mayor had gone to the table. 'Be careful!' he called.

She looked up. Her blue eyes were wide. 'What is it? What's on the film?'

'An experimental drug. I –' Andrew glanced at Lydia – '*we* think it affects telomeres, the caps of chromosomes. During cell replication, they get shorter, you see, and –'

Lydia touched Andrew's arm. The mayor was looking bemused. 'It's a chemical that kills all the cells in your body.'

'I see.' The mayor clasped her hands behind her back.

Portofino faced Andrew. 'You said a man called Broadstairs was behind this. Where is he?'

Andrew pointed to the open French door. 'He went out that way.'

'How long ago?'

Andrew checked his watch. 'Maybe seven minutes.'

'He could be anywhere!' Portofino reached for his phone.

'Wait. Will has gone after him – and Gaia, our friend. I can ask them where he is.'

Portofino watched as Andrew grabbed a key fob from his pocket and hit a black button.

His eyes widened as Andrew spoke into thin air: 'Will, Gaia, DI Portofino's here, and de Souza's in custody. Where are you? Do you have Broadstairs? Are you all right?'

Will didn't answer.

He was finding it hard enough to breathe, never mind speak.

After leaping over the railings, Broadstairs had sprinted down a path towards Circular Quay and scaled a gate. Will and Gaia had raced after him.

At the quay, they'd seen him make straight for the wooden jetties – and steal a water taxi. The driver had been chatting to a girl at one of the ticket kiosks.

Will and Gaia hadn't missed a beat. They'd kept on running, heading back past the ferry terminals, weaving through the crowd, to the MCA. The microlight was safely tied up. It bobbed in the water.

As Will jumped down into the front seat, he noticed a piece of paper stuck to the windscreen. He snatched it up.

Under a blue-and-white logo were the words:

Sydney Harbour Authority:
Mooring Violation Code 113A
Fine: $1100

Then details of how to pay.

'What's that?' Gaia gasped as she climbed in. Her lungs felt like wool. She couldn't get enough air. Her heart was pounding so hard she could feel it in her back.

Will only shook his head. He screwed up the fine and dropped it at his feet. Then he started up the engine and flicked on the avionics.

Behind him, Gaia searched for the taxi. At last, she spotted it. Broadstairs was passing the Opera House. Then he disappeared into darkness.

And they heard:

'Will, Gaia, DI Portofino's here and de Souza's in custody. Where are you? Do you have Broadstairs? Are you all right?'

Will tried to catch his breath. Failed. He yanked the mooring rope free and hit the accelerator. At once, the microlight skated away from the wall.

'We're OK,' Gaia managed. 'We're in the microlight. Broadstairs has stolen a water taxi. We're going after him.'

'Going after him *where?*'

'I don't know!' Gaia took a deep breath and felt sick. She'd never run that fast before. 'East from Circular Quay. Use my contact lens.'

'I am,' Andrew said. 'But I can only see black. It's too dark. You'll have to update me over the toothphone.'

Will revved the engine, and Gaia gripped her seat. The floats seared across the water.

He kept his eyes on their speed. Twenty-five knots. They veered around a ferry. Red and green boating lights blinked all around them. Will straightened their course. Pressed his foot on the accelerator. *Thirty. Thirty-three.*

Just a little more speed . . .

He nudged the nose up, and they took off.

Wind blasted Gaia's face. She saw black sky, and a pale moon. Then the microlight banked, and she made out Fort Denison. *Where was he?* Her gaze skidded over two kayaks and a tourist cruiser strung with white fairy lights – to a small, yellow boat.

The wake reflected the moonlight. It left a glittering trail that led right to Broadstairs.

If he maintained that course, eventually he'd reach North and South Head – and the Pacific Ocean. They couldn't let that happen.

The microlight was much faster than the taxi, so they'd catch him easily. But they were up in the air. Intercepting him could be difficult.

'Will, how exactly are we going to stop him?' she said, and she shivered. Her clothes were still damp. She was starting to cool down rapidly.

'We've got Sam,' Will replied.

But a sonar strike would stop Broadstairs for only a few minutes, Gaia thought. Would that be long enough for them to land the microlight and taxi to the boat? And then what? They'd have to restrain him. Or keep hitting him with the sonar until the police arrived.

Suddenly Broadstairs was behind them. Will pulled back with his right arm, to bring them around.

'I've got another idea,' she said. 'Those taxis have got inflatable sides. If we can get close, I could drop my last two bags of nanotubes and we could use Sam's torch to ignite them.'

There was a pause. 'Use the microlight as a bomber, you mean?'

She heard the excitement in his voice.

Andrew exclaimed through the toothphone: 'Gaia, that's genius!'

'Broadstairs shouldn't have a gun,' she went on. 'There'd have been no reason to try to take one into Government House. If we can get low enough to blast a decent hole, the sides will collapse. He'll have to hold on to the centreboard, or swim. That should give the police time to get here.'

'Portofino is already on his way,' Andrew said. 'Apparently there's a police launch down at Circular Quay.'

Gaia peered over the side of the cockpit, craning her neck.

There was Broadstairs. Near the Botanic Gardens.

'Gaia, get the bags ready,' Will called. 'I'll bank down on three. One. Two –'

'Mr Chen.'

Mei's voice was urgent.

'Report,' Chen barked.

'Something has gone wrong. Target three is still alive. Broadstairs has fled the scene. He is on the harbour, heading east. I am in pursuit.'

Chen stiffened. He could hardly believe what he was hearing.

Still alive?

Sudden anger seized his heart.

Broadstairs had *failed*?

How?

He clenched his frail fists. 'In pursuit how?'

With the help of her ceramic gun, Mei had just liberated a black powerboat from two British tourists. Now she was searing across the water. 'I have a boat, Mr Chen.' And her eyes shot up to the microlight. Coincidence? Or was it also trailing Broadstairs?

'The police are there?'

'Not yet,' Mei said. 'But I think I have company. Aerial. Unidentified.'

Chen coughed. Broadstairs, he thought, you fool!

How long before the police or Mei's *unidentified company* caught up with him?

Would Broadstairs spill his secrets?

There was a chance.

'I will follow your signal, and stay as close to the water as possible,' Chen said. 'I want those methods! But if necessary, you must eliminate Broadstairs. He cannot talk to the police!'

'Understood.'

Chen flopped back against the seat.

He wanted nothing more than to get his hands on the techniques. But Broadstairs could not be allowed an opportunity to betray him. If that became likely, Broadstairs would have to be killed!

Beside him, his viper raised her yellow head. Chen met his snake's cold eyes.

'Perhaps you would have the honour, my beauty,' he said.

'*Three!*'

The microlight dipped, and Gaia was thrown forward. Wind buffeted her face. This wasn't going to be easy.

'I'm going to come around at him from the south,' Will said. 'When I'm as low and as slow as I can get, I'll tell you. But I can't go too slow or we risk stalling. You'll have to judge when to drop. I'll have Sam ready.'

'Thirty knots,' Gaia called. 'Don't go below thirty knots!'

'I know!'

They were descending fast. Suddenly they were below the level of the skyscrapers.

The wind blew stronger, and the microlight rocked. With one hand, Gaia held the bags against her stomach. With the other, she clutched the side of the cockpit. They veered hard to the left. Will traced a half-circle through the night.

Gaia held her breath and scanned the water.

Where was he?

There! To the south-east. Approaching a finger-shaped wharf. Restaurant tables spilled out on to the pavement.

Now they were only about ten metres above the water.

One hand on the accelerator, Will watched their speed. And he lifted their nose. 'Thirty-four knots,' he called. 'Thirty-two.'

They still seemed to be flying fast, Gaia thought. And to hit Broadstairs, she'd have to take into account their speed, and the boat's, and the wind's.

'Gaia? Are you ready?'

She took a deep breath. 'Yeah.'

She stuck her head into the wind. It made her eyes sting. She was freezing cold, but her hands were sweaty. She *had* to get the bags over the boat.

Every split second, the yellow taxi came closer.

Gaia made out Broadstairs's head. It was shiny black in the moonlight.

'*Thirty-one knots,*' Will called. 'I can't go any slower!'

Then she saw Broadstairs glance up. She even saw the whites of his eyes. '*Now!*'

The first bag plummeted.

A six-watt beam pierced the darkness.

They flew right past, and Gaia's head shot round.

She saw a flash – and then nothing. Black water.

Will glanced over his shoulder. 'You missed.'

Gaia exhaled hard. They were flying fast. Broadstairs was a tiny moving target. 'Maybe it's not possible –' she started.

'*No*. You just have to focus. It's like hitting a cricket ball. You can't *think* about it.'

'I've never hit a cricket ball in my life.'

'Well, I have.'

'Then maybe you should drop the bag.'

'I've got Sam. You can do it, Gaia! Trust me.'

Trust me. She took a deep breath.

'You've got another bag, haven't you? I'll bring us back around.'

The microlight suddenly sloped to the left. Gaia felt her stomach drag behind – and catch up. They were curling back hard. The cockpit was juddering.

Will's shoulders ached as he struggled to keep the control bar steady. Then he brought them out of their loop and he fixed his eyes on the taxi.

'Remember – don't *think*,' he called. He checked their speed. 'Thirty-four knots. Thirty-two . . .'

Gaia's pulse throbbed. This was their last chance. They *had* to hit him.

Again, she made out Broadstairs's black head.

And she swallowed hard. She played hockey and netball at school. She wasn't bad. But she wasn't exactly good.

Now they were closing in fast.

Gaia held her breath. She glued her eyes to Broadstairs, and she told herself: *Relax. Relax . . .*

Then she felt her arm twitch.

'Now!'

She released the bag.

At the same instant, Sam's beam shot out.

And flames burst out below them. Smoke billowed up into the air.

Gaia twisted in her seat. She couldn't see the taxi. *Had they hit it?*

Will swung his weight to the left, to bring the microlight around.

At last, the boat emerged from the smoke. Its left side was in tatters. Burning yellow streamers hissed as they hit the water.

'*Yes!*' Andrew called through the toothphone.

'You did it,' Will said. He looked round, and grinned.

And Gaia breathed. The taxi was keeling badly. Already it was starting to fill.

But it was limping on.

Suddenly it swerved to the right – towards the shore. Gaia tensed. She followed its trajectory. And she saw another wharf, with two shadowy frigates, painted combat grey. A crane rose above them, stark against the night.

'Will, he's heading for the dockyard.'

But beyond the dock, he saw trees and narrow streets. If Broadstairs made it that far, it would be impossible to track from the air.

'We'll have to land to follow him,' he called.

'Yeah,' Gaia said. Her triumph began to evaporate.

But she'd hit him, she told herself. Surely it would be easier for the police to catch him on foot.

She glanced back in the direction of Circular Quay. She saw only a ferry, the tourist cruiser and a black powerboat, close to the shore. 'Andrew, where's Portofino?'

A pause. It seemed to last forever.

'Gaia, I just talked to his colleague, PC Taylor. Apparently he's at his boat. He's on his way. And he's called for a helicopter. So don't take any risks.'

'What – us?' Will said.

'I mean it, Will!'

Will fixed his gaze on the black water ahead.

To their right, Broadstairs was closing in on the dock.

He gripped the accelerator lever. 'Gaia, hold on,' he called. 'We're going down!'

Mei eased up on the throttle of her powerboat.

The intentions of the microlight were no longer in any doubt. It had just tried to bomb Broadstairs from the water! But her target had survived. He was still in her sights.

'Mr Chen,' she said, 'Broadstairs is approaching a wharf. It looks like a naval dockyard.'

'I will meet you,' he barked. 'Remember, *I* want to deal with Broadstairs.'

'Understood.'

Mei looked up.

The microlight was slowing. Was it preparing to land? And who was on board? Clearly not the police. Surely not the two kids she'd spotted running after Broadstairs as he'd fled Government House . . .

Whoever it was, they seemed determined to stop Broadstairs. Which meant they might get in the way. She could either run that risk. Or she could get rid of them.

Right now.

30

Forty knots.

Will kept one eye on their speed and the other on Broadstairs. The taxi was smoking as it crawled towards the dock

Then his head turned. What *was* that?

He'd noticed the powerboat in the background as they'd zeroed in on Broadstairs. Now it was heading away from the shore, towards them. A dark-haired woman was standing with one hand on the wheel. She was raising the other –

'Gaia, *get down*!'

Will swung his body hard to the left.

Too late.

At the last moment, he'd seen the white gun.

Now he heard a sharp ripping sound. And another. The control bar juddered.

'*Will!*'

Gaia stared up at the right wing. Two bullets had just torn through it. It was flapping violently.

The microlight lurched.

'Will!' she cried again.

'*What's happening?*' Andrew called.

'Our wing just got *shot*! Will –'

'I know!' Air rushed through the holes. Will was holding tight to the control bar, trying to stabilize them. But it was shaking badly.

Suddenly the cockpit see-sawed.

Gaia yelled out.

And Will saw something fall. A flash of silver. There was a tiny splash below them. He cursed.

'What was that?' Gaia called.

'Sam!' The robot had been on his lap.

She squeezed her eyes shut. They'd just been shot. Now they'd lost their only weapon.

In the front, Will checked the avionics. They were losing altitude and speed fast. The harbour whirled around them. He saw black water. Then stars. 'We're going down!'

He banked to the left. The microlight tipped so far over, the horizon was almost vertical.

Gaia wanted to scream. She clamped her mouth shut. Her eyes were fixed on the holes in the wing. She could see the trails left by the air streaming through.

Again, the cockpit jerked. 'The other *wing*!' she cried.

'Yeah!' Will said.

They were tilting badly to the left. If he couldn't get them straight, the wing would hit the water first. It could snap. They'd be sent hurtling across the harbour.

'Someone tell me what's happening!' Andrew demanded.

Will glanced over the cockpit. The left float was five metres above the surface. He shifted his entire body-weight to the right.

Four metres.

'Gaia, lean right!'

She obeyed. The undercarriage swung.

Three metres.

And at last, they began to level out. Wind screamed through the bullet holes. The control bar wrenched at Will's arms. It tore at his shoulders. He gritted his teeth. He couldn't hold on much longer.

One metre.

He let go.

Slam.

The floats hit the water and bounced. The microlight rocked to the left.

We're going over, Gaia thought. *We're going over –*

Then they rocked back to the right.

Both floats were in the water. Plumes of white spray shot into the air. As the drag kicked in, Will breathed.

They were in bad shape, but they were down.

'Gaia?'

Gaia's stomach had clammed up. Now waves of nausea rushed out.

'*Gaia?*'

'Gaia, are you all right?' Andrew cried.

'Yeah,' she said.

The right wing was sagging as the harbour rushed

past, and she was about to vomit, she was sure of it, but they were holding steady. They were safe.

Then she looked over the side of the cockpit. And she thought: *not for long.*

Outside Government House, Andrew stared at the images streaming from Gaia's contact lens camera.

'Who do you think shot at them?' Lydia whispered, her eyes wide.

They were beside the portico, waiting for the police car that PC Taylor said was coming to take them to the station. De Souza was nowhere to be seen. She'd been escorted from the dining room by two security guards and was already in a cell, Andrew guessed.

Taylor had been tight-lipped. He'd only said she was being 'dealt with'. Then he'd told them to wait and hurried back to the mayor, muttering something about detective work.

'*Andrew?*' Lydia said.

'I have no idea,' he replied. He'd been wondering the same thing. 'I suppose it could be another of Broadstairs's accomplices. But if so, why didn't they pick him up when his boat got hit?'

'Perhaps that's what's happening now.'

Andrew nodded, and sighed. The screen had turned black, with an occasional flicker of light. Being a spectator was frustrating enough. But when the picture was this bad, it was excruciating!

'Gaia, please tell me what you're doing,' he whispered.

No answer.

'Gaia –'

Then he heard: *'Andrew. Shh.'*

Gaia reached the top of the ladder and she crouched, panting.

Where was Broadstairs?

They were a minute behind him. No more.

From the microlight, she'd seen him arrive at the wharf. By the time they'd pulled in beside the battered taxi, he'd disappeared over the top of a ladder that ran up between the two frigates. His right leg had dragged. *Injured.* Caught by the nanotubes, Gaia realized.

Now, concealed by the shadows of the boats, Gaia's heart pounded. Next to her, Will's eyes strained.

The dockyard was badly lit. Scattered across the scrubby ground were chains, pallets, a forklift truck and three huge metal cargo crates. Beyond were dense trees, and then a tall fence topped with barbed wire.

Andrew asked what they were doing.

'Andrew. Shh.'

'There!' Will hissed.

Gaia tensed. Broadstairs had just emerged from behind one of the crates. He was twenty metres away, heading for the trees. And he was limping.

'Andrew,' Will whispered. 'Broadstairs is in the

dockyard. Tell the police!' Then he turned to Gaia. 'That first crate – go!'

Thirty metres away, Chen Jianguo stepped out of his limousine.

'Wait here,' he called to the driver.

And he hobbled towards a black gate. Through it, he could see pine trees, their branches waving. The jutting outline of the top section of a boat, beyond the dock wall. And a woman in a black suit, her back to a palm tree.

'I am here,' he whispered now. 'I can see you.'

Mei's head shot round.

After shooting the microlight, she'd steered in along the wharf.

Instead of following Broadstairs, she had found another ladder, past the boats. She'd climbed it, and discovered the gate. She'd blasted the lock. And she had spotted Broadstairs. He was moving slowly. It would be a simple matter to head him off.

Now she darted over to the gate. She swung it open.

'Where is he?' Chen demanded.

Mei spun. 'He should be—'

Chen finished her sentence. 'Right there.'

The best-laid plans, Broadstairs knew, could go wrong.

But there was *wrong*. And there was *utter disaster*.

What had happened? The $100 million had been his. Chen had wanted proof, and he'd given it to him twice. Yu had been as good as dead.

Then the kids had shown up. He'd escaped. They'd followed him. They'd just tried to kill him! Again, he'd escaped. He'd made it to the dock.

And now, out of the shadows of a fig tree, stepped a slim woman in a suit. She had a round face and tiny black eyes. At her side was an old man with a hunch and scraps of white hair.

Disbelief. Pain. Anger. They merged in Broadstairs's body, an explosive mix.

He had met Chen once, two years ago, in New York.

There was no forgetting the hollow cheeks, the shrunken lips, the filmy eyes. Then there was the snake. The Russell's viper. Chen's trademark.

It was draped around the old man's neck.

Chen Jianguo.

He was here in Sydney.

And his black-suited companion was raising her *gun.*

Chen coughed. Blood spattered into the air. He took two steps forward.

Broadstairs didn't budge.

Partly because he would never willingly concede ground to a man like Chen. Partly because the pain in his injured leg was getting worse. There was a deep gash in his thigh. Burning plastic had left a weal across his shin.

He told himself to ignore the white barrel aiming at his chest.

'Chen,' Broadstairs said coolly. 'I was going to call you.'

Behind the crate, Gaia glanced at Will. The old man *was* Chen, and it was his assassin who'd tried to kill them!

So here, she thought, was the creator of the Ex-Prize. He was barely five feet tall. Emaciated. Withered. His face was sunken, the flesh almost gone. It was as though his skull was trying to shed its skin, like a *snake*.

'Will – around his neck!'

'I've seen it,' he whispered. And he frowned. Chen had just said something. Now Broadstairs was speaking:

'But your presence makes this even easier. My people have the first two techniques. I have the third.' Broadstairs had stuffed de Souza's purse into his jacket pocket. He pulled it out.

Will and Gaia saw a ruby flash. Again, she glanced at Will. But he was focused on Chen.

'The third technique,' Chen said, and arched his eyebrow. 'Which *failed.*'

'No. The technique works.'

'Then the failure –'

'Was due to the necessity of trusting my chemist! It seems I was betrayed.'

Which was true, Broadstairs thought. Though surely not by de Souza. He reached for his leg. The pain throbbed. Blood was soaking his trousers. And he resisted the urge to glance back.

He'd seen the microlight go down. But after what had happened in Government House, surely the police would be searching for him.

His gaze flickered. What was that – beyond Chen and Mei – past the figs? Was it a *gate*?

'Chen, we are businessmen,' he said. 'I have what you want. Give me two hours. You transfer the money and I will bring all three techniques to you. There is no reason why the deal should not still be done.'

Chen's rheumy eyes narrowed. And he tensed. Was that a siren, coming from out the harbour? The police! Were they looking for Broadstairs?

But within his grasp was the third method, at least. If he could not curse and kill all three men who would take his place, at least he could kill one – and without the need to spend $100 million. Perhaps there was a chance he could still become a god!

Chen whispered in Mei's ear. The breeze picked up. It lifted white wisps of his hair.

'The deal has changed, Broadstairs,' he rasped. 'You will give the purse to Mei, and I will let you live.'

Broadstairs frowned. He'd heard the siren too.

And Chen had jabbed a bony finger at Mei.

Slowly, Broadstairs raised the purse to his chest. As he did so, he undid the clasp. Mei kept coming. Now she was ten paces away. Her elbow was crooked, the gun aiming right at him.

She held out her hand.

Broadstairs extended his arm slightly. Two fingers were inside the purse.

Four paces.

Mei reached out.

Holding the perfume bottle, Broadstairs let the purse fall. It dropped with a clunk. He saw Mei's black eyes widen, and he hit her with a burst of the drug. The deadly spray enveloped her face.

Forty-six seconds. That's what de Souza had told him. Easily long enough for Mei to shoot him.

She blinked, and raised the gun. But Broadstairs was already there. He lunged for her arm. She tried to spin away, and he punched her hard in the stomach. Mei staggered backwards, towards the edge of the dock.

Behind her, Chen hissed: '*Mei!*'

Again, she tried to level the gun.

Broadstairs's fist connected with her face. He felt her nose crunch. It was an ugly sound. And hitting women wasn't usually his style – unless, of course, they were trying to kill him.

'*Broadstairs!*' Chen cried.

But Broadstairs's eyes were on Mei. Blood was trickling down her chin.

Now her arm shook.

Sweat slicked her forehead. A hideous grimace grabbed her face, torturing her features. She clawed at her chest, and gasped. Her lungs caught. She could not breathe. She cried out, and the cry became a sickening groan.

Suddenly she stumbled.

'Mei, the gun!' Chen hissed.

And she toppled sideways, off the wall. The gun fell with her.

Silence. Then a splash.

Gaia stared.

Rapid-ageing. It had worked.

Broadstairs had killed someone with his drug.

And Broadstairs and Chen were facing each other.

The siren was still faint.

What would happen now?

31

Broadstairs took a deep breath. He turned to Chen.

The old man was hunched right over, his fists clenched. His filmy eyes were almost closed.

Chen Jianguo. King of the Shanghai underworld. He was trembling like the leaves in the fig tree behind him.

'Now,' Broadstairs said, 'call your banker, transfer the money, and I will let you live.'

Chen snarled. His snake curled her tail. Then he opened his right fist. Silver flashed.

Chen aimed the scorpion's mouth at Broadstairs's chest.

He flicked the tail, and a tiny silver dart shot through the air. It was arrow-headed. Coated in death.

Broadstairs ducked sideways. The dart hit a branch and bounced. Another flick.

What was Chen doing?

Suddenly a hail of darts needled the air. Broadstairs had no idea what was on them. But this was *Chen*.

He cursed. And he ran to the left, towards trees. Adrenalin dulled the pain in his leg. Broadstairs hit a pine. He swerved around it. A dart thwacked into the trunk. Another skewered a leaf.

Broadstairs glimpsed Chen's face. His lips were curled in a snarl, his hand raised.

At this distance, his perfume bottle was useless. 'Chen, I still have what you want. We can talk!'

But the old man kept coming. Broadstairs scoured the ground, looking for something to use as a shield. Saw nothing. He pressed a hand against his thigh. Hot blood was running down his shin.

'The red scorpion!' Chen screeched. 'How will it feel to die by its venom!'

Broadstairs gritted his teeth. He made for the next tree.

Will touched Gaia's arm. They couldn't let Broadstairs out of their sight. 'The forklift,' he said.

Broadstairs was weaving between the trees. Chen was following, his back to them.

Don't turn round, Will thought.

And he saw something red, by a pallet. De Souza's purse. It had fallen hard. He snatched it up, and he felt something inside. There was no time to look now. He pushed it into his pocket.

When he reached the forklift, he crouched. Gaia threw herself to the ground behind him.

Will peered around the side of the cabin – and he saw Chen. Hobbling *backwards*.

What was wrong?

Chen tugged at the silver tail. But nothing was happening.

Had he run out of darts?

If so, surely he must have hit Broadstairs!

'*Chen.*'

His fingers fumbled. He dropped the scorpion.

And there was Broadstairs, moving out from the trees. Dragging his leg. But *still alive*.

Chen stared in disbelief. He rubbed at his eyes. If Mei were here –

But Mei was dead.

And Broadstairs was coming towards him. The glass bottle glinted in his hand.

A red haze descended over Chen's brain. Anger made his body shake. Nine hundred and thirty-nine murderous henchmen, and he was facing an enemy – facing *death* at the hands of a man like Broadstairs – *alone*.

Not quite.

Chen's hand rose to his snake. He stroked her cool, soft skin.

'My beauty,' he murmured.

'*Chen,*' Broadstairs said again.

The man was close now. His grey eyes were cold as bullets. His hair was black, his face ghostly white. Broadstairs had no colour. He seemed inhuman. But no, Chen thought, he was living. And what was living could *die*.

Chen unhooked the golden muzzle. He seized his

viper by the neck. As Broadstairs took one more step towards him, he hurled her.

She shot through the air.

Chen saw her tail flick, and her jaws open. Her white fangs gleamed –

And she smacked to the ground. She hissed and seethed.

Broadstairs had thrown himself out of danger! He was on the leaves, gripping his leg. Still he held the bottle in his hand.

Pure fury powered through Chen's blood. His bowed legs were weak but they would carry him to his snake. The muzzle was gone, but she was *his* and this time, he would not miss!

As Broadstairs scrambled up, Chen darted forward. He reached down.

'My beauty,' he murmured.

The viper's head snapped back. Chen grabbed her.

And she struck.

Chen's right hand had clasped around her body. Her tongue had flickered. Suddenly he'd seen his fury reflected in her cold eyes. Then her yellow body had become a blur!

Now Chen froze.

Every nerve in his body screamed out.

His viper's head was clamped around *his own wrist*.

Twin pulses of pain shot from her fangs. 'No!' he whispered. '*No!*'

She let go. Her yellow body dropped to the ground,

and Chen heard her slither away into the undergrowth. The dealer's notes swam in front of his eyes.

A viper can tailor the dose of venom to the prey.
Muscles behind the fangs control the volume
expelled. A Daboia russelii *can inject up to 250 mg.*
The lethal dose for a man is fifty.

The pain swelled. Chen's veins felt weak. His blood pressure was falling. His heart rate was dropping.

He wheeled. Anger contorted his face.

Broadstairs was watching him.

Chen fell.

The deadly venom merged with his blood. With every beat of his heart, it spread further around his body. He could feel it in his hands, in his toes. In his heart.

Dark thoughts started to batter Chen's dying brain.

He would not make the Meeting of the Tigers.

The Giraffe or the Dung Beetle would take *his* place.

He would not be a god.

And Broadstairs was *free.*

Then, in Chen's last moment, his right eye flickered open.

What he saw gave him some comfort.

A blur in the sky, to the west.

Will and Gaia heard it before they saw it.

A helicopter. It was still in the distance, but it was heading right at them. Police, surely.

And there, coming across the water, was a flashing blue light. Portofino at last. He'd be at the dock in minutes.

Will's gaze swerved to Broadstairs.

He was gripping his leg, but he was on the move. Already, he'd passed Chen's body. He was heading towards the black gate. If he made it out of the dock, it wouldn't be difficult for him to escape. They couldn't let him.

But what could they do? If only he had Sam.

'Will,' Gaia said. 'Will, we have to do something!'

He nodded. 'I'm thinking!'

Suddenly she jumped up. She yelled: 'Broadstairs!' And she ran.

'*Gaia!*' Will hissed. 'Wait!'

She ignored him. They *had* to make Broadstairs stop. She could use herself as bait. To hold him for a few more moments. To stop him running through that gate. The police would be here.

'Broadstairs!'

Broadstairs glanced back – and he staggered to a halt. Gaia stopped.

He was twenty metres away. His eyes glowed. They looked hot with fury. They ran down her. Trying to see if she was armed, she guessed.

Then he looked over her shoulder. And Gaia saw him stiffen. The whirr of the rotor was getting louder.

Every second she could keep Broadstairs occupied would bring the police closer, she thought.

A twig snapped back behind her. Will, she guessed. Coming after her.

Then Broadstairs thundered: '*Stop!*'

The girl, he thought.

The girl and the boy from Government House.

His brain boiled. He'd killed Mei. He'd killed Chen. And now these kids were here. They thought they could stop him?

He'd kill them. He'd –

He swallowed. The helicopter was approaching the next wharf. And he could see a blue light closing in on the dock. Police. They'd swarm the place. He had to get away. He had to –

The boy was walking towards him.

'*Stop!*' Broadstairs yelled.

Again, he glanced up at the helicopter. Then he bolted. Not towards the gate.

But at Gaia.

For a moment, surprise froze Gaia's muscles.

Then they thawed. She darted to the left, towards the trees. What was Broadstairs thinking? He was injured. The police were coming. She'd expected him to run *away*.

She veered in between two trees, her heart racing. She hit a branch, and stumbled. She glanced back – and Broadstairs was *there*.

His hand was reaching for her shoulder. His fingers touched her. They pinched her flesh.

Gaia shot out with her elbow.

He grunted. But he didn't let go.

Suddenly his arm was under her neck. He squeezed it tight. She retched.

Split seconds. What had happened?

She kicked hard at his leg. He flinched. Then she saw a flash of glass by her cheek. The perfume bottle.

'*Gaia.*'

She coughed. She couldn't breathe. She pulled at Broadstairs's arm.

'Gaia, stay still.'

Out of the corner of her eye, she saw Will. He was in the trees. Then Broadstairs's grip tightened, and white stars punctured her vision.

Broadstairs adjusted his grip. Gaia took a deep breath, and wheezed. Fear was coursing through her blood. She felt faint.

He held the bottle against her face. 'Do as your friend says,' he hissed. 'If this liquid touches your skin –'

'I'll turn old like you then die!' The words tore at her throat.

Broadstairs bent his head to her face. The metallic eyes glared. 'If I knew as much as you, I'd have been tempted to keep my mouth shut in case there was an off-chance I'd let you live. Now that off-chance is decidedly *off.*'

Then he shouted to Will: 'She's coming with me. And when the police get here, I advise you to point them in the wrong direction because if I get caught, I will kill her. Do you understand?'

Will took a deep breath. He nodded.

And Andrew's voice came through his toothphone: 'Will, you have to stop him. He'll kill her! Will!'

Broadstairs turned. Dragging Gaia, he headed away, towards the figs – and the gate.

Will's brain raced. He had to do something. But *what*? He didn't even have Sam.

And he remembered de Souza's purse. *What was inside?*

His hands fumbling, Will pulled it from his pocket. He reached in, and his fingers touched plastic. He pulled out an auto-inject syringe. *Insulin glargine* was typed on the label. Insulin was for treating diabetes. But he'd bet anything that liquid wasn't insulin.

Broadstairs would have wanted to be sure of Yu's death. This had to be another dose of the drug.

If I get caught, I will kill her.

But Broadstairs *would* be caught. He was injured. The police were coming.

And if somehow he escaped? He'd killed Mei. He'd have killed Chen. Would he really let Gaia live?

Will fixed his eyes on Broadstairs. They were almost at the gate.

'Broadstairs!' he called.

But he kept moving.

'Will!' Andrew cried in his ear. 'He's getting away! Do something! Will!'

Will took two steps forward. He thought of Chen's darts. He'd bowled a cricket ball thousands of times. This would be different. But it was still throwing.

There was no time to think. If he was going to do this, he thought, he had to do it now.

But it was dark. And Broadstairs was holding Gaia right up against him. If he missed, he'd kill Gaia.

He had to get Broadstairs to turn around.

He had to make him let go of Gaia.

He had to make Broadstairs want to kill him more than he wanted to kill her.

How?

Will sprinted after them, and he shouted: 'James Parramore. We know who you are!'

33

Will was in among the figs. Silver moonlight lit the leaves.

He stopped.

Broadstairs was turning.

Fury and confusion gripped his face. He was still holding Gaia. Was it him? Will thought.

'St Petersburg,' Will called. 'You remember that? Your revolutionary weapon? Do you know who we are?'

'St Petersburg?' Broadstairs whispered.

And Will's blood rushed. Andrew had been right!

'Parramore!' Andrew exclaimed in his ear. 'It really is him!'

James Parramore. He was a murderer and a dangerous psychopath. MI6 had hunted him for weeks. *STORM had found him.* But at what cost? *Not Gaia's life.* He *could not* let that happen.

'We stopped you then,' Will said. 'We blew up your base.'

Parramore's eyes narrowed. They were molten pinpricks of grey.

'And here, we got inside your computers. We got into

Phoenix House. We found out about the Viper Club. And Chen. We stopped you. *I* stopped you.'

'*You!*' Parramore spat the word.

Will's gaze flicked to Gaia. She'd been motionless, her face white. But now she staggered, as Parramore let go.

'*Will*,' she whispered.

Parramore raised the bottle. Gaia could feel the anger burn from his body. And she saw something fly through the air.

The world fragmented.

Gaia felt the breeze on her face.

From what seemed like hundreds of miles away, she heard a shout. '*DI Portofino! Will Knight? Gaia Carella? Are you here?*'

The helicopter's blades rustled the leaves. It was coming in to land.

She saw Parramore's eyes widen.

And the syringe strike home.

Right in his chest.

Her eyes shot to Will.

He was standing there. Not moving. *Stunned.*

Will's heart hammered in his body. The syringe was designed to auto-inject. The plunger would have fired on impact, he thought. *The drug was in Parramore's blood.*

He'd been holding his breath. Now he gasped. 'Gaia,' he said quietly. '*Get back.*'

She took two cautious steps.

But Parramore seemed oblivious. He was gazing down. His fingers opened. He dropped the bottle. It smashed.

Gaia covered her face. And she watched him reach for the syringe. He plucked it out. And he looked at Will.

A boy, he thought. Killed by this boy.

St Petersburg. Sydney. *They* had destroyed his weapon? *They* had robbed him of $100 million. *They* had killed him. *Children.*

And by this – *his drug.* Mei's face flashed into his mind. He had witnessed her agony. How many seconds did he have left?

Parramore coughed. His breath caught. His heart palpitated.

His face spasmed. His money, his power. *Gone.*

A throbbing knot of pain was building in the core of his body. He could feel it sucking in his life. Growing and swelling. His own hideous black hole.

As the pain exploded, Parramore collapsed, the boy's face fixed in his mind.

Will stared.

Blood pounded in sickening waves through his head.

Parramore was on his back, limp.

Gaia was watching him. *She was alive.*

But he'd just killed Parramore.

He'd just killed a man.

Light. It burned Will's eyes. He lay on his back on the hard bunk.

Time had passed, but he wasn't sure how much. He'd been in shock. Perhaps he still was. He felt numb.

Parramore's dying seconds replayed constantly. He saw the silver eyes, fixed open. Saw Parramore stagger, and fall.

And he heard Gaia's voice as DI Portofino had reached them, and asked what had happened.

'He tried to kill me,' she'd said. 'So I had to kill him. Didn't I, Will? *I killed him.*'

Then four officers had jogged over. They'd arrived in the helicopter, Will guessed. Portofino said something to them. And they hustled him and Gaia out of the dock-yard, to a waiting car.

Later, when they were on the move, Andrew whispered:

'Will, Gaia. I know you can't talk. *Parramore.* I can still hardly believe it . . .'

He cleared his throat.

'Now, you have to listen. Lydia and I are at the

station. We're waiting to be interviewed. So we have to get our stories straight. Will, I saw that you killed Parramore. I know it was to save Gaia.

'Gaia, I heard you tell Portofino you did it, and I imagine you did that because you were afraid Will wasn't acting strictly in self-defence. Anyway, Gaia, I saw Will pick up a purse. It was de Souza's – the one she had in Government House.

'Will took out the syringe, and of course he threw it at Parramore. But if you say Parramore had the purse and while you were struggling, you managed to get hold of the syringe, and you used it on him, that should do it . . . Gaia? Will?'

No response.

Will squeezed his eyes shut.

Two hours later, Will had been taken from a cell to an interview room.

It had grey walls, a grey desk, two plastic chairs and a digital recorder.

Portofino was waiting. He told him Andrew had said something about Broadstairs being a man called Parramore. He'd need more detail about why they thought that. But it could come later. First, he wanted Will to describe exactly what had happened at the dockyard.

Will wanted to tell the truth. But Gaia had already told them –

Yes, she'd already told them she had killed Parramore. And if he hadn't killed Parramore in self-defence, then what was it? Manslaughter?

He couldn't be locked up. He *had* to get back to London. He was waiting for information about his father.

But it wasn't just that.

Gaia, and Andrew. He couldn't be without them.

So, in broken sentences, Will had repeated Andrew's story.

Now, lying on his back in the bunk, he felt sick.

He'd killed someone and lied about it. *What would Dad have thought?*

The cell door clanged open.

A middle-aged woman with blonde hair in a bun walked in. Marjorie Blaxted. Their contact at the British Embassy.

Will didn't move.

'I've spoken to Mr Barrington,' Blaxted said calmly. 'And now you must come with me.'

Will rolled his head. He looked past her, waiting for Portofino or another officer to come in.

She realized what he was thinking. 'It's all right, Will, you're free to go.'

He couldn't help feeling surprised. 'Gaia –'

'Is also being released. Andrew is waiting with your Australian friend. Now if you don't mind, I'd like to get out of here too. Four hours has been quite enough.'

'Four hours . . . what time is it?'

'Time to get you to the airport before you miss your flight. Come along.'

Marjorie Blaxted led the way along the corridor to the waiting room.

'*Will!*'

Andrew and Lydia had been sitting on plastic chairs. Now Andrew jumped up. Lydia rose, unsure what to do.

'Are you all right?' Andrew asked. 'Will?'

Will still felt numb. Slowly he nodded.

Andrew smiled. His blue eyes blinked in the bright strip light. Then he turned.

Another door had swung open.

Gaia. She looked ashen. She saw Will and her expression didn't change.

Portofino was right behind her. He ran a hand through his hair. And wished he hadn't. It felt even thinner. *Stress,* he told himself. And Taylor was desperate to be a detective!

'Right,' he said, 'I have your statements, and you're free to go with Mrs Blaxted. But she's agreed on your behalf that you'll cooperate fully with what will probably be a drawn-out investigation.

'We'll need you to testify against de Souza,' he went on, 'and go through how Broadstairs – or rather, Parramore – died, as well as Mr Chen and his accomplice. But we might be able to set up a video link with London, so you won't have to come back to Sydney. Unless you want to.'

Will noticed Andrew's gaze slide to Lydia.

'So we can go now?' Gaia asked quietly.

Portofino nodded. 'But before you do, there's some-one who wants to talk to you. Don't look so alarmed. It's nothing to worry about.' Through the open door, he shouted: 'Taylor, could you ask Mr Yu to come in?'

A few moments later, Yu Jichei strode into the wait-ing room.

His smart suit looked unruffled.

Close up, Andrew thought, he was even taller and broader than he'd seemed in Government House.

'Now I'll leave you to it,' Portofino said. 'The mayor's requested a meeting, and I'm late.'

When Portofino had gone, Yu held out his hand. Solemnly, he shook Andrew's, then Lydia's, then Gaia's, and Will's.

As he let go of Will's hand, he said: 'I understand that I owe you all my life.'

Silence.

'You're welcome,' Lydia said at last.

Yu smiled slightly. 'That is gracious of you. But you *saved my life.* By the way, my bodyguard sends his apologies.' He looked at Will. 'The scar in his cheek will remind him of his mistake. Now, tell me, how can I repay you?'

Gaia glanced at Will. He still looked dazed. But what had Andrew said? Yu was a rising star in Chinese poli-tics. He was powerful and influential. This was Will's chance. Didn't he see it?

'Will's father, Jonathan Knight, was a field officer with MI6,' Gaia said.

Yu raised an eyebrow.

'Last September, he was killed near a place called Xidi, in eastern China. He was investigating a secret research institute. And he was meant to be working with a CIA officer, but the CIA say their man never existed. We want to know what happened to Will's father. What was going on at the institute? Who killed him?'

Out of the corner of her eye, Gaia noticed Marjorie Blaxted frown. Andrew was nodding. Lydia was looking at Will, whose expression had hardened. He was watching Yu.

Yu was quiet. He'd probably been expecting a request for money, Gaia thought. Or a trip to China. Not this.

At last, Yu inclined his head. He glanced at Will, but addressed Gaia.

'Give me forty-eight hours. I will do what I can. You have my word.'

'Matt Walker?'

Walker was waiting impatiently in a bright white corridor. With no time to change, he was still in his checked shirt and his RM Williams trousers. There were three scorch holes in one leg, and a jagged tear in his sleeve. His face was smeared with dust and soot.

He'd been lucky: in the explosion, he hadn't suffered any serious injuries. But his head was splitting. When he and Marshall had finally nabbed Simpkin and shoved him into their car, it had ached. On the long journey to Adelaide – during which Simpkin had refused to speak – it started to throb.

They'd hustled Simpkin straight to a local jail. Then, after taking a scraping from the inside of his cheek, they'd driven to the forensics lab.

Two hours ago, MI6 Operations Control had forwarded the DNA profile of Sir James Parramore. According to the records, it had been collected from a hair left behind after a meeting in a Vienna coffee house in 1998.

Marshall had taken the profile through to the lab, and gone off in search of pizza.

Now the technician was at one end of the corridor, holding a piece of paper. Marshall had just appeared at the other, with a stack of three boxes.

When the man called his name, Walker jumped up. Simpkin was Parramore. He and Marshall were both sure of it. They had their man. All they needed was the final confirmation.

'There's no match,' the technician said.

'. . . No match?'

Walker looked round as three pizza boxes hit the floor.

'There has to be!' Marshall said.

The man shuffled. 'I'm afraid not.'

And Walker closed his eyes. He'd been *sure*. They'd both been sure.

'Could there be a mistake?' Marshall asked. 'Could you have got the result wrong?'

The technician shook his head. 'I'm sorry.'

'Not as bloody sorry as we are,' Marshall said.

35

Trafalgar Square, London, 10 September. 10.12

The sun was bright. It made the fountains sparkle.

Will watched tourists take photos of each other by Nelson's Column. Beyond the square, he saw Big Ben and Admiralty Arch.

Gaia sat beside him with her arms folded. Andrew was strolling around, hands in the pockets of a tight brown jacket, head in the clouds.

He checked his watch. Barrington was two minutes late. And it was just over forty-seven hours since they'd been released from the custody of the New South Wales police.

Will still felt hazy. But it was getting better.

When Gaia had asked Yu about his father, he'd had to concentrate hard to hear her. Then, as Blaxted had been escorting the three of them to a waiting car and Andrew had suddenly run back to Lydia, seized her shoulders and kissed her goodbye, Will had felt nothing.

It had been four or five hours before that numbness started to ebb away.

He'd killed a man. Nothing could change that.

But there had been justification. An urgent reason *why*.

At the airport, Andrew busy texting Lydia, and Blaxted off buying coffee, Gaia had touched his arm.

'I haven't said thank you yet,' she said.

Will had looked at her. 'For killing someone to stop them killing you?' He held her gaze. 'I'd do it a hundred times. I'd never hesitate. Would you?'

'Lydia says hello!'

Will looked up. Trafalgar Square rushed back.

Andrew was waving his phone. He smiled as he headed over to the bench. 'She might be coming to London next spring.'

'That's great,' Gaia said.

'Though she's a bit upset about having to sign the official secrets act, which of course means she can't actually write about any of this.'

Gaia nodded. She was very fond of Andrew, and she was pleased about Lydia, but he was becoming obsessed. He wouldn't even take off her jacket – which, he insisted, Lydia had told him to keep.

On the flight home, Andrew had grilled her. Had Lydia said anything about him to her? Had she done as he'd asked, and talked him up?

Gaia had felt bad. 'I would have done, but there was so much going on. I didn't get a chance.'

Andrew had looked crestfallen.

'But you didn't need talking up – did you?'

And he'd understood her implication: Lydia's apparently positive feelings about him had developed of their own accord.

Andrew had smiled to himself. And he'd hardly stopped.

Since their farewell, they'd exchanged forty-seven texts.

Lydia sent him constant updates. Her dad had been furious, then proud. There was a police cordon around Phoenix House. The *Australian* had reported the mysterious discovery of a deadly Russell's viper in a restaurant at Woollomolloo wharf.

Was so tempted to call them, she texted. *Bloody official secrets act.*

As he sat down next to Gaia on the bench in Trafalgar Square, Andrew decided spring was too long to wait. Perhaps she could come out for Christmas. He was about to text her to suggest she stayed with him. But a low voice called:

'Will, Andrew, Gaia. *G'day!*'

Shute Barrington strode across the square.

His customary leather jacket and black jeans had gone. Instead, he wore a neat grey suit and a tie. His curly brown hair had been closely cut.

He reached a fountain and stopped, leaning against

it. With one hand, he shielded his eyes. Will, Andrew and Gaia joined him.

'You're probably sick of the sunshine, aren't you?' he said.

'You call this sunshine?' Andrew asked. 'We've been waiting half an hour and we're still not burnt.'

Barrington smiled. Was Andrew trying to be funny or factual?

'First things first,' he said. He faced Will. 'I'm sorry, there's no more news. But one of our senior diplomats in Beijing is trying to arrange a meeting with a local man who apparently did some construction at the institute. Perhaps we'll turn up something.'

Will nodded. He couldn't help feeling disappointed. So, he thought, Barrington's promised 'unusual channels' still weren't working.

'Now, to events in Sydney,' Barrington said. 'I've been through all your police statements. Very interesting they are too. *Sir James Parramore.* You actually caught him! Walker and Marshall's man turned out to be a run of the mill murderer. They're suitably miserable. And while – of course – I believed your statements, we've just had biological verification.

'When the Australian police searched Phoenix House, they found a safe protected by a biometric access mechanism. An iris scanner, in fact. Four hours ago they sent us an image of the iris required to open that safe. I compared it with our records. And they match!'

Gaia nodded. Will looked at the ground.

Andrew managed a faint smile. Of course, he was pleased. But he couldn't be happy when clearly Will was suffering. The last thing Will would probably want was more questions, he realized. 'So if you've read our statements,' Andrew said, 'you know everything we did.'

Barrington snorted. 'I wouldn't go that far. For starters, how did you really find out about the Viper Club and the prize – and that Chen had ordered Broadstairs to kill three people? Your statements were pretty vague and not *entirely* convincing. Did you really overhear explicit conversations about all this while you were inside Phoenix House, as you told DI Portofino?'

'Ah,' Andrew said. He couldn't really lie about this to Barrington. He hadn't wanted to lie to Portofino either, but he'd also wanted to get home. 'Well, actually I – I wrote some software.'

'I see. And the reason you didn't tell Portofino about this would be?'

Andrew hesitated.

'Something to do with breaking who knows how many laws? Of course, I should report and deport you, but *just* this once . . .' Barrington smiled.

'Barrington, we have a few questions,' Will said. 'What happened to de Souza? Have the police searched her lab?'

'De Souza's in custody,' Barrington replied. 'She's been charged with conspiracy to murder and attempted murder. Phoenix House has been raided. The forensic chemists have found a drug that actually seems to reverse cellular ageing – while the drug that killed Broadstairs did the opposite, as you know. I've requested samples of both, but it might be some time before we get our hands on the compounds.'

'What about de Bruyn and Collins?' Will asked. 'We think they used a microwave weapon to kill de Bruyn, but we don't know what they did to Collins.'

Barrington glanced over his shoulder. Two Japanese tourists had stopped behind him, and were embracing for a photograph. He scowled at them until they left.

'A microwave weapon built into a briefcase *was* found on the person of a man who'd been employed at Phoenix House,' Barrington said. 'He confessed to shooting de Bruyn. And immediately shopped his colleague, who posed as a waiter and slipped the crushed kernels of *Cerbera odollam* into a canapé he gave to Collins.'

So they'd been right, Andrew thought. It *had* been the waiter. '*Cerbera odollam*? And it was another guard who killed him!'

'Shh,' Barrington said, glancing over his shoulder. 'Walls have ears, I understand, so I don't see why fountains shouldn't.

'It's a plant that grows in India,' he went on. 'It contains a potent heart toxin. It seems the locals have known about it some time, but it was only "discovered" last month by a bio-prospector who works out of Delhi.'

335

Andrew nodded slowly. If he and Lydia had arrived five minutes earlier – or if he'd called out to try to warn Collins – would Collins still be alive? But they thought he'd been safe. He couldn't think like that now.

'So what did Parramore have to do with Phoenix House?' Gaia asked. 'How did he know de Souza?'

'Ah. Well, that bit of the jigsaw has just been slotted into place,' Barrington said. 'That's why I was late. It seems that for the past three years, Parramore has been funding de Souza's work to the tune of half a million dollars a year. She's been offering the anti-ageing treatment for a year or so, but it seems she's also been trying to improve on it.

'Last month, she sent an email to Parramore with "bad news" about the results of a trial. The compound had done the opposite of what they'd hoped. But when Chen announced his prize, Parramore must have remembered that email – and so he went to Sydney to see if he could use the drug.'

Andrew was surprised. 'So he was paying for her research even before she created the ageing drug? I thought Parramore was into weapons and oil, and that sort of thing. Not rejuvenation therapies.'

'One of our operatives found a deleted email dated just after the payments started,' Barrington said. 'Like the other members of the Viper Club, Parramore was clearly obsessed with death. But this email suggests he couldn't bear the thought of it for himself. He hoped de Souza would extend his life.'

Barrington looked at Gaia. 'The truth is, you did the world a great favour. Parramore was hugely dangerous, and reckless. He personally killed forty-three people. And remember Russia. He was involved in research that could have murdered thousands.'

'Stealth Teens Overthrow Reckless Maniac,' Andrew said, and smiled.

Neither Will nor Gaia were smiling, Barrington noticed. His expression become serious. 'It was self-defence,' he said to Gaia. 'You had no choice. I'd have done exactly the same. Anyone would.'

And Will felt shame and anger rush through his body. He wanted to tell Barrington exactly what had happened.

But how could he? It was too late for that. He'd lied. And that lie was part of him now.

What would Dad say? Will didn't want to know the answer.

'So what happens to the other members of the Viper Club?' Andrew asked, to change the subject.

Barrington shrugged. 'Being interested in death isn't a crime in itself. But this case does justify a closer look at those members' activities. At least, it does in my book. Oh, and while we're on the subject of crime, Mrs Blaxted has forwarded a bill from the owner of Watson's Retreat for a hefty mooring fine, and a new microlight. Given the circumstances, I've decided to take care of it.'

Now Barrington took a moment to survey the three faces. He could understand why Gaia was subdued.

Will still looked utterly miserable, and even Andrew had lost his smile. But they'd caught Parramore. They'd done well.

'On a happier note,' Barrington said, 'I'm told the New South Wales police are giving Lydia Michalitsianos an award.' He fixed his gaze on Andrew. 'I thought you'd like to know.'

Andrew coloured.

'And it's not only walls and fountains that have ears,' Barrington said, a gleam creeping back into his eye. 'So apparently does Marjorie Blaxted. She saw – and tell me if I've somehow got this wrong – but she says she saw you *kiss* Lydia Michalitsianos and she said it was one of the loudest –'

'*Really*,' Andrew said. His hand flew to his glasses. His cheeks burned crimson.

Barrington grinned. 'Now, with loving and leaving in mind, I'm afraid I must be off.' He began to turn away, and stopped. The grin slipped. 'Look, I'm not going to give you *advice*, but I am going to suggest this: go home, do some homework, play computer games, hang out in malls. Do *normal* stuff for a while. OK?'

He didn't wait for an answer. He whirled, and strode back towards Admiralty Arch.

Gaia watched him go. *Hang out in malls?* she thought. And she looked round.

Will's mobile was ringing.

He checked the caller ID. *No Number*. He hit the answer button.

'Will Knight?'

Suddenly Trafalgar Square vanished. He knew that voice. 'Mr Yu?'

Gaia and Andrew exchanged glances.

'I have mixed news,' Yu said. 'I have not been able to discover the nature of the research at the institute or the name of any person that might have killed your father.'

Will waited, trying to stop disappointment welling up again. Mixed news. What was to come?

'However,' Yu said, 'I do have a name for the man who was calling himself a CIA officer and purporting to work with your father. I also have an address. I will text both to you. I am sorry that I could not be of more assistance. If you are ever in China, do visit my office. And again, thank you for saving my life. *Xiexie*. Good bye.'

A name. An address. It wasn't what he'd hoped for. But it was something. It was more than Barrington had come up with.

He realized Andrew and Gaia were watching him. 'The CIA officer *wasn't* a CIA officer,' he said quickly. 'Yu has his name and address. He's texting them to me.'

'That's fantastic!' Andrew said.

Will's phone beeped. He took a deep breath. Opened the text. Read:

Fraser McCann, Room M103, the Queen Mary, Long Beach, Los Angeles.

'Los Angeles . . .' Will said.

He read the message again.

Fraser McCann. This man had pretended to work with

his father. He had to know *something* about who'd killed him.

He had to.

Andrew looked at Gaia: 'I just need to pack a few things. I can be ready in half an hour. How about you?'

She nodded. 'Yeah.'

Will raised his head. 'You're coming with me?'

'What else would we do?' Andrew said, surprised. 'That is – if you want us?'

For a moment, Will didn't speak. Not because he didn't know the answer. But because his throat felt so tight, he wasn't sure he'd be able to get the word out.

His heart was pounding. Every beat made his thoughts rush.

His dad. He *had* to know the truth. Gaia and Andrew would help him.

'Yes.'

Author's Note

1. Spy Seeds: researchers at Lockheed Martin's Advanced Technology Laboratories in New Jersey are developing Nano Air Vehicles modelled on a maple seed. The single blade will have a tiny rocket thruster in the tip.

2. Will's synthetic gills are based on research by an Israeli inventor called Alon Bodner.

3. The swimming pool at the Australian Institute of Sports Research is modelled on the Aquatics Testing Training and Research Unit of the Australian Institute of Sport (AIS) in Canberra. The boxing kit was also developed by scientists at the AIS.

4. The microlight described in this book is based on a model manufactured by Australian company Airborne.

5. Researchers at the Swiss Federal Institute of Technology in Lausanne have created a simple robot modelled on the spine of a salamander. The robot can swim, run and crawl. 'Sam' is much smaller, and made from different materials – including a shape memory alloy. There are three main types of shape memory alloy, and all can 'remember' their original shape.

6. Artificial muscles have been created (and are being further developed) by various teams. For example, researchers at the University of Texas have made artificial muscles that are 100 times stronger than the real thing. These muscles use a chemical fuel, such as hydrogen or methanol.

7. Ultrasound and high-power, low-frequency sonar can stun divers.

8. A contact lens with an inbuilt camera is under development by a team in Israel.

9. The fact that carbon nanotubes can ignite when lit with a bright light was discovered by accident by a student at the Rensselaer Polytechnic Institute in New York, US.

Notes on the science

1 Telomeres and ageing: various researchers have shown that telomerase keeps telomeres intact – and that this can make a cell immortal. Scientists expect tests of anti-ageing drugs based on telomerase to take place on people soon. However, while in theory a drug that suddenly obliterated a person's telomeres would kill them, it would take longer than the drug described in this book – and no such drug exists. This part of the book is fiction. *Protein composition of catalytically active human telomerase from immortal cells* was published in *Science* in 2007.

2. *Cerbera odollam* is known as the 'suicide tree' in India. The kernels contain a potent heart toxin. But the death appears natural, and a pathologist would not suspect murder (or suicide) unless there was evidence the person had eaten the plant.

3. An electromagnetic (EM) weapon (generating high-power microwaves, for example) could in theory trigger a heart attack remotely, by interfering with the electrical signals in the heart. Researchers at the Trymas Engineering Centre in Moscow, for instance, are investigating the impact of radio waves on nerves and hearts. However, current high-power EM weapons are large, and would burn the skin.

4. Australian researchers have found that people are more open to being persuaded by an argument after two cups of coffee.

*

Sydney's Government House does exist, though the interior is not quite as described. There are rumours that an emergency escape tunnel was built from the house down to the harbour – but officials deny that any exists.

NAME SAM

INTENTION: AMPHIBIAN SURVEILLANCE & RETRIEVAL

SPECS:

Based on a salamander.
Nickel-titanium shape-memory alloy body (so if bent, bounces back into shape). Artificial muscles made from shape-memory wires coated in platinum (methanol, oxygen and hydrogen gas fuel).
Fitted with visible and infrared camera, microphone and 6-watt torch.
Sticky foot-pads let it scale walls like a gecko. Navigates — and defends itself — using sonar.

CREATED:
Submarine Research Lab,
Sutton Hall

TESTED:
Watson's Bay, Sydney

POTENTIAL MODIFICATIONS:

Make foot-pads noiseless?
Increase sonar power?

(Great name! - Andrew P.S. Like the 'defends itself' bit. Obviously that's what it was doing when it hit de Souza's Indian contact. And the security guard at the gallery . . .)

NAME

SPY SEEDS

INTENTION: Aerial reconnaissance

SPECS:

Inspired by sycamore seed. Dacron wing.
5 cm long. Tiny rocket in wing tip blasts
seed up at 10 m/second to height of 1 km.
As seed descends, wing spins, slowing its
velocity. Built-in camera streams back
footage of the ground.

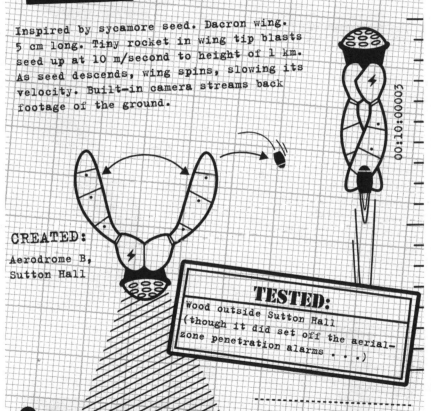

00:10:00003

CREATED:

Aerodrome B,
Sutton Hall

TESTED:

Wood outside Sutton Hall
(though it did set off the aerial-
zone penetration alarms . . .)

POTENTIAL MODIFICATIONS:

Reduce camera weight?

(So *not actually*
designed for shooting
at people who get in
the way then? Andrew)

NAME

SECOND SIGHT

INTENTION: To enable someone else to see exactly what you see

SPECS: Contact lens fitted with miniature camera. Camera streams footage to hand-held display

CREATED: Sutton Hall

TESTED:

Sutton. (Persuaded Charlie Spicer to wear one to a STASIS social night at the local pub. Saw the tortured expressions on everyone's faces when Spicer sang karaoke.)

(Resolution often non-existent, especially at night. Though I did see the flames when you bombed Broadstairs! Andrew)

POTENTIAL MODIFICATIONS:

Poor resolution in low light. Improve.

NAME

BREATHE EASY

CREATED: Bedroom, London and Sutton Hall

INTENTION: To breathe like a fish

SPECS:

Seawater flows into tubes in vest. Pressure is lowered so air dissolved in the water turns back into a gas. Air piped to diver's mouthpiece. Battery-powered.

TESTED:

Research Lake 2, Sutton Hall (after checking with Charlie Spicer that none of his creations were present) and Watson's Bay, Sydney

POTENTIAL MODIFICATIONS:

Increase airflow for high-demand situations

(Breathe easy? Yes, that's exactly what I was doing in the flooded tunnel with the rats. Seriously though, if you hadn't invented it, Yu probably wouldn't be breathing at all. Andrew)

FUTURE INVENTIONS?

1 Good to see what someone else sees. But what if you could read their thoughts?

2 Adapt some of Sam's defences to Ratty? (Sam v useful, but not quite the same.) And need new non-lethal weapons. Have to be able to stop people like Broadstairs without seriously hurting them.

THE INFINITY CODE

E. L. YOUNG

**Will Knight, 14: Inventive genius.
Creates cutting-edge gadgets (S.T.O.R.M.-sceptic)**

**Andrew Minkel, 14: Software millionaire
(and fashion disaster). Founder of S.T.O.R.M.**

**Gaia Carella, 14: Brilliant chemist with a habit of
blowing stuff up (usually schools).**

**Caspian Baraban, 14: Gifted astrophysicist.
Obsessed with the immense forces of space
(equally immense ego).**

Will mocks S.T.O.R.M.'s plan to combat global problems, but then they uncover a plot to create a revolutionary weapon. Will swallows his doubts as they race to Russia to confront the scientific psychopath with a deadly power at his fingertips.

The first book in the S.T.O.R.M. series, *The Infinity Code* is a gadget-packed high-adrenalin adventure.

S.T.O.R.M.

THE GHOSTMASTER

E. L. YOUNG

Two high-profile burglaries have hit the headlines in Venice, and CCTV footage sent to S.T.O.R.M. shows a strange spectral form at the crime scenes. The thefts are dubbed the work of *Il Fantasma* – The Ghost – but who is really behind them? When their contact goes missing, S.T.O.R.M. head to Venice to investigate. They soon find themselves in deep water, on the trail of an unknown criminal genius who plans to plunge the world into chaos.

Armed with brilliant brains, top-spec speedboats and Will's cutting-edge gadgets, can S.T.O.R.M. find the mind behind the mayhem – the sinister Ghostmaster?

THE BLACK SPHERE

E. L. YOUNG

Six scientists were working on Project FIREball. Now five are dead and one is missing. Carrying plans for a world-changing technology, he is wanted by MI6, the CIA and a ruthless megalomaniac.

S.T.O.R.M. join the high-stakes manhunt, heading into the heart of the sinister Black Sphere and deep into mortal danger . . .

Don't miss S.T.O.R.M.'s final heart-stopping mission, coming soon

S.T.O.R.M.
THE DEATH WEB

E. L. YOUNG

The first title in the Nathan Fox series

NATHAN
FOX
Dangerous Times

L. BRITTNEY

Nathan is an actor in the same company as Will Shakespeare.
A skilled acrobat with many other talents, he catches the
eye of England's Spymaster General. Recruited as an agent
– and partnered with fearless spy John Pearce – Nathan is
trained at a School of Defence in the arts that will keep him
alive.

His first mission takes Nathan Fox to Venice – into the eye
of an explosive situation involving the formidable General
Othello . . .

A selected list of titles available from Macmillan Children's Books

The prices shown below are correct at the time of going to press. However, Macmillan Publishers reserves the right to show new retail prices on covers, which may differ from those previously advertised.

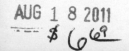